EX LIBRIS
PACE COLLEGE

PACE COLLEGE PLAZA
NEW YORK

D1226348

THE GLORIOUS HUSSAR

Titles in the Companion Book series:

THE GLORIOUS HUSSAR *by Sir Arthur Conan Doyle*

SABRES OF FRANCE *by James Finn*

WITH WOLFE IN CANADA *by G. A. Henty*

BATTLE IN THE WILDERNESS *by Konrad Kellen*

IN THE AZTEC TREASURE HOUSE *by Thomas A. Janvier*

THE WORLD OF THE AZTECS *by Elizabeth Gresham*

THE KNIGHTS AT BAY *by Philip Lindsay*

THE FIGHTING MONKS *by Richard Horchler*

THE GLORIOUS

The Best of the

WALKER AND COMPANY

New York

HUSSAR

Exploits and Adventures of the Brigadier Gerard

by SIR ARTHUR CONAN DOYLE

Published by permission of the Sir Arthur
Conan Doyle estates. The special features of
this edition copyright © 1961 by Walker
and Company. All rights reserved.

Library of Congress
Catalog Card No. 61-16991

Published simultaneously in Canada
by George J. McLeod Ltd., Toronto

MANUFACTURED IN
THE UNITED STATES OF AMERICA IN 1961

PZ
·7.
D76Gl
7–10

Author's Preface

READERS OF MARBOT, DE GONNEVILLE, COIGNET, de Fezenac, Bourgogne, and the other French soldiers who have recorded their reminiscences of the Napoleonic campaigns will recognise the fountain from which I have drawn the adventures of Etienne Gerard. It was an extraordinary age, and produced extraordinary types. For twenty-three years France was at war, with one short breathing space of a few months. To Frenchmen war had become the normal and natural state. Children were born in war, grew up in war, fought in the war, and died in the same endless war without ever knowing what peace was like. Yet, as we read the memoirs of these fighting men, or if we consult the descriptions left by those who, like our own Napier, had met them in the field, we find that they were by no means brutalised by this strange experience, and that among them were knightly and gentle souls, playfully gallant, whose actions recall the very spirit of chivalry. A better knight than Marbot never rode in the lists, and what shall we say of that dragoon, described by Napier, who raised his sword, saluted and passed, on perceiving that his English antagonist in a fierce *mêlée* had only one arm, or that madcap officer of the cavalry who charged the whole English army single-handed. These are the men, glorious in their youth, and pathetic in their useless and poverty-stricken old age, of whom I desired to draw a type, noble, *debonnaire*, capable, self-sufficient, human, and garrulous. I may add that there has been some attempt to keep the military and historical detail correct.

A preface had always seemed to me an unnecessary impertinence, until I found by experience how easily one may be

This Preface by Sir Arthur Conan Doyle is taken from his Preface to the limited 'Author's Edition' of his works published by Smith Elder (1902).

misunderstood, and so before I stand aside I am emboldened to say a few words as to my own conception of the art of fiction. That conception is that our treatment may be as wide as the heavens and as broad as the earth, if it does but attain the essential end of *interest*. All methods and schools, romance and realism, symbolism and naturalism, have the one object in view—to interest. They are all good so far as they attain that, and all useless when they cease to do so. The weary workers or the more weary idlers turn to the writer and demand to have their thoughts drawn away from themselves and the routine of their own lives. Within the bounds of morality all methods are legitimate by which we can effect this. Every school is right in claiming that it is justified, and every school is wrong when it tries to prove that its rival is unjustified. You are right to make your book adventurous, you are right to make it theological, you are right to make it informative or controversial or idyllic, or humorous or grave or what you will, but you *must* make it interesting. That is essential—all the rest is detail. There is nothing inconsistent in the same writer using every method in turn, so long as he can in each hold his reader and take his thoughts from his own selfish interests.

But there comes the obvious retort, 'You say "interesting"—interesting to *whom*?' The difficulty is not really a great one. The higher and more permanent work has always been interesting to all. The work which is the cult of a clique, too precious for general use, must be wanting in some quality. We know cases where obscurity of style has retarded the recognition of really great writers—but obscurity of style is not a virtue, and they were great in spite of it. Take the most honoured names in our literature, Scott, Thackeray, Dickens, Reade, Poe, they do not interest one or other social stratum, but they appeal equally to all educated readers. If you were to make a list of the works of fiction which have proved their greatness by their permanence and by the common consensus of mankind, you would find that no narrow formula would cover them. *Tom Jones, Don Quixote, Gulliver's Travels, Madame Bovary, Esmond, Pride and Prejudice, Notre Dame,* which shall we rule out as inartistic? And yet the only point which they have in common is that each of them holds the attention of every reader.

It is just this power of holding the attention which forms the art of story-telling—an art which may be developed and improved but cannot be imitated. It is the power of sympathy, the sense of the dramatic. There is no more capricious and indefinable quality. The professor in his study may have no trace of it, while the Irish nurse in the attic can draw out the very souls of his children with her words. It is imagination—and it is the power of conveying imagination. But we do not know what imagination is, and so all our definitions and explanations become mere juggling with words.

And still critics are found to write, 'The book is interesting, but we confess that we are unable to say what useful purpose it serves.' As if interest were not in itself the essential purpose! Ask the sleepless man worn with insomnia, the watcher beside the sick-bed, the man of business whose very sanity depends upon getting his thoughts out of one weary groove, the tired student, the woman whose only escape from an endless sordid life is that one window of imagination which leads out into the enchanted country—ask all these if interest serves any useful purpose. The life of a writer of fiction has its own troubles, the weary waiting for ideas, the blank reaction when they have been used, worst of all the despair when the thought which had seemed so bright and new goes dull and dark in the telling. But surely he has in return some claim to hope that if he can but interest his readers he fulfils the chief end of man in leaving others a little happier than he found them.

A. CONAN DOYLE

Undershaw, Hindhead

Contents

I. How the Brigadier Came to the
   Castle of Gloom   1

II. How the Brigadier Slew the
    Brothers of Ajaccio   23

III. How the Brigadier Captured
     Saragossa   44

IV. How the Brigadier Slew the
    Fox   64

V. How the Brigadier Took the
   Field Against the Marshal Millefleurs   77

VI. How the Brigadier Rode to Minsk   100

VII. How the Brigadier Won His Medal   119

VIII. How the Brigadier Was Tempted
      by the Devil   142

IX. How the Brigadier Bore Himself
    at Waterloo   164

X. The Last Adventure of the
   Brigadier   199

1807

I. How the Brigadier Came to the Castle of Gloom

YOU DO very well, my friends, to treat me with some little reverence, for in honoring me you are honoring both France and yourselves. It is not merely an old, grey-moustached officer whom you see eating his omelette or draining his glass, but it is a fragment of history. In me you see one of the last of those wonderful men, the men who were veterans when they were yet boys, who learned to use a sword earlier than a razor, and who during a hundred battles had never once let the enemy see the color of their knapsacks. For twenty years we were teaching Europe how to fight, and even when they had learned their lesson it was only the thermometer, and never the bayonet, which could break the Grand Army down. Berlin, Naples, Vienna, Madrid, Lisbon, Moscow—we stabled our horses in them all. Yes, my friends, I say again that you do well to send your children to me with flowers, for these ears have heard the trumpet calls of France, and these eyes have seen her standards in lands where they may never be seen again.

Even now, when I doze in my arm-chair, I can see those great warriors stream before me—the green-jacketed chasseurs, the giant cuirassiers, Poniatowski's lancers, the white-mantled dragoons, the nodding bearskins of the horse grenadiers. And then there comes the thick, low rattle of the drums, and through wreaths of dust and smoke I see the line of high bonnets, the row of brown faces, the swing and toss of the long, red plumes amid the sloping lines of steel. And there rides Ney with his red head, and Lefebvre with his bulldog jaw, and

Lannes with his Gascon swagger; and then amidst the gleam
of brass and the flaunting feathers I catch a glimpse of *him*,
the man with the pale smile, the rounded shoulders, and the
far-off eyes. There is an end of my sleep, my friends, for up
I spring from my chair, with a cracked voice calling and a
silly hand outstretched, so that Madame Titaux has one more
laugh at the old fellow who lives among the shadows.

Although I was a full Chief of Brigade when the wars came
to an end, and had every hope of soon being made a General
of Division, it is still rather to my earlier days that I turn
when I wish to talk of the glories and the trials of a soldier's
life. For you will understand that when an officer has so many
men and horses under him, he has his mind full of recruits and
remounts, fodder and farriers, and quarters, so that even when
he is not in the face of the enemy, life is a very serious matter
for him. But when he is only a lieutenant or a captain, he has
nothing heavier than his epaulettes upon his shoulders, so that
he can clink his spurs and swing his dolman, drain his glass
and kiss his girl, thinking of nothing save enjoying a gallant
life. That is the time when he is likely to have adventures, and
it is often to that time that I shall turn in the stories which
I may have for you. So it will be tonight when I tell you of
my visit to the Castle of Gloom; of the strange mission of Sub-
Lieutenant Duroc, and of the horrible affair of the man who
was once known as Jean Carabin, and afterwards as the Baron
Straubenthal.

You must know, then, that in the February of 1807, im-
mediately after the taking of Danzig, Major Legendre and I
were commissioned to bring four hundred remounts from
Prussia into Eastern Poland.

The hard weather, and especially the great battle at Eylau,
had killed so many of the horses that there was some danger
of our beautiful Tenth of Hussars becoming a battalion of
light infantry. We knew, therefore, both the Major and I,
that we should be very welcome at the front. We did not
advance very rapidly, however, for the snow was deep, the
roads detestable, and we had but twenty returning invalids
to assist us. Besides, it is impossible, when you have a daily
change of forage, and sometimes none at all, to move horses
faster than a walk. I am aware that in the story-books the cavalry whirls past at the maddest of gallops; but for my own
part, after twelve campaigns, I should be very satisfied to

know that my brigade could always walk upon the march and
trot in the presence of the enemy. This I say of the hussars
and chasseurs, mark you, so that it is far more the case with
cuirassiers or dragoons.

For myself I am fond of horses, and to have four hundred
of them, of every age and shade and character, all under my
own hands, was a very great pleasure to me. They were from
Pomerania for the most part, though some were from Nor-
mandy and some from Alsace, and it amused us to notice that
they differed in character as much as the people of those prov-
inces. We observed also, what I have often proved since, that
the nature of a horse can be told by his color, from the co-
quettish light bay, full of fancies and nerves, to the hardy
chestnut, and from the docile roan to the pig-headed rusty-
black. All this has nothing in the world to do with my story,
but how is an officer of cavalry to get on with his tale when
he finds four hundred horses waiting for him at the outset?
It is my habit, you see, to talk of that which interests myself
and so I hope that I may interest you.

We crossed the Vistula opposite Marienwerder, and had
got as far as Riesenberg, when Major Legendre came into my
room in the post-house with an open paper in his hand.

"You are to leave me," said he, with despair upon his face.

It was no very great grief to me to do that, for he was, if
I may say so, hardly worthy to have such a subaltern. I saluted,
however, in silence.

"It is an order from General Lasalle," he continued; "you
are to proceed to Rossel instantly, and to report yourself at
the headquarters of the regiment."

No message could have pleased me better. I was already
very well thought of by my superior officers. It was evident
to me, therefore, that this sudden order meant that the regiment was about to see service once more, and that Lasalle understood how incomplete my squadron would be without me.
It is true that it came at an inconvenient moment, for the
keeper of the post-house had a daughter—one of those ivory-
skinned, black-haired Polish girls—with whom I had hoped to
have some further talk. Still, it is not for the pawn to argue
when the fingers of the player move him from the square; so
down I went, saddled my big black charger, Rataplan, and set
off instantly upon my lonely journey.

My word, it was a treat for those poor Poles and Jews, who

have so little to brighten their dull lives, to see such a picture as that before their doors! The frosty morning air made Rataplan's great black limbs and the beautiful curves of his back and sides gleam and shimmer with every gambade. As for me, the rattle of hoofs upon a road, and the jingle of bridle chains which comes with every toss of a saucy head, would even now set my blood dancing through my veins. You may think, then, how I carried myself in my five-and-twentieth year—I, Etienne Gerard, the picked horseman and surest blade in the ten regiments of hussars. Blue was our colour in the Tenth—a sky-blue dolman and pelisse with a scarlet front—and it was said of us in the army that we could set a whole population running, the women towards us, and the men away. There were bright eyes in the Riesenberg windows that morning which seemed to beg me to tarry; but what can a soldier do, save to kiss his hand and shake his bridle as he rides upon his way?

It was a bleak season to ride through the poorest and ugliest country in Europe, but there was a cloudless sky above, and a bright, cold sun, which shimmered on the huge snow-fields. My breath reeked into the frosty air, and Rataplan sent up two feathers of steam from his nostrils, while the icicles drooped from the side-irons of his bit. I let him trot to warm his limbs, while for my own part I had too much to think of to give much heed to the cold. To north and south stretched the great plains, mottled over with dark clumps of fir and lighter patches of larch. A few cottages peeped out here and there, but it was only three months since the Grand Army had passed that way, and you know what that meant to a country. The Poles were our friends, it was true, but out of a hundred thousand men, only the Guard had waggons, and the rest had to live as best they might. It did not surprise me, therefore, to see no signs of cattle and no smoke from the silent houses. A weal had been left across the country where the great host had passed, and it was said that even the rats were starved wherever the Emperor had led his men.

By midday I had got as far as the village of Saalfeldt, but as I was on the direct road for Osterode, where the Emperor was wintering, and also for the main camp of the seven divisions of infantry, the highway was choked with carriages and carts. What with artillery caissons and waggons and couriers, and the ever-thickening stream of recruits and stragglers, it seemed to me that it would be a very long time before I should join my comrades. The plains, however, were five feet deep in snow, so there was nothing for it but to plod upon our way. It was with joy, therefore, that I found a second road which branched away from the other, trending through a fir-wood towards the north. There was a small auberge at the cross-roads, and a patrol of the Third Hussars of Conflans—the very regiment of which I was afterwards colonel—were mounting their horses at the door. On the steps stood their officer, a slight, pale young man, who looked more like a young priest from a seminary than a leader of the devil-may-care rascals before him.

"Good-day, sir," said he, seeing that I pulled up my horse.

"Good-day," I answered. "I am Lieutenant Etienne Gerard, of the Tenth."

I could see by his face that he had heard of me. Everybody had heard of me since my duel with the six fencing-masters. My manner, however, served to put him at his ease with me.

"I am Sub-Lieutenant Duroc, of the Third," said he.

"Newly joined?" I asked.

"Last week."

I had thought as much, from his white face and from the way in which he let his men lounge upon their horses. It was not so long, however, since I had learned myself what it was like when a schoolboy has to give orders to veteran troopers. It made me blush, I remember, to shout abrupt commands to men who had seen more battles than I had years, and it would have come more natural for me to say, "With your permission, we shall now wheel into line," or, "If you think it best, we shall trot." I did not think the less of the lad, therefore, when I observed that his men were somewhat out of hand, but I gave them a glance which stiffened them in their saddles.

"May I ask, monsieur, whether you are going by this northern road?" I asked.

"My orders are to patrol it as far as Arensdorf," said he.

"Then I will, with your permission, ride so far with you," said I. "It is very clear that the longer way will be the faster."

So it proved, for this road led away from the army into a country which was given over to Cossacks and marauders, and it was as bare as the other was crowded. Duroc and I rode

in front, with our six troopers clattering in the rear. He was a good boy, this Duroc, with his head full of the nonsense that they teach at St. Cyr, knowing more about Alexander and Pompey than how to mix a horse's fodder or care for a horse's feet. Still, he was, as I have said, a good boy, unspoiled as yet by the camp. It pleased me to hear him prattle away about his sister Marie and about his mother in Amiens. Presently we found ourselves at the village of Hayenau. Duroc rode up to the post-house and asked to see the master.

"Can you tell me," said he, "whether the man who calls himself the Baron Straubenthal lives in these parts?"

The postmaster shook his head, and we rode upon our way. I took no notice of this, but when, at the next village, my comrade repeated the same question, with the same result, I could not help asking him who this Baron Straubenthal might be.

"He is a man," said Duroc, with a sudden flush upon his boyish face, "to whom I have a very important message to convey."

Well, this was not satisfactory, but there was something in my companion's manner which told me that any further questioning would be distasteful to him. I said nothing more, therefore, but Duroc would still ask every peasant whom we met whether he could give him any news of the Baron Straubenthal.

For my own part I was endeavoring, as an officer of light cavalry should, to form an idea of the lay of the country, to note the course of the streams, and to mark the places where there should be fords. Every step was taking us farther from the camp round the flanks of which we were traveling. Far to the south a few plumes of grey smoke in the frosty air marked the position of some of our outposts. To the north, however, there was nothing between ourselves and the Russian winter quarters. Twice on the extreme horizon I caught a glimpse of the glitter of steel, and pointed it out to my companion. It was too distant for us to tell whence it came, but we had little doubt that it was from the lance-heads of marauding Cossacks.

The sun was just setting when we rode over a low hill and saw a small village upon our right, and on our left a high black castle, which jutted out from amongst the pine-woods.

A farmer with his cart was approaching us—a matted-haired, downcast fellow, in a sheepskin jacket.

"What village is this?" asked Duroc.

"It is Arensdorf," he answered, in his barbarous German dialect.

"Then here I am to stay the night," said my young companion. Then, turning to the farmer, he asked his eternal question, "Can you tell me where the Baron Straubenthal lives?"

"Why, it is he who owns the Castle of Gloom," said the farmer, pointing to the dark turrets over the distant fir forest.

Duroc gave a shout like the sportsman who sees his game rising in front of him. The lad seemed to have gone off his head—his eyes shining, his face deathly white, and such a grim set about his mouth as made the farmer shrink away from him. I can see him now, leaning forward on his brown horse, with his eager gaze fixed upon the great black tower.

"Why do you call it the Castle of Gloom?" I asked.

"Well, it's the name it bears upon the country-side," said the farmer. "By all accounts there have been some black doings up yonder. It's not for nothing that the wickedest man in Poland has been living there these fourteen years past."

"A Polish nobleman?" I asked.

"Nay, we breed no such men in Poland," he answered.

"A Frenchman, then?" cried Duroc.

"They say that he came from France."

"And with red hair?"

"As red as a fox."

"Yes, yes, it is my man," cried my companion, quivering all over in his excitement. "It is the hand of Providence which has led me here. Who can say that there is not justice in this world? Come, Monsieur Gerard, for I must see the men safely quartered before I can attend to this private matter."

He spurred on his horse, and ten minutes later we were at the door of the inn of Arensdorf, where his men were to find their quarters for the night.

Well, all this was no affair of mine, and I could not imagine what the meaning of it might be. Rossel was still far off, but I determined to ride on for a few hours and take my chance of some wayside barn in which I could find shelter for Rataplan and myself. I had mounted my horse, therefore, after tossing off a cup of wine, when young Duroc came running out of the door and laid his hand upon my knee.

"Monsieur Gerard," he panted, "I beg of you not to abandon me like this!"

"My good sir," said I, "if you would tell me what is the matter and what you would wish me to do, I should be better able to tell you if I could be of any assistance to you."

"You can be of the very greatest," he cried. "Indeed, from all that I have heard of you, Monsieur Gerard, you are the one man whom I should wish to have by my side tonight."

"You forget that I am riding to join my regiment."

"You cannot, in any case, reach it tonight. Tomorrow will bring you to Rossel. By staying with me you will confer the very greatest kindness upon me, and you will aid me in a matter which concerns my own honor and the honor of my family. I am compelled, however, to confess to you that some personal danger may possibly be involved."

It was a crafty thing for him to say. Of course, I sprang from Rataplan's back and ordered the groom to lead him back into the stables.

"Come into the inn," said I, "and let me know exactly what it is that you wish me to do."

He led the way into a sitting-room, and fastened the door lest we should be interrupted. He was a well-grown lad, and as he stood in the glare of the lamp, with the light beating upon his earnest face and upon his uniform of silver grey, which suited him to a marvel, I felt my heart warm towards him. Without going so far as to say that he carried himself as I had done at his age, there was at least similarity enough to make me feel in sympathy with him.

"I can explain it all in a few words," said he. "If I have not already satisfied your very natural curiosity, it is because the subject is so painful a one to me that I can hardly bring myself to allude to it. I cannot, however, ask for your assistance without explaining to you exactly how the matter lies.

"You must know, then, that my father was the well-known banker, Christophe Duroc, who was murdered by the people during the September massacres. As you are aware, the mob took possession of the prisons, chose three so-called judges to pass sentence upon the unhappy aristocrats, and then tore them to pieces when they were passed out into the street. My father had been a benefactor of the poor all his life. There were many to plead for him. He had the fever, too, and was carried in, half-dead, upon a blanket. Two of the judges were in favor of acquitting him; the third, a young Jacobin, whose huge body and brutal mind had made him a leader among these wretches, dragged him, with his own hands, from the litter, kicked him again and again with his heavy boots, and hurled him out of the door, where in an instant he was torn limb from limb under circumstances which are too horrible for me to describe. This, as you perceive, was murder, even under their own unlawful laws, for two of their own judges had pronounced in my father's favor.

"Well, when the days of order came back again, my elder brother began to make inquiries about this man. I was only a child then, but it was a family matter, and it was discussed in my presence. The fellow's name was Carabin. He was one of Sansterre's Guard, and a noted duelist. A foreign lady named the Baroness Straubenthal having been dragged before the Jacobins, he had gained her liberty for her on the promise that she with her money and estates should be his. He had married her, taken her name and title, and escaped out of France at the time of the fall of Robespierre. What had become of him we had no means of learning.

"You will think, doubtless, that it would be easy for us to find him, since we had both his name and his title. You must remember, however, that the Revolution left us without money, and that without money such a search is very difficult. Then came the Empire, and it became more difficult still, for, as you are aware, the Emperor considered that the 18th Brumaire brought all accounts to a settlement, and that on that day a veil had been drawn across the past. None the less, we kept our own family story and our own family plans.

"My brother joined the army, and passed with it through all Southern Europe, asking everywhere for the Baron Straubenthal. Last October he was killed at Jena, with his mission still unfulfilled. Then it became my turn, and I have the good fortune to hear of the very man of whom I am in search at one of the first Polish villages which I have to visit, and within a fortnight of joining my regiment. And then, to make the matter even better, I find myself in the company of one whose name is never mentioned throughout the army save in connection with some daring and generous deed."

This was all very well, and I listened to it with the greatest interest, but I was none the clearer as to what young Duroc wished me to do.

"How can I be of service to you?" I asked.

"By coming up with me."

"To the Castle?"

"Precisely."

"When?"

"At once."

"But what do you intend to do?"

"I shall know what to do. But I wish you to be with me, all the same."

Well, it was never in my nature to refuse an adventure, and, besides, I had every sympathy with the lad's feelings. It is very well to forgive one's enemies, but one wishes to give them something to forgive also. I held out my hand to him, therefore.

"I must be on my way for Rossel tomorrow morning, but tonight I am yours," said I.

We left our troopers in snug quarters, and, as it was but a mile to the Castle, we did not disturb our horses. To tell the truth, I hate to see a cavalry man walk, and I hold that just as he is the most gallant thing upon earth when he has his saddle-flaps between his knees, so he is the most clumsy when he has to loop up his sabre and his sabre-tache in one hand and turn in his toes for fear of catching the rowels of his spurs. Still, Duroc and I were of the age when one can carry things off, and I dare swear that no woman at least would have quarrelled with the appearance of the two young hussars, one in blue and one in grey, who set out that night from the Arensdorf post-house. We both carried our swords, and for my own part I slipped a pistol from my holster into the side of my pelisse, for it seemed to me that there might be some wild work before us.

The track which led to the Castle wound through a pitch-black fir-wood, where we could see nothing save the ragged patch of stars above our head. Presently, however, it opened up, and there was the Castle right in front of us, about as far as a carbine would carry. It was a huge, uncouth place, and bore every mark of being exceedingly old, with turrets at every corner, and a square keep on the side which was nearest to us. In all its great shadow there was no sign of light save from a single window, and no sound came from it. To me there was something awful in its size and its silence, which corresponded so well with its sinister name. My companion pressed on eagerly, and I followed him along the ill-kept path which led to the gate.

There was no bell or knocker upon the great iron-studded door, and it was only by pounding with the hilts of our sabres that we could attract attention. A thin, hawk-faced man, with a beard up to his temples, opened it at last. He carried a lantern in one hand, and in the other a chain which held an enormous black hound. His manner at the first moment was threatening, but the sight of our uniforms and of our faces turned it into one of sulky reserve.

"The Baron Straubenthal does not receive visitors at so late an hour," said he, speaking in very excellent French.

"You can inform Baron Straubenthal that I have come eight hundred leagues to see him, and that I will not leave until I have done so," said my companion. I could not myself have said it with a better voice and manner.

The fellow took a sidelong look at us and tugged at his black beard in his perplexity.

"To tell the truth, gentlemen," said he, "the Baron has a cup or two of wine in him at this hour, and you would certainly find him a more entertaining companion if you were to come again in the morning."

He had opened the door a little wider as he spoke, and I saw by the light of the lamp in the hall behind him that three other rough fellows were standing there, one of whom held another of these monstrous hounds. Duroc must have seen it also, but it made no difference to his resolution.

"Enough talk," said he, pushing the man to one side. "It is with your master that I have to deal."

The fellows in the hall made way for him as he strode in among them, so great is the power of one man who knows what he wants over several who are not sure of themselves. My companion tapped one of them upon the shoulder with as much assurance as though he owned him.

"Show me to the Baron," said he.

The man shrugged his shoulders, and answered something in Polish. The fellow with the beard, who had shut and barred the front door, appeared to be the only one among them who could speak French.

"Well, you shall have your way," said he, with a sinister

smile. "You shall see the Baron. And perhaps, before you have finished, you will wish that you had taken my advice."

We followed him down the hall, which was stone-flagged and very spacious, with skins scattered upon the floor, and the heads of wild beasts upon the walls. At the farther end he threw open a door, and we entered.

It was a small room, scantily furnished, with the same marks of neglect and decay which met us at every turn. The walls were hung with discolored tapestry, which had come loose at one corner, so as to expose the rough stonework behind. A second door, hung with a curtain, faced us upon the other side. Between lay a square table, strewn with dirty dishes and the sordid remains of a meal. Several bottles were scattered over it. At the head of it, and facing us, there sat a huge man with a lion-like head and a great shock of orange-colored hair. His beard was of the same glaring hue; matted and tangled and coarse as a horse's mane. I have seen some strange faces in my time, but never one more brutal than that, with its small, vicious, blue eyes, its white, crumpled cheeks, and the thick, hanging lip which protruded over his monstrous beard. His head swayed about on his shoulders, and he looked at us with the vague, dim gaze of a drunken man. Yet he was not so drunk but that our uniforms carried their message to him.

"Well, my brave boys," he hiccoughed. "What is the latest news from Paris, eh? You're going to free Poland, I hear, and have meantime all become slaves yourselves—slaves to a little aristocrat with his grey coat and his three-cornered hat. No more citizens either, I am told, and nothing but monsieur and madame. My faith, some more heads will have to roll into the sawdust basket some of these mornings."

Duroc advanced in silence, and stood by the ruffian's side.

"Jean Carabin," said he.

The Baron started, and the film of drunkenness seemed to be clearing from his eyes.

"Jean Carabin," said Duroc, once more.

He sat up and grasped the arms of his chair.

"What do you mean by repeating that name, young man?" he asked.

"Jean Carabin, you are a man whom I have long wished to meet."

"Supposing that I once had such a name, how can it concern you, since you must have been a child when I bore it?"

"My name is Duroc."

"Not the son of——?"

"The son of the man you murdered."

The Baron tried to laugh, but there was terror in his eyes.

"We must let bygones be bygones, young man," he cried. "It was our life or theirs in those days: the aristocrats or the people. Your father was of the Gironde. He fell. I was of the mountain. Most of my comrades fell. It was all the fortune of war. We must forget all this and learn to know each other better, you and I." He held out a red, twitching hand as he spoke.

"Enough," said young Duroc. "If I were to pass my sabre through you as you sit in that chair, I should do what is just and right. I dishonor my blade by crossing it with yours. And yet you are a Frenchman, and have even held a commission under the same flag as myself. Rise, then, and defend yourself!"

"Tut, tut!" cried the Baron. "It is all very well for you young bloods——"

Duroc's patience could stand no more. He swung his open hand into the center of the great orange beard. I saw a lip fringed with blood, and two glaring blue eyes above it.

"You shall die for that blow."

"That is better," said Duroc.

"My sabre!" cried the other. "I will not keep you waiting, I promise you!" and he hurried from the room.

I have said that there was a second door covered with a curtain. Hardly had the Baron vanished when there ran from behind it a woman, young and beautiful. So swiftly and noiselessly did she move that she was between us in an instant, and it was only the shaking curtains which told us whence she had come.

"I have seen it all," she cried. "Oh, sir, you have carried yourself splendidly." She stooped to my companion's hand, and kissed it again and again ere he could disengage it from her grasp.

"Nay, madame, why should you kiss my hand?" he cried.

"Because it is the hand which struck him on his vile, lying mouth. Because it may be the hand which will avenge my mother. I am his step-daughter. The woman whose heart he broke was my mother. I loathe him, I fear him. Ah, there is his step!" In an instant she had vanished as suddenly as she

had come. A moment later, the Baron entered with a drawn sword in his hand, and the fellow who had admitted us at his heels.

"This is my secretary," said he. "He will be my friend in this affair. But we shall need more elbow-room than we can find here. Perhaps you will kindly come with me to a more spacious apartment."

It was evidently impossible to fight in a chamber which was blocked by a great table. We followed him out, therefore, into the dimly-lit hall. At the farther end a light was shining through an open door.

"We shall find what we want in here," said the man with the dark beard. It was a large, empty room, with rows of barrels and cases round the walls. A strong lamp stood upon a shelf in the corner. The floor was level and true, so that no swordsman could ask for more. Duroc drew his sabre and sprang into it. The Baron stood back with a bow and motioned me to follow my companion. Hardly were my heels over the threshold when the heavy door crashed behind us and the key screamed in the lock. We were taken in a trap.

For a moment we could not realize it. Such incredible baseness was outside all our experiences. Then, as we understood how foolish we had been to trust for an instant a man with such a history, a flush of rage came over us, rage against his villainy and against our own stupidity. We rushed at the door together, beating it with our fists and kicking with our heavy boots. The sound of our blows and of our execrations must have resounded through the Castle. We called to this villain, hurling at him every name which might pierce even into his hardened soul. But the door was enormous—such a door as one finds in mediæval castles—made of huge beams clamped together with iron. It was as easy to break as a square of the Old Guard. And our cries appeared to be of as little avail as our blows, for they only brought for answer the clattering echoes from the high roof above us. When you have done some soldiering, you soon learn to put up with what cannot be altered. It was I, then, who first recovered my calmness, and prevailed upon Duroc to join with me in examining the apartment which had become our dungeon.

There was only one window, which had no glass in it, and was so narrow that one could not so much as get one's head through. It was high up, and Duroc had to stand upon a barrel in order to see from it.

"What can you see?" I asked.

"Fir-woods and an avenue of snow between them," said he. "Ah!" he gave a cry of surprise.

I sprang upon the barrel beside him. There was, as he said, a long, clear strip of snow in front. A man was riding down it, flogging his horse and galloping like a madman. As we watched, he grew smaller and smaller, until he was swallowed up by the black shadows of the forest.

"What does that mean?" asked Duroc.

"No good for us," said I. "He may have gone for some brigands to cut our throats. Let us see if we cannot find a way out of this mouse-trap before the cat can arrive."

The one piece of good fortune in our favor was that beautiful lamp. It was nearly full of oil, and would last us until morning. In the dark our situation would have been far more difficult. By its light we proceeded to examine the packages and cases which lined the walls. In some places there was only a single line of them, while in one corner they were piled nearly to the ceiling. It seemed that we were in the storehouse of the Castle, for there were a great number of cheeses, vegetables of various kinds, bins full of dried fruits, and a line of wine barrels. One of these had a spigot in it, and as I had eaten little during the day, I was glad of a cup of claret and some food. As to Duroc, he would take nothing, but paced up and down the room in a fever of anger and impatience. "I'll have him yet!" he cried, every now and then. "The rascal shall not escape me!"

This was all very well, but it seemed to me, as I sat on a great round cheese eating my supper, that this youngster was thinking rather too much of his own family affairs and too little of the fine scrape into which he had got me. After all, his father had been dead fourteen years, and nothing could set that right; but here was Etienne Gerard, the most dashing lieutenant in the whole Grand Army, in imminent danger of being cut off at the very outset of his brilliant career. Who was ever to know the heights to which I might have risen if I were knocked on the head in this hole-and-corner business, which had nothing whatever to do with France or the Emperor? I could not help thinking what a fool I had been, when

I had a fine war before me and everything which a man could desire, to go off on a hare-brained expedition of this sort, as if it were not enough to have a quarter of a million Russians to fight against, without plunging into all sorts of private quarrels as well.

"That is all very well," I said at last, as I heard Duroc muttering his threats. "You may do what you like to him when you get the upper hand. At present the question rather is, what is *he* going to do to us?"

"Let him do his worst!" cried the boy. "I owe a duty to my father."

"That is mere foolishness," said I. "If you owe a duty to your father, I owe one to my mother, which is to get out of this business safe and sound."

My remark brought him to his senses.

"I have thought too much of myself!" he cried. "Forgive me, Monsieur Gerard. Give me your advice as to what I should do."

"Well," said I, "it is not for our health that they have shut us up here among the cheeses. They mean to make an end of us if they can. That is certain. They hope that no one knows that we have come here, and that none will trace us if we remain. Do your hussars know where you have gone to?"

"I said nothing."

"Hum! It is clear that we cannot be starved here. They must come to us if they are to kill us. Behind a barricade of barrels we could hold our own against the five rascals whom we have seen. That is, probably, why they have sent that messenger for assistance."

"We must get out before he returns."

"Precisely, if we are to get out at all."

"Could we not burn down this door?" he cried.

"Nothing could be easier," said I. "There are several casks of oil in the corner. My only objection is that we should ourselves be nicely toasted, like two little oyster *pâtés*."

"Can you not suggest something?" he cried, in despair. "Ah, what is that?"

There had been a low sound at our little window, and a shadow came between the stars and ourselves. A small, white hand was stretched into the lamplight. Something glittered between the fingers.

"Quick! quick!" cried a woman's voice.

We were on the barrel in an instant.

"They have sent for the Cossacks. Your lives are at stake. Ah, I am lost! I am lost!"

There was the sound of rushing steps, a hoarse oath, a blow, and the stars were once more twinkling through the window. We stood helpless upon the barrel with our blood cold with horror. Half a minute afterward we heard a smothered scream, ending in a choke. A great door slammed somewhere in the silent night.

"Those ruffians have seized her. They will kill her," I cried.

Duroc sprang down with the inarticulate shouts of one whose reason has left him. He struck the door so frantically with his naked hands that he left a blotch of blood with every blow.

"Here is the key!" I shouted, picking one from the floor. "She must have thrown it in at the instant that she was torn away."

My companion snatched it from me with a shriek of joy. A moment later he dashed it down upon the boards. It was so small that it was lost in the enormous lock. Duroc sank upon one of the boxes with his head between his hands. He sobbed in his despair. I could have sobbed, too, when I thought of the woman and how helpless we were to save her.

But I am not easily baffled. After all, this key must have been sent to us for a purpose. The lady could not bring us that of the door, because this murderous stepfather of hers would most certainly have it in his pocket. Yet this other must have a meaning, or why should she risk her life to place it in our hands? It would say little for our wits if we could not find out what that meaning might be.

I set to work moving all the cases out from the wall, and Duroc, gaining new hope from my courage, helped me with all his strength. It was no light task, for many of them were large and heavy. On we went, working like maniacs, slinging barrels, cheeses, and boxes pell-mell into the middle of the room. At last there only remained one huge barrel of vodka, which stood in the corner. With our united strength we rolled it out, and there was a little low wooden door in the wainscot behind it. The key fitted, and with a cry of delight we saw it swing open before us. With the lamp in my hand, I squeezed my way in, followed by my companion.

We were in the powder-magazine of the Castle—a rough,

walled cellar, with barrels all around it, and one with the top staved in in the center. The powder from it lay in a black heap upon the floor. Beyond there was another door, but it was locked.

"We are no better off than before," cried Duroc. "We have no key."

"We have a dozen!" I cried.

"Where?"

I pointed to the line of powder barrels.

"You would blow this door open?"

"Precisely."

"But you would explode the magazine."

It was true, but I was not at the end of my resources.

"We will blow open the store-room door," I cried.

I ran back and seized a tin box which had been filled with candles. It was about the size of my busby—large enough to hold several pounds of powder. Duroc filled it while I cut off the end of a candle. When we had finished it, it would have puzzled a colonel of engineers to make a better petard. I put three cheeses on the top of each other and placed it above them, so as to lean against the lock. Then we lit our candle-end and ran for shelter, shutting the door of the magazine behind us.

It is no joke, my friends, to be among all those tons of powder, with the knowledge that if the flame of the explosion should penetrate through one thin door our blackened limbs would be shot higher than the Castle keep. Who could have believed that a half-inch of candle could take so long to burn? My ears were straining all the time for the thudding of the hoofs of the Cossacks who were coming to destroy us. I had almost made up my mind that the candle must have gone out when there was a smack like a bursting bomb, our door flew to bits, and pieces of cheese, with a shower of turnips, apples, and splinters of cases, were shot in among us. As we rushed out we had to stagger through an impenetrable smoke, with all sorts of débris beneath our feet, but there was a glimmering square where the dark door had been. The petard had done its work.

In fact, it had done more for us than we had even ventured to hope. It had shattered gaolers as well as gaol. The first thing that I saw as I came out into the hall was a man with a butcher's axe in his hand, lying flat upon his back, with a gaping wound across his forehead. The second was a huge dog, with two of its legs broken, twisting in agony upon the floor. As it raised itself up I saw the two broken ends flapping like flails. At the same instant I heard a cry, and there was Duroc, thrown against the wall, with the other hound's teeth in his throat. He pushed it off with his left hand, while again and again he passed his sabre through its body, but it was not until I blew out its brains with my pistol that the iron jaws relaxed, and the fierce, bloodshot eyes were glazed in death.

There was no time for us to pause. A woman's scream from in front—a scream of mortal terror—told us that even now we might be too late. There were two other men in the hall, but they cowered away from our drawn swords and furious faces. The blood was streaming from Duroc's neck and dyeing the grey fur of his pelisse. Such was the lad's fire, however, that he shot in front of me, and it was only over his shoulder that I caught a glimpse of the scene as we rushed into the chamber in which we had first seen the master of the Castle of Gloom.

The Baron was standing in the middle of the room, with his tangled mane bristling like an angry lion. He was, as I have said, a huge man with enormous shoulders; and as he stood there, with his face flushed with rage and his sword advanced, I could not but think that, in spite of all his villainies, he had a proper figure for a grenadier. The lady lay cowering in a chair behind him. A weal across one of her white arms and a dog-whip upon the floor were enough to show that our escape had hardly been in time to save her from his brutality. He gave a howl like a wolf as we broke in, and was upon us in an instant, hacking and driving, with a curse at every blow.

I have already said that the room gave no space for swordsmanship. My young companion was in front of me in the narrow passage between the table and the wall, so that I could only look on without being able to aid him. The lad knew something of his weapon, and was as fierce and active as a wildcat, but in so narrow a space the weight and strength of the giant gave him the advantage. Besides, he was an admirable swordsman. His parade and riposte were as quick as lightning. Twice he touched Duroc upon the shoulder, and then, as the lad slipped on a lunge, he whirled up his sword to finish him before he could recover his feet. I was quicker than he, however, and took the cut upon the pommel of my sabre.

"Excuse me," said I, "but you have still to deal with Etienne Gerard."

He drew back and leaned against the tapestry-covered wall, breathing in little, hoarse gasps, for his foul living was against him.

"Take your breath," said I. "I will await your convenience."

"You have no cause of quarrel against me," he panted.

"I owe you some little attention," said I, "for having shut me up in your store-room. Besides, if all other were wanting, I see cause enough upon that lady's arm."

"Have your way, then!" he snarled, and leaped at me like a madman. For a minute I saw only the blazing blue eyes, and the red-glazed point which stabbed and stabbed, rasping off to right or to left, and yet ever back at my throat and my breast. I had never thought that such good sword-play was to be found at Paris in the days of the Revolution. I do not suppose that in all my little affairs I have met six men who had a better knowledge of their weapon. But he knew that I was his master. He read death in my eyes, and I could see that he read it. The flush died from his face. His breath came in shorter and in thicker gasps. Yet he fought on, even after the final thrust had come, and died still hacking and cursing, with foul cries upon his lips, and his blood clotting upon his orange beard. I, who speak to you, have seen so màny battles, that my old memory can scarce contain their names, and·yet of all the terrible sights which these eyes have rested upon, there is none which I care to think of less than of that orange beard with the crimson stain in the center, from which I had drawn my sword-point.

It was only afterward that I had time to think of all this. His monstrous body had hardly crashed down upon the floor before the woman in the corner sprang to her feet, clapping her hands together and screaming out in her delight. For my part I was disgusted to see a woman take such delight in a deed of blood, and I gave no thought as to the terrible wrongs which must have befallen her before she could so far forget the gentleness of her sex. It was on my tongue to tell her sharply to be silent, when a strange, choking smell took the

breath from my nostrils, and a sudden yellow glare brought out the figures upon the faded hangings.

"Duroc, Duroc!" I shouted, tugging at his shoulder. "The Castle is on fire!"

The boy lay senseless upon the ground, exhausted by his wounds. I rushed out into the hall to see whence the danger came. It was our explosion which had set alight the dry framework of the door. Inside the store-room some of the boxes were already blazing. I glanced in, and as I did so my blood was turned to water by the sight of the powder barrels beyond, and of the loose heap upon the floor. It might be seconds, it could not be more than minutes, before the flames would be at the edge of it. These eyes will be closed in death, my friends, before they cease to see those crawling lines of fire and the black heap beyond.

How little I can remember what followed. Vaguely I can recall how I rushed into the chamber of death, how I seized Duroc by one limp hand and dragged him down the hall, the woman keeping pace with me and pulling at the other arm. Out of the gateway we rushed, and on down the snow-covered path until we were on the fringe of the fir forest. It was at that moment that I heard a crash behind me, and glancing round, saw a great spout of fire shoot up into the wintry sky. An instant later there seemed to come a second crash, far louder than the first. I saw the fir trees and the stars whirling round me, and I fell unconscious across the body of my comrade.

It was some weeks before I came to myself in the post-house of Arensdorf, and longer still before I could be told all that had befallen me. It was Duroc, already able to go soldiering, who came to my bedside and gave me an account of it. He it was who told me how a piece of timber had struck me on the head and laid me almost dead upon the ground. From him, too, I learned how the Polish girl had run to Arensdorf, how she had roused our hussars, and how she had only just brought them back in time to save us from the spears of the Cossacks who had been summoned from their bivouac by that same black-bearded secretary whom we had seen galloping so swiftly over the snow. As to the brave lady who had twice saved our lives, I could not learn very much about her at that moment from Duroc, but when I chanced to meet him in Paris two years later, after the campaign of Wagram, I was not very much surprised to find that I needed no introduction to his bride, and that by the queer turns of fortune he had himself, had he chosen to use it, that very name and title of the Baron Straubenthal, which showed him to be the owner of the blackened ruins of the Castle of Gloom.

1807

II. *How the Brigadier Slew the Brothers of Ajaccio*

WHEN the Emperor needed an agent he was always very ready to do me the honor of recalling the name of Etienne Gerard, though it occasionally escaped him when rewards were to be distributed. Still, I was a colonel at twenty-eight, and the chief of a brigade at thirty-one, so that I have no reason to be dissatisfied with my career. Had the wars lasted another two or three years I might have grasped my bâton, and the man who had his hand upon that was only one stride from a throne. Murat had changed his hussar's cap for a crown, and another light cavalry man might have done as much. However, all those dreams were driven away by Waterloo, and, although I was not able to write my name upon history, it is sufficiently well known by all who served with me in the great wars of the Empire.

What I want to tell you tonight is about the very singular affair which first started me upon my rapid upward course, and which had the effect of establishing a secret bond between the Emperor and myself.

There is just one little word of warning which I must give you before I begin. When you hear me speak, you must always bear in mind that you are listening to one who has seen history from the inside. I am talking about what my ears have heard and my eyes have seen, so you must not try to confute me by quoting the opinions of some student or man of the pen, who has written a book of history or memoirs. There is much which is unknown by such people, and much which never will be known by the world. For my own part, I could 23 tell you some very surprising things were it discreet to do so. The facts which I am about to relate to you tonight were kept secret by me during the Emperor's lifetime, because I gave him my promise that it should be so, but I do not think that there can be any harm now in my telling the remarkable part which I played.

You must know, then, that at the time of the Treaty of Tilsit I was a simple lieutenant in the Tenth Hussars, without money or interest. It is true that my appearance and my gallantry were in my favor, and that I had already won a reputation as being one of the best swordsmen in the army; but among the host of brave men who surrounded the Emperor it needed more than this to insure a rapid career. I was confident, however, that my chance would come, though I never dreamed that it would take so remarkable a form.

When the Emperor returned to Paris, after the declaration of peace in the year 1807, he spent much of his time with the Empress and the Court at Fontainebleau. It was the time when he was at the pinnacle of his career. He had in three successive campaigns humbled Austria, crushed Prussia, and made the Russians very glad to get upon the right side of the Niemen. The old Bulldog over the Channel was still growling, but he could not get very far from his kennel. If we could have made a perpetual peace at that moment, France would have taken a higher place than any nation since the days of the Romans. So I have heard the wise folk say, though for my part I had other things to think of. All the girls were glad to see the army back after its long absence, and you may be sure that I had my share of any favors that were going. You may judge how far I was a favorite in those days when I say that even now, in my sixtieth year—but why should I dwell upon that which is already sufficiently well known?

Our regiment of hussars was quartered with the horse chasseurs of the guard at Fontainebleau. It is, as you know, but a little place, buried in the heart of the forest, and it was wonderful at this time to see it crowded with Grand Dukes and Electors and Princes, who thronged round Napoleon like puppies round their master, each hoping that some bone might be thrown to him. There was more German than French to be heard in the street, for those who had helped us in the later war had come to beg for a reward, and those who had opposed us had come to try and escape their punishment.

And all the time our little man, with his pale face and his cold, grey eyes, was riding to the hunt every morning, silent and brooding, all of them following in his train, in the hope that some word would escape him. And then, when the humor seized him, he would throw a hundred square miles to that man or tear as much off the other, round off one kingdom by a river, or cut off another by a chain of mountains. That was how he used to do business, this little artilleryman, whom we had raised so high with our sabres and our bayonets. He was very civil to us always, for he knew where his power came from. We knew also, and showed it by the way in which we carried ourselves. We were agreed, you understand, that he was the finest leader in the world, but we did not forget that he had the finest men to lead.

Well, one day I was seated in my quarters playing cards with young Morat, of the horse chasseurs, when the door opened and in walked Lasalle, who was our Colonel. You know what a fine, swaggering fellow he was, and the sky-blue uniform of the Tenth suited him to a marvel. My faith, we youngsters were so taken by him that we all swore and diced and drank and played the deuce whether we like it or no, just that we might resemble our Colonel! We forgot that it was not because he drank or gambled that the Emperor was going to make him the head of the light cavalry, but because he had the surest eye for the nature of a position or for the strength of a column, and the best judgment as to when infantry could be broken, or whether guns were exposed, of any man in the army. We were too young to understand all that, however, so we waxed our moustaches and clinked our spurs and let the ferrules of our scabbards wear out by trailing them along the pavement in the hope that we should all become Lasalles. When he came clanking into my quarters, both Morat and I sprang to our feet.

"My boy," said he, clapping me on the shoulder, "the Emperor wants to see you at four o'clock."

The room whirled round me at the words, and I had to lean my hands upon the edge of the cardtable.

"What?" I cried. "The Emperor!"

"Precisely," said he, smiling at my astonishment.

"But the Emperor does not know of my existence, Colonel," I protested. "Why should he send for me?"

"Well, that's just what puzzles me," cried Lasalle, twirling

his moustache. "If he wanted the help of a good sabre, why should he descend to one of my lieutenants when he might have found all that he needed at the head of the regiment? However," he added, clapping me on the shoulder again in his hearty fashion, "every man has his chance. I have had mine, otherwise I should not be Colonel of the Tenth. I must not grudge you yours. Forwards, my boy, and may it be the first step towards changing your busby for a cocked hat."

It was but two o'clock, so he left me, promising to come back to accompany me to the palace. My faith, what a time I passed, and how many conjectures did I make as to what it was that the Emperor could want of me! I paced up and down my little room in a fever of anticipation. Sometimes I thought that perhaps he had heard of the guns which we had taken at Austerlitz; but, then, there were so many who had taken guns at Austerlitz, and two years had passed since the battle. Or it might be that he wished to reward me for my affair with the *aide-de-camp* of the Russian Emperor. But then again a cold fit would seize me, and I would fancy that he had sent for me to reprimand me. There were a few duels which he might have taken in ill part, and there were one or two little jokes in Paris since the peace.

But, no! I considered the words of Lasalle. "If he had need of a brave man," said Lasalle.

It was obvious that my Colonel had some idea of what was in the wind. If he had not known that it was to my advantage, he would not have been so cruel as to congratulate me. My heart glowed with joy as this conviction grew upon me, and I sat down to write to my mother and to tell her that the Emperor was waiting, at that very moment, to have my opinion upon a matter of importance. It made me smile as I wrote it to think that, wonderful as it appeared to me, it would probably only confirm my mother in her opinion of the Emperor's good sense.

At half-past three I heard a sabre come clanking against every step of my wooden stair. It was Lasalle, and with him was a lame gentleman, very neatly dressed in black with dapper ruffles and cuffs. We did not know many civilians, we of the army, but, my word, this was one whom we could not afford to ignore! I had only to glance at those twinkling eyes, the comical, upturned nose, and the straight, precise mouth, to know that I was in the presence of the one man in France whom even the Emperor had to consider.

"This is Monsieur Etienne Gerard, Monsieur de Talleyrand," said Lasalle.

I saluted, and the statesman took me in from the top of my panache to the rowel of my spur, with a glance that played over me like a rapier point.

"Have you explained to the lieutenant the circumstances under which he is summoned to the Emperor's presence?" he asked, in his dry, creaking voice.

They were such a contrast, these two men, that I could not help glancing from one to the other of them: the black, sly politician, and the big, sky-blue hussar with one fist on his hip and the other on the hilt of his sabre. They both took their seats as I looked, Talleyrand without a sound, and Lasalle with a clash and a jingle like a prancing charger.

"It's this way, youngster," said he, in his brusque fashion: "I was with the Emperor in his private cabinet this morning when a note was brought in to him. He opened it, and as he did so he gave such a start that it fluttered down on to the floor. I handed it up to him again, but he was staring at the wall in front of him as if he had seen a ghost. 'Fratelli dell' Ajaccio,' he muttered; and then again, 'Fratelli dell' Ajaccio.' I don't pretend to know more Italian than a man can pick up in two campaigns, and I could make nothing of this. It seemed to me that he had gone out of his mind; and you would have said so also, Monsieur de Talleyrand, if you had seen the look in his eyes. He read the note, and then he sat for half an hour or more without moving."

"And you?" asked Talleyrand.

"Why, I stood there not knowing what I ought to do. Presently he seemed to come back to his senses.

" 'I suppose, Lasalle,' said he, 'that you have some gallant young officers in the Tenth?'

" 'They are all that, sire,' I answered.

" 'If you had to pick one who was to be depended upon for action, but who would not think too much—you understand me, Lasalle—which would you select?' he asked.

" 'I have one,' said I, 'who is all spurs and moustaches, with never a thought beyond women and horses.'

" 'That is the man I want,' said Napoleon. 'Bring him to my private cabinet at four o'clock.'

"So, youngster, I came straight away to you at once, and mind that you do credit to the Tenth Hussars."

I was by no means flattered by the reasons which had led

to my Colonel's choice, and I must have shown as much in my face, for he roared with laughter and Talleyrand gave a dry chuckle also.

"Just one word of advice before you go, Monsieur Gerard," said he: "you are now coming into troubled waters, and you might find a worse pilot than myself. We have none of us any idea as to what this little affair means, and, between ourselves, it is very important for us, who have the destinies of France upon our shoulders, to keep ourselves in touch with all that goes on. You understand me, Monsieur Gerard?"

I had not the least idea what he was driving at, but I bowed and tried to look as if it was clear to me.

"Act very guardedly, then, and say nothing to anybody," said Talleyrand. "Colonel de Lasalle and I will not show ourselves in public with you, but we will await you here, and we will give you our advice when you have told us what has passed between the Emperor and yourself. It is time that you started now, for the Emperor never forgives unpunctuality."

Off I went on foot to the palace, which was only a hundred paces off. I made my way to the antechamber, where Duroc, with his grand new scarlet and gold coat, was fussing about among the crowd of people who were waiting. I heard him whisper to Monsieur de Caulaincourt that half of them were German Dukes who expected to be made Kings, and the other half German Dukes who expected to be made paupers. Duroc, when he heard my name, showed me straight in, and I found myself in the Emperor's presence.

I had, of course, seen him in camp a hundred times, but I had never been face to face with him before. I have no doubt that if you had met him without knowing in the least who he was, you would simply have said that he was a sallow little fellow with a good forehead and fairly well-turned calves. His tight white cashmere breeches and white stockings showed off his legs to advantage. But even a stranger must have been struck by the singular look of his eyes, which could harden into an expression which would frighten a grenadier. It is said that even Augereau, who was a man who had never known what fear was, quailed before Napoleon's gaze, at a time, too, when the Emperor was but an unknown soldier. He looked mildly enough at me, however, and motioned me to remain by the door. De Meneval was writing to his dictation, looking up at him between each sentence with his spaniel eyes.

"That will do. You can go," said the Emperor, abruptly.
Then, when the secretary had left the room, he strode across
with his hands behind his back, and he looked me up and
down without a word. Though he was a small man himself,
he was very fond of having fine-looking fellows about him,
and so I think that my appearance gave him pleasure. For my
own part, I raised one hand to the salute and held the other
upon the hilt of my sabre, looking straight ahead of me, as a
soldier should.

"Well, Monsieur Gerard," said he, at last, tapping his forefinger upon one of the Brandenburgs of gold braid upon the
front of my pelisse, "I am informed that you are a very deserv-
ing young officer. Your Colonel gives me an excellent account
of you."

I wished to make a brilliant reply, but I could think of nothing save Lasalle's phrase that I was all spurs and moustaches,
so it ended in my saying nothing at all. The Emperor watched
the struggle which must have shown itself upon my features,
and when, finally, no answer came he did not appear to be
displeased.

"I believe that you are the very man that I want," said he.
"Brave and clever men surround me upon every side. But a
brave man who——" He did not finish his sentence, and for
my own part I could not understand what he was driving at.
I contented myself with assuring him that he could count
upon me to the death.

"You are, as I understand, a good swordsman?" said he.

"Tolerable, sire," I answered.

"You were chosen by your regiment to fight the champion of the Hussars of Chambarant?" said he.

I was not sorry to find that he knew so much of my exploits.

"My comrades, sire, did me that honor," said I.

"And for the sake of practice you insulted six fencing
masters in the week before your duel?"

"I had the privilege of being out seven times in as many
days, sire," said I.

"And escaped without a scratch?"

"The fencing master of the 23rd Light Infantry touched
me on the left elbow, sire."

"Let us have no more child's play of the sort, monsieur,"
he cried, turning suddenly to that cold rage of his which was
so appalling. "Do you imagine that I place veteran soldiers in

these positions that you may practice quarte and tierce upon them? How am I to face Europe if my soldiers turn their points upon each other? Another word of your duellings, and I break you between these fingers."

I saw his plump white hands flash before my eyes as he spoke, and his voice had turned to the most discordant hissing and growling. My word, my skin pringled all over as I listened to him, and I would gladly have changed my position for that of the first man in the steepest and narrowest breach that ever swallowed up a storming party. He turned to the table, drank off a cup of coffee, and then when he faced me again every trace of this storm had vanished, and he wore that singular smile which came from his lips but never from his eyes.

"I have need of your services, Monsieur Gerard," said he. "I may be safer with a good sword at my side, and there are reasons why yours should be the one which I select. But first of all I must bind you to secrecy. Whilst I live what passes between us today must be known to none but ourselves."

I thought of Talleyrand and of Lasalle, but I promised.

"In the next place, I do not want your opinions or conjectures, and I wish you to do exactly what you are told."

I bowed.

"It is your sword that I need, and not your brains. I will do the thinking. Is that clear to you?"

"Yes, sire."

"You know the Chancellor's Grove, in the forest?"

I bowed.

"You know also the large double fir-tree where the hounds assembled on Tuesday?"

Had he known that I met a girl under it three times a week, he would not have asked me. I bowed once more without remark.

"Very good. You will meet me there at ten o'clock tonight."

I had got past being surprised at anything which might happen. If he had asked me to take his place upon the Imperial throne I could only have nodded my busby.

"We shall then proceed into the wood together," said the Emperor. "You will be armed with a sword, but not with pistols. You must address no remark to me, and I shall say nothing to you. We will advance in silence. You understand?"

"I understand, sire."

"After a time we shall see a man, or more probably two men, under a certain tree. We shall approach them together. If I signal to you to defend me, you will have your sword ready. If, on the other hand, I speak to these men, you will wait and see what happens. If you are called upon to draw, you must see that neither of them, in the event of there being two, escapes from us. I shall myself assist you."

"Sire," I cried, "I have no doubt that two would not be too many for my sword; but would it not be better that I should bring a comrade than that you should be forced to join in such a struggle?"

"Ta, ta, ta," said he. "I was a soldier before I was an Emperor. Do you think, then, that artillerymen have not swords as well as the hussars? But I ordered you not to argue with me. You will do exactly what I tell you. If swords are once out, neither of these men is to get away alive."

"They shall not, sire," said I.

"Very good. I have no more instructions for you. You can go."

I turned to the door, and then an idea occurring to me I turned.

"I have been thinking, sire——" said I.

He sprang at me with the ferocity of a wild beast. I really thought he would have struck me.

"Thinking!" he cried. "You, *you!* Do you imagine I chose you out because you could think? Let me hear of your doing such a thing again! You, the one man—but, there! You meet me at the fir-tree at ten o'clock."

My faith, I was right glad to get out of the room. If I have a good horse under me, and a sword clanking against my stirrup-iron, I know where I am. And in all that relates to green fodder or dry, barley and oats and rye, and the handling of squadrons upon the march, there is no one who can teach me very much. But when I meet a Chamberlain and a Marshal of the Palace, and have to pick my words with an Emperor, and find that everybody hints instead of talking straight out, I feel like a troop-horse who has been put in a lady's *calèche*. It is not my trade, all this mincing and pretending. I have learned the manners of a gentleman, but never those of a courtier. I was right glad then to get into the fresh air again, and I ran away up to my quarters like a schoolboy who has just escaped from the seminary master.

But as I opened the door, the very first thing that my eye rested upon was a long pair of sky-blue legs with hussar boots, and a short pair of black ones with knee breeches and buckles. They both sprang up together to greet me.

"Well, what news?" they cried, the two of them.

"None," I answered.

"The Emperor refused to see you?"

"No, I have seen him."

"And what did he say?"

"Monsieur de Talleyrand," I answered, "I regret to say that it is quite impossible for me to tell you anything about it. I have promised the Emperor."

"Pooh, pooh, my dear young man," said he, sidling up to me, as a cat does when it is about to rub itself against you. "This is all among friends, you understand, and goes no farther than these four walls. Besides, the Emperor never meant to include me in this promise."

"It is but a minute's walk to the palace, Monsieur de Talleyrand," I answered; "if it would not be troubling you too much to ask you to step up to it and bring back the Emperor's written statement that he did not mean to include you in this promise, I shall be happy to tell you every word that passed."

He showed his teeth to me then like the old fox that he was.

"Monsieur Gerard appears to be a little puffed up," said he. "He is too young to see things in their just proportion. As he grows older he may understand that it is not always very discreet for a subaltern of cavalry to give such very abrupt refusals."

I did not know what to say to this, but Lasalle came to my aid in his downright fashion.

"The lad is quite right," said he. "If I had known that there was a promise I should not have questioned him. You know very well, Monsieur de Talleyrand, that if he had answered you, you would have laughed in your sleeve and thought as much about him as I think of the bottle when the burgundy is gone. As for me, I promise you that the Tenth would have had no room for him, and that we should have lost our best swordsman if I had heard him give up the Emperor's secret."

But the statesman became only the more bitter when he saw that I had the support of my Colonel.

"I have heard, Colonel de Lasalle," said he, with an icy dignity, "that your opinion is of great weight upon the subject of light cavalry. Should I have occasion to seek information about that branch of the army, I shall be very happy to apply to you. At present, however, the matter concerns diplomacy, and you will permit me to form my own views upon that question. As long as the welfare of France and safety of the Emperor's person are largely committed to my care, I will use every means in my power to secure them, even if it should be against the Emperor's own temporary wishes. I have the honor, Colonel de Lasalle, to wish you a very good day!"

He shot a most unamiable glance in my direction, and, turning upon his heel, he walked with little, quick, noiseless steps out of the room.

I could see from Lasalle's face that he did not at all relish finding himself at enmity with the powerful Minister. He rapped out an oath or two, and then, catching up his sabre and his cap, he clattered away down the stairs. As I looked out of the window I saw the two of them, the big blue man and the limping black one, going up the street together. Talleyrand was walking very rigidly, and Lasalle was waving his hands and talking, so I suppose he was trying to make his peace.

The Emperor had told me not to think, and I endeavored to obey him. I took up the cards from the table where Morat had left them, and I tried to work out a few combinations at écarte. But I could not remember which were trumps, and I threw them under the table in despair. Then I drew my sabre and practiced giving point until I was weary, but it was all of no use at all. My mind *would* work, in spite of myself. At ten o'clock I was to meet the Emperor in the forest. Of all extraordinary combinations of events in the whole world, surely this was the last which would have occurred to me when I rose from my couch that morning. But the responsibility—the dreadful responsibility! It was all upon my shoulders. There was no one to halve it with me. It made me cold all over. Often as I have faced death upon the battlefield, I have never known what real fear was until that moment. But then I considered that after all I could but do my best like a brave and honorable gentleman, and above all obey the orders which I had received, to the very letter. And, if all went well, this would surely be the foundation of my fortunes. Thus, swaying between my fears and my hopes, I spent the long, long evening until it was time to keep my appointment.

I put on my military overcoat, as I did not know how much of the night I might have to spend in the woods, and I fastened my sword outside it. I pulled off my hussar boots also, and wore a pair of shoes and gaiters, that I might be lighter upon my feet. Then I stole out of my quarters and made for the forest, feeling very much easier in my mind, for I am always at my best when the time of thought has passed and the moment for action arrived.

I passed the barracks of the Chasseurs of the Guards, and the line of cafés all filled with uniforms. I caught a glimpse as I went by of the blue and gold of some of my comrades, amid the swarm of dark infantry coats and the light green of the Guides. There they sat, sipping their wine and smoking their cigars, little dreaming what their comrade had on hand. One of them, the chief of my squadron, caught sight of me in the lamplight, and came shouting after me into the street. I hurried on, however, pretending not to hear him, so he, with a curse at my deafness, went back at last to his wine bottle.

It is not very hard to get into the forest at Fontainebleau. The scattered trees steal their way into the very streets, like the tirailleurs in front of a column. I turned into a path, which led to the edge of the woods, and then I pushed rapidly forward towards the old fir-tree. It was a place which, as I have hinted, I had my own reasons for knowing well, and I could only thank the Fates that it was not one of the nights upon which Léonie would be waiting for me. The poor child would have died of terror at the sight of the Emperor. He might have been too harsh with her—and worse still, he might have been too kind.

There was a half moon shining, and, as I came up to our trysting-place, I saw that I was not the first to arrive. The Emperor was pacing up and down, his hands behind him and his face sunk somewhat forward upon his breast. He wore a grey great-coat with a capote over his head. I had seen him in such a dress in our winter campaign in Poland, and it was said that he used it because the hood was such an excellent disguise. He was always fond, whether in the camp or in Paris, of walking round at night, and overhearing the talk in the cabarets or round the fires. His figure, however, and his way of carrying his head and his hands were so well known that he was always recognized, and then the talkers would say whatever they thought would please him best.

My first thought was that he would be angry with me for having kept him waiting, but as I approached him, we heard the big church clock of Fontainebleau clang out the hour of ten. It was evident, therefore, that it was he who was too soon, and not I too late. I remembered his order that I should make no remark, so contented myself with halting within four paces of him, clicking my spurs together, grounding my sabre, and saluting. He glanced at me, and then without a word he turned and walked slowly through the forest, I keeping always about the same distance behind him. Once or twice he seemed to me to look apprehensively to right and to left, as if he feared that someone was observing us. I looked also, but although I have the keenest sight, it was quite impossible to see anything except the ragged patches of moonshine between the great black shadows of the trees. My ears are as quick as my eyes, and once or twice I thought that I heard a twig crack; but you know how many sounds there are in a forest at night, and how difficult it is even to say what direction they come from.

We walked for rather more than a mile, and I knew exactly what our destination was, long before we got there. In the center of one of the glades, there is the shattered stump of what must at some time have been a most gigantic tree. It is called the Abbott's Beech, and there are so many ghostly stories about it that I know many a brave soldier who would not care about mounting sentinel over it. However, I cared as little for such folly as the Emperor did, so we crossed the glade and made straight for the old broken trunk. As we approached, I saw that two men were waiting for us beneath it.

When I first caught sight of them they were standing rather behind it, as if they were not anxious to be seen, but as we came nearer they emerged from its shadow and walked forward to meet us. The Emperor glanced back at me, and slackened his pace a little so that I came within arm's length of him. You may think that I had my hilt well to the front, and that I had a very good look at these two people who were approaching us.

The one was tall, remarkably so, and of very spare frame, while the other was rather below the usual height, and had a brisk, determined way of walking. They each wore black cloaks, which were slung right across their figures, and hung down upon one side, like the mantles of Murat's dragoons. They had flat black caps, like those I have since seen in Spain, which threw their faces into darkness, though I could see the gleam of their eyes from beneath them. With the moon behind them and their long black shadows walking in front, they were such figures as one might expect to meet at night near the Abbot's Beech. I can remember that they had a stealthy way of moving, and that as they approached, a moonshine formed two white diamonds between their legs and the legs of their shadows.

The Emperor had paused, and these two strangers came to a stand also within a few paces of us. I had drawn up close to my companion's elbow, so that the four of us were facing each other without a word spoken. My eyes were particularly fixed upon the taller one, because he was slightly the nearer to me, and I became certain as I watched him that he was in the last state of nervousness. His lean figure was quivering all over, and I heard a quick, thin panting like that of a tired dog. Suddenly one of them gave a short, hissing signal. The tall man bent his back and his knees like a diver about to spring, but before he could move, I had jumped with drawn sabre in front of him. At the same instant the smaller man bounded past me, and buried a long poniard in the Emperor's heart.

My God! the horror of that moment! It is a marvel that I did not drop dead myself. As in a dream, I saw the grey coat whirl convulsively round, and caught a glimpse in the moonlight of three inches of red point which jutted out from between the shoulders. Then down he fell with a dead man's gasp upon the grass, and the assassin, leaving his weapon buried in his victim, threw up both his hands and shrieked with joy. But I—I drove my sword through his midriff with such frantic force, that the mere blow of the hilt against the end of his breast-bone sent him six paces before he fell, and left my reeking blade ready for the other. I sprang round upon him with such a lust for blood upon me as I had never felt, and never have felt, in all my days. As I turned, a dagger flashed before my eyes, and I felt the cold wind of it pass my neck and the villain's wrist jar upon my shoulder. I shortened my sword, but he winced away from me, and an instant afterwards was in full flight, bounding like a deer across the glade in the moonlight.

But he was not to escape me thus. I knew that the murderer's poniard had done its work. Young as I was, I had seen enough of war to know a mortal blow. I paused but for an instant to touch the cold hand.

"Sire! Sire!" I cried, in an agony; and then as no sound came back and nothing moved, save an ever-widening dark circle in the moonlight, I knew that all was indeed over. I sprang madly to my feet, threw off my great-coat, and ran at the top of my speed after the remaining assassin.

Ah, how I blessed the wisdom which had caused me to come in shoes and gaiters! And the happy thought which had thrown off my coat. He could not get rid of his mantle, this wretch, or else he was too frightened to think of it. So it was that I gained upon him from the beginning. He must have been out of his wits, for he never tried to bury himself in the darker parts of the woods, but he flew on from glade to glade, until he came to the heath-land which leads up to the great Fontainebleau quarry. There I had him in full sight, and knew that he could not escape me. He ran well, it is true—ran as a coward runs when his life is the stake. But I ran as Destiny runs when it gets behind a man's heels. Yard by yard I drew in upon him. He was rolling and staggering. I could hear the rasping and crackling of his breath. The great gulf of the quarry suddenly yawned in front of his path, and glancing at me over his shoulder, he gave a shriek of despair. The next instant he had vanished from my sight.

Vanished utterly, you understand. I rushed to the spot, and gazed down into the black abyss. Had he hurled himself over? I had almost made up my mind that he had done so, when a gentle sound rising and falling came out of the darkness beneath me. It was his breathing once more, and it showed me where he must be. He was hiding in the tool-house.

At the edge of the quarry and beneath the summit there is a small platform upon which stands a wooden hut for the use of the laborers. It was into this, then, that he had darted. Perhaps he had thought, the fool, that, in the darkness, I would not venture to follow him. He little knew Etienne Gerard. With a spring I was on the platform, with another I was through the doorway, and then, hearing him in the corner, I hurled myself down upon the top of him.

He fought like a wildcat, but he never had a chance with

his shorter weapon. I think that I must have transfixed him with that first mad lunge, for, though he struck and struck, his blows had no power in them, and presently his dagger tinkled down upon the floor. When I was sure that he was dead, I rose up and passed out into the moonlight. I climbed on to the heath again, and wandered across it as nearly out of my mind as a man could be.

With the blood singing in my ears, and my naked sword still clutched in my hand, I walked aimlessly on until, looking round me, I found that I had come as far as the glade of the Abbot's Beech, and saw in the distance that gnarled stump which must ever be associated with the most terrible moment of my life. I sat down upon a fallen trunk with my sword across my knees and my head between my hands, and I tried to think about what had happened and what would happen in the future.

The Emperor had committed himself to my care. The Emperor was dead. Those were the two thoughts which clanged in my head, until I had no room for any other ones. He had come with me and he was dead. I had done what he had ordered when living. I had revenged him when dead. But what of all that? The world would look upon me as responsible. They might even look upon me as the assassin. What could I prove? What witnesses had I? Might I not have been the accomplice of these wretches? Yes, yes, I was eternally dishonored—the lowest, most despicable creature in all France. This, then, was the end of my fine military ambitions—of the hopes of my mother. I laughed bitterly at the thought. And what was I to do now? Was I to go into Fontainebleau, to wake up the palace, and to inform them that the great Emperor had been murdered within a pace of me? I could not do it—no, I could not do it! There was but one course for an honorable gentleman whom Fate had placed in so cruel a position. I would fall upon my dishonored sword, and so share, since I could not avert, the Emperor's fate. I rose with my nerves strung to this last piteous deed, and as I did so, my eyes fell upon something which struck the breath from my lips. The Emperor was standing before me!

He was not more than ten yards off, with the moon shining straight upon his cold, pale face. He wore his grey overcoat, but the hood was turned back, and the front open, so that I could see the green coat of the Guides and the white breeches. His hands were clasped behind his back, and his chin sunk forward upon his breast, in the way that was usual with him.

"Well," said he, in his hardest and most abrupt voice, "what account do you give of yourself?"

I believe that, if he had stood in silence for another minute, my brain would have given way. But those sharp military accents were exactly what I needed to bring me to myself. Living or dead, here was the Emperor standing before me and asking me questions. I sprang to the salute.

"You have killed one, I see," said he, jerking his head towards the beech.

"Yes, sire."

"And the other escaped?"

"No, sire, I killed him also."

"What!" he cried. "Do I understand that you have killed them both?" He approached me as he spoke with a smile which set his teeth gleaming in the moonlight.

"One body lies there, sire," I answered. "The other is in the tool-house at the quarry."

"Then the Brothers of Ajaccio are no more," he cried, and after a pause, as if speaking to himself: "The shadow has passed me forever." Then he bent forward and laid his hand upon my shoulder.

"You have done very well, my young friend," said he. "You have lived up to your reputation."

He was flesh and blood, then, this Emperor. I could feel the little, plump palm that rested upon me. And yet I could not get over what I had seen with my own eyes, and so I stared at him in such bewilderment that he broke once more into one of his smiles.

"No, no, Monsieur Gerard," said he, "I am not a ghost, and you have not seen me killed. You will come here, and all will be clear to you."

He turned as he spoke, and led the way towards the great beech stump.

The bodies were still lying upon the ground, and two men were standing beside them. As we approached I saw from the turbans that they were Roustem and Mustafa, the two Mameluke servants. The Emperor paused when he came to the gray figure upon the ground, and turning back the hood which shrouded the features, he showed a face which was very different from his own.

"Here lies a faithful servant who has given up his life for his master," said he. "Monsieur de Goudin resembles me in figure and in manner, as you must admit."

What a delirium of joy came upon me when these few words made everything clear to me. He smiled again as he saw the delight which urged me to throw my arms round him and to embrace him, but he moved a step away, as if he had divined my impulse.

"You are unhurt?" he asked.

"I am unhurt, sire. But in another minute I should in my despair——"

"Tut, tut!" he interrupted. "You did very well. He should himself have been more on his guard. I saw everything which passed."

"You saw it, sire!"

"You did not hear me follow you through the wood, then? I hardly lost sight of you from the moment that you left your quarters until poor De Goudin fell. The counterfeit Emperor was in front of you and the real one behind you. You will now escort me back to the palace."

He whispered an order to his Mamelukes, who saluted in silence and remained where they were standing. For my part, I followed the Emperor with my pelisse bursting with pride. My word, I have always carried myself as a hussar should, but Lasalle himself never strutted and swung his dolman as I did that night. Who should clink his spurs and clatter his sabre if it were not I—I, Etienne Gerard—the confidant of the Emperor, the chosen swordsman of the light cavalry, the man who slew the would-be assassins of Napoleon? But he noticed my bearing and turned upon me like a blight.

"Is that the way you carry yourself on a secret mission?" he hissed, with that cold glare in his eyes. "Is it thus that you will make your comrades believe that nothing remarkable has occurred? Have done with this nonsense, monsieur, or you will find yourself transferred to the sappers, where you would have harder work and duller plumage."

That was the way with the Emperor. If ever he thought that anyone might have a claim upon him, he took the first opportunity to show him the gulf that lay between. I saluted and was silent, but I must confess to you that it hurt me after all that had passed between us. He led on to the palace, where we passed through the side door and up into his own cabinet. There were a couple of grenadiers at the staircase, and their eyes started out from under their fur caps, I promise you, when they saw a young lieutenant of hussars going up to the Emperor's room at midnight. I stood by the door, as I had done in the afternoon, while he flung himself down in an armchair, and remained silent so long that it seemed to me that he had forgotten all about me. I ventured at last upon a slight cough to remind him.

"Ah, Monsieur Gerard," said he, "you are very curious, no doubt, as to the meaning of all this?"

"I am quite content, sire, if it is your pleasure not to tell me," I answered.

"Ta, ta, ta," said he, impatiently. "These are only words. The moment that you were outside that door you would begin making inquiries about what it means. In two days your brother officers would know about it, in three days it would be all over Fontainebleau, and it would be in Paris on the fourth. Now, if I tell you enough to appease your curiosity, there is some reasonable hope that you may be able to keep the matter to yourself."

He did not understand me, this Emperor, and yet I could only bow and be silent.

"A few words will make it clear to you," said he, speaking very swiftly and pacing up and down the room. "They were Corsicans, these two men. I had known them in my youth. We had belonged to the same society—Brothers of Ajaccio, as we called ourselves. It was founded in the old Paoli days, you understand, and we had some strict rules of our own, which were not infringed with impunity."

A very grim look came over his face as he spoke, and it seemed to me that all that was French had gone out of him, and that it was the pure Corsican, the man of strong passions and of strange revenges, who stood before me. His memory had gone back to those early days of his, and for five minutes, wrapped in thought, he paced up and down the room with his quick little tiger steps. Then with an impatient wave of his hands he came back to his palace and to me.

"The rules of such a society," he continued, "are all very well for a private citizen. In the old days there was no more loyal brother than I. But circumstances change, and it would be neither for my welfare nor for that of France that I should now submit myself to them. They wanted to hold me to it, and so brought their fate upon their own heads. These were the two chiefs of the order, and they had come from Corsica to summon me to meet them at the spot which they named. I knew what such a summons meant. No man had ever returned from obeying one. On the other hand, if I did not go, I was sure that disaster would follow. I am a brother myself, you remember, and I know their ways."

Again there came that hardening of his mouth and cold glitter of his eyes.

"You perceive my dilemma, Monsieur Gerard," said he. "How would you have acted yourself, under such circumstances?"

"Given the word to the Tenth Hussars, sire," I cried. "Patrols could have swept the woods from end to end, and brought these two rascals to your feet."

He smiled, but he shook his head.

"I had very excellent reasons why I did not wish them taken alive," said he. "You can understand that an assassin's tongue might be as dangerous a weapon as an assassin's dagger. I will not disguise from you that I wished to avoid scandal at all cost. That was why I ordered you to take no pistols with you. That also is why my Mamelukes will remove all traces of the affair, and nothing more will be heard about it. I thought of all possible plans, and I am convinced that I selected the best one. Had I sent more than one guard with De Goudin into the woods, then the brothers would not have appeared. They would not change their plans nor miss their chance for the sake of a single man. It was Colonel Lasalle's accidental presence at the moment when I received the summons which led to my choosing one of his hussars for the mission. I selected you, Monsieur Gerard, because I wanted a man who could handle a sword, and who would not pry more deeply into the affair than I desired. I trust that, in this respect, you will justify my choice as well as you have done in your bravery and skill."

"Sire," I answered, "you may rely upon it."

"As long as I live," said he, "you never open your lips upon this subject."

"I dismiss it entirely from my mind, sire. I will efface it

from my recollection as if it had never been. I will promise
you to go out of your cabinet at this moment exactly as I was
when I entered it at four o'clock."

"You cannot do·that," said the Emperor, smiling. "You
were a lieutenant at that time. You will permit me, Captain,
to wish you a very good-night."

1809

III. How the Brigadier Captured Saragossa

HAVE I ever told you, my friends, the circumstances connected with my joining the Hussars of Conflans at the time of the siege of Saragossa, and the very remarkable exploit which I performed in connection with the taking of that city? No? Then you have indeed something still to learn. I will tell it to you exactly as it occurred. Save for two or three men and a score or two of women, you are the first who have ever heard the story.

You must know, then, that it was in the Tenth Hussars that I served as a lieutenant and as a captain. At the time I speak of I was only twenty-seven years of age, as reckless and desperate a man as any in that great army. It chanced that the war had come to a halt in Germany, while it was still raging in Spain; so the Emperor, wishing to reinforce the Spanish army, transferred me as senior captain to the Hussars of Conflans, which were at that time in the Fifth Army Corps under Marshal Lannes.

It was a long journey from Berlin to the Pyrenees. My new regiment formed part of the force which, under Marshal Lannes, was then besieging the Spanish town of Saragossa. I turned my horse's head in that direction, therefore, and behold me a week or so later at the French headquarters, whence I was directed to the camp of the Hussars of Conflans.

You have read, no doubt, of this famous siege of Saragossa, and I will only say that no general could have had a harder task than that with which Marshal Lannes was confronted. 44 The immense city was crowded with a horde of Spaniards—

soldiers, peasants, priests—all filled with the most furious hatred of the French, and the most savage determination to perish before they would surrender. There were eighty thousand men in the town and only thirty thousand to besiege them. Yet we had a powerful artillery, and our Engineers were of the best. There was never such a siege, for it is usual that when the fortifications are taken the city falls; but here it was not until the fortifications were taken that the real fighting began. Every house was a fort and every street a battlefield, so that slowly, day by day, we had to work our way inwards, blowing up the houses with their garrisons until more than half the city had disappeared. Yet the other half was as determined as ever, and in a better position for defense, since it consisted of enormous convents and monasteries with walls like the Bastille, which could not be so easily brushed out of our way. This was the state of things at the time that I joined the army.

I will confess to you that cavalry are not of much use in a siege, although there was a time when I would not have permitted any one to have made such an observation. The Hussars of Conflans were encamped to the south of the town, and it was their duty to throw out patrols and to make sure that no Spanish force was advancing from that quarter. The colonel of the regiment was not a good soldier, and the regiment was at that time very far from being in the high condition which it afterwards attained. Even in that one evening I saw several things which shocked me; for I had a high standard, and it went to my heart to see an ill-arranged camp, an ill-groomed horse, or a slovenly trooper. That night I supped with twenty-six of my new brother-officers, and I fear that in my zeal I showed them only too plainly that I found things very different from what I was accustomed to in the army of Germany. There was silence in the mess after my remarks, and I felt that I had been indiscreet when I saw the glances that were cast at me. The colonel especially was furious, and a great major named Olivier, who was the fire-eater of the regiment, sat  opposite to me curling his huge black moustaches, and staring at me as if he would eat me. However, I did not resent his attitude, for I felt that I had indeed been indiscreet, and that it would give a bad impression if upon this my first evening I quarreled with my superior officer.

So far I admit that I was wrong, but now I come to the

sequel. Supper over, the colonel and some other officers left the room, for it was in a farmhouse that the mess was held. There remained a dozen or so, and a goat-skin of Spanish wine having been brought in, we all made merry. Presently this Major Olivier asked me some questions concerning the army of Germany and as to the part which I had myself played in the campaign. Flushed with wine, I was drawn on from story to story. It was not unnatural, my friends. You will sympathize with me. Up there I had been the model for every officer of my years in the army. I was the first swordsman, the most dashing rider, the hero of a hundred adventures. Here I found myself not only unknown, but even disliked. Was it not natural that I should wish to tell these brave comrades what sort of man it was that had come among them? Was it not natural that I should wish to say, "Rejoice, my friends, rejoice! It is no ordinary man who has joined you tonight, but it is I, *the* Gerard, the hero of Ratisbon, the victor of Jena, the man who broke the square at Austerlitz"? I could not say all this. But I could at least tell them some incidents which would enable them to say it for themselves. I did so. They listened unmoved. I told them more. At last, after my tale of how I had guided the army across the Danube, one universal shout of laughter broke from them all. I sprang to my feet, flushed with shame and anger. They had drawn me on. They were making game of me. They were convinced that they had to do with a braggart and a liar. Was this my reception in the Hussars of Conflans? I dashed the tears of mortification from my eyes, and they laughed the more at the sight.

"Do you know, Captain Pelletan, whether Marshal Lannes is still with the army?" asked the major.

"I believe that he is, sir," said the other.

"Really, I should have thought that his presence was hardly necessary now that Captain Gerard has arrived."

Again there was a roar of laughter. I can see the ring of faces, the mocking eyes, the open mouths—Olivier with his great black bristles, Pelletan thin and sneering, even the young sub-lieutenants convulsed with merriment. Heavens, the indignity of it! But my rage had dried my tears. I was myself again, cold, quiet, self-contained, ice without and fire within.

"May I ask, sir," said I to the major, "at what hour the regiment is paraded?"

"I trust, Captain Gerard, that you do not mean to alter our hours," said he, and again there was a burst of laughter, which died away as I looked slowly round the circle.

"What hour is the assembly?" I asked, sharply, of Captain Pelletan.

Some mocking answer was on his tongue, but my glance kept it there. "The assembly is at six," he answered.

"I thank you," said I. I then counted the company, and found that I had to do with fourteen officers, two of whom appeared to be boys fresh from St. Cyr. I could not condescend to take any notice of their indiscretion. There remained the major, four captains, and seven lieutenants.

"Gentlemen," I continued, looking from one to the other of them, "I should feel myself unworthy of this famous regiment if I did not ask you for satisfaction for the rudeness with which you have greeted me, and I should hold you to be unworthy of it if on any pretext you refused to grant it."

"You will have no difficulty upon that score," said the major. "I am prepared to waive my rank and to give you every satisfaction in the name of the Hussars of Conflans."

"I thank you," I answered. "I feel, however, that I have some claim upon these other gentlemen who laughed at my expense."

"Whom would you fight, then?" asked Captain Pelletan.

"All of you," I answered.

They looked in surprise from one to the other. Then they drew off to the other end of the room, and I heard the buzz of their whispers. They were laughing. Evidently they still thought that they had to do with some empty braggart. Then they returned.

"Your request is unusual," said Major Oliver, "but it will be granted. How do you propose to conduct such a duel? The terms lie with you."

"Sabres," said I. "And I will take you in order of seniority, beginning with you, Major Olivier, at five o'clock. I will thus be able to devote five minutes to each before the assembly is blown. I must, however, beg you to have the courtesy to name the place of meeting, since I am still ignorant of the locality."

They were impressed by my cold and practical manner. Already the smile had died away from their lips. Olivier's face was no longer mocking, but it was dark and stern.

"There is a small open space behind the horse lines," said

he. "We have held a few affairs of honor there, and it has done very well. We shall be there, Captain Gerard, at the hour you name."

I was in the act of bowing to thank them for their acceptance when the door of the mess-room was flung open and the colonel hurried into the room, with an agitated face.

"Gentlemen," said he, "I have been asked to call for a volunteer from among you for a service which involves the greatest possible danger. I will not disguise from you that the matter is serious in the last degree, and that Marshal Lannes has chosen a cavalry officer because he can be better spared than an officer of infantry or of Engineers. Married men are not eligible. Of the others, who will volunteer?"

I need not say that all the unmarried officers stepped to the front. The colonel looked round in some embarrassment. I could see his dilemma. It was the best man who should go, and yet it was the best man whom he could least spare.

"Sir," said I, "may I be permitted to make a suggestion?"

He looked at me with a hard eye. He had not forgotten my observations at supper. "Speak!" said he.

"I would point out, sir," said I, "that this mission is mine both by right and by convenience."

"Why so, Captain Gerard?"

"By right, because I am the senior captain. By convenience, because I shall not be missed in the regiment, since the men have not yet learned to know me."

The colonel's features relaxed.

"There is certainly truth in what you say, Captain Gerard," said he. "I think that you are indeed best fitted to go upon this mission. If you will come with me I will give you your instructions."

I wished my new comrades good-night as I left the room, and I repeated that I should hold myself at their disposal at five o'clock next morning. They bowed in silence, and I thought that I could see, from the expression of their faces, that they had already begun to take a more just view of my character.

I had expected that the colonel would at once inform me what it was that I had been chosen to do, but instead of that he walked on in silence, I following behind him. We passed through the camp and made our way across the trenches and over the ruined heaps of stones which marked the old wall of the town. Within there was a labyrinth of passages, formed among the débris of the houses which had been destroyed by the mines of the Engineers. Acres and acres were covered with splintered walls and piles of brick which had once been a populous suburb. Lanes had been driven through it and lanterns placed at the corners with inscriptions to direct the wayfarer. The colonel hurried onwards until at last, after a long walk, we found our way barred by a high grey wall which stretched right across our path. Here behind a barricade lay our advanced guard. The colonel led me into a roofless house, and there I found two general officers, a map stretched over a drum in front of them, they kneeling beside it and examining it carefully by the light of a lantern. The one with the clean-shaven face and the twisted neck was Marshal Lannes, the other was General Razout, the head of the Engineers.

"Captain Gerard has volunteered to go," said the colonel.

Marshal Lannes rose from his knees and shook me by the hand.

"You are a brave man, sir," said he. "I have a present to make to you," he added, handing me a very tiny glass tube. "It has been specially prepared by Dr. Fardet. At the supreme moment you have but to put it to your lips and you will be dead in an instant."

This was a cheerful beginning. I will confess to you, my friends, that a cold chill passed up my back and my hair rose upon my head.

"Excuse me, sir," said I, as I saluted, "I am aware that I have volunteered for a service of great danger, but the exact details have not yet been given to me."

"Colonel Perrin," said Lannes severely, "it is unfair to allow this brave officer to volunteer before he has learned what the perils are to which he will be exposed."

But already I was myself once more.

"Sir," said I, "permit me to remark that the greater the danger the greater the glory, and that I could only repent of volunteering if I found that there were no risks to be run."

It was a noble speech, and my appearance gave force to my words. For the moment I was an heroic figure. As I saw Lannes's eyes fixed in admiration upon my face it thrilled me to think how splendid was the début which I was making in the army of Spain. If I died that night my name would not be

forgotten. My new comrades and my old, divided in all else, would still have a point of union in their love and admiration of Etienne Gerard.

"General Razout, explain the situation!" said Lannes, briefly.

The Engineer officer rose, his compasses in his hand. He led me to the door and pointed to the high grey wall which towered up amongst the débris of the shattered houses.

"That is the enemy's present line of defense," said he. "It is the wall of the great Convent of the Madonna. If we can carry it the city must fall, but they have run countermines all round it, and the walls are so enormously thick that it would be an immense labor to breach it with artillery. We happen to know, however, that the enemy have a considerable store of powder in one of the lower chambers. If that could be exploded the way would be clear for us."

"How can it be reached?" I asked.

"I will explain. We have a French agent within the town named Hubert. This brave man has been in constant communication with us, and he had promised to explode the magazine. It was to be done in the early morning, and for two days running we have had a storming party of a thousand Grenadiers waiting for the breach to be formed. But there has been no explosion, and for these two days we have had no communication from Hubert. The question is, what has become of him?"

"You wish me to go and see?"

"Precisely. Is he ill, or wounded, or dead? Shall we still wait for him, or shall we attempt the attack elsewhere? We cannot determine this until we have heard from him. This is a map of the town, Captain Gerard. You perceive that within this ring of convents and monasteries are a number of streets which branch off from a central square. If you come so far as this square you will find the cathedral at one corner. In that corner is the street of Toledo. Hubert lives in a small house between a cobbler's and a wine-shop, on the right-hand side as you go from the cathedral. Do you follow me?"

"Clearly."

"You are to reach that house, to see him, and to find out if his plan is still feasible or if we must abandon it." He produced what appeared to be a roll of dirty brown flannel.

"This is the dress of a Franciscan friar," said he. "You will find it the most useful disguise."

I shrank away from it.

"It turns me into a spy," I cried. "Surely I can go in my uniform?"

"Impossible! How could you hope to pass through the streets of the city? Remember, also, that the Spaniards take no prisoners, and that your fate will be the same in whatever dress you are taken."

It was true, and I had been long enough in Spain to know that that fate was likely to be something more serious than mere death. All the way from the frontier I had heard grim tales of torture and mutilation. I enveloped myself in the Franciscan gown.

"Now I am ready."

"Are you armed?"

"My sabre."

"They will hear it clank. Take this knife and leave your sword. Tell Hubert that at four o'clock before dawn the storming party will again be ready. There is a sergeant outside who will show you how to get into the city. Good-night, and good luck!"

Before I had left the room the two generals had their cocked hats touching each other over the map. At the door an under-officer of Engineers was waiting for me. I tied the girdle of my gown, and taking off my busby I drew the cowl over my head. My spurs I removed. Then in silence I followed my guide.

It was necessary to move with caution, for the walls above were lined by the Spanish sentries, who fired down continually at our advanced posts. Slinking along under the very shadow of the great convent, we picked our way slowly and carefully among the piles of ruins until we came to a large chestnut tree. Here the sergeant stopped.

"It is an easy tree to climb," said he. "A scaling ladder would not be simpler. Go up it, and you will find that the top branch will enable you to step upon the roof of that house. After that it is your guardian angel who must be your guide, for I can help you no more."

Girding up the heavy brown gown, I ascended the tree as directed. A half-moon was shining brightly, and the line of roof stood out dark and hard against the purple, starry sky. The tree was in the shadow of the house. Slowly I crept from branch to branch until I was near the top. I had but to climb along a stout limb in order to reach the wall. But suddenly my ears caught the patter of feet, and I cowered against the trunk and tried to blend myself with its shadow. A man was coming towards me on the roof. I saw his dark figure creeping along, his body crouching, his head advanced, the barrel of his gun protruding. His whole bearing was full of caution and suspicion. Once or twice he paused, and then came on again until he had reached the edge of the parapet within a few yards of me. Then he knelt down, levelled his musket, and fired.

I was so astonished at this sudden crash at my very elbow that I nearly fell out of the tree. For an instant I could not be sure that he had not hit me. But when I heard a deep groan from below, and the Spaniard leaned over the parapet and laughed aloud, I understood what had occurred. It was my poor, faithful sergeant who had waited to see the last of me. The Spaniard had seen him standing under the tree and had shot him. You will think that it was good shooting in the dark, but these people use *trebucos*, or blunderbusses, which are filled up with all sorts of stones and scraps of metal, so that they will hit you as certainly as I have hit a pheasant on a branch. The Spaniard stood peering down through the darkness, while an occasional groan from below showed that the sergeant was still living. The sentry looked round and everything was still and safe. Perhaps he thought that he would like to finish off this accursed Frenchman, or perhaps he had a desire to see what was in his pockets; but whatever his motive he laid down his gun, leaned forward, and swung himself into the tree. The same instant I buried my knife in his body, and he fell with a loud crashing through the branches and came with a thud to the ground. I heard a short struggle below and an oath or two in French. The wounded sergeant had not waited long for his vengeance.

For some minutes I did not dare to move, for it seemed certain that someone would be attracted by the noise. However, all was silent save for the chimes striking midnight in the city. I crept along the branch and lifted myself on to the roof. The Spaniard's gun was lying there, but it was of no service to me, since he had the powder-horn at his belt. At the same time, if it were found it would warn the enemy that something had happened, so I thought it best to drop it over the wall. Then I looked round for the means of getting off the roof and down into the city.

It was very evident that the simplest way by which I could get down was that by which the sentinel had got up, and what this was soon became evident. A voice along the roof called "Manuelo! Manuelo!" several times, and, crouching in the shadow, I saw in the moonlight a bearded head, which protruded from a trap-door. Receiving no answer to his summons the man climbed through, followed by three other fellows all armed to the teeth. You will see here how important it is not to neglect small precautions, for had I left the man's gun where I found it a search must have followed, and I should certainly have been discovered. As it was, the patrol saw no sign of their sentry and thought, no doubt, that he had moved along the line of the roofs. They hurried on, therefore, in that direction, and I, the instant that their backs were turned, rushed to the open trap-door and descended the flight of steps which led from it. The house appeared to be an empty one, for I passed through the heart of it and out, by an open door, into the street beyond.

It was a narrow and deserted lane, but it opened into a broader road, which was dotted with fires, round which a great number of soldiers and peasants were sleeping. The smell within the city was so horrible that one wondered how people could live in it, for during the months that the siege had lasted there had been no attempt to cleanse the streets or to bury the dead. Many people were moving up and down from fire to fire, and among them I observed several monks. Seeing that they came and went unquestioned, I took heart and hurried on my way in the direction of the great square. Once a man rose from beside one of the fires and stopped me by seizing my sleeve. He pointed to a woman who lay motionless upon the road, and I took him to mean that she was dying, and that he desired me to administer the last offices of the Church. I sought refuge, however, in the very little Latin that was left to me. "*Ora pro nobis,*" said I, from the depths of my cowl. "*Te deum laudamus. Ora pro nobis.*" I raised my hand as I spoke and pointed forwards. The fellow released my sleeve and shrank back in silence, while I, with a solemn gesture, hurried upon my way.

As I had imagined, this broad boulevard led out into the central square, which was full of troops and blazing with fires. I walked swiftly onwards, disregarding one or two people who addressed remarks to me. I passed the cathedral and followed the street which had been described to me. Being upon the side of the city which was farthest from our attack, there were no troops encamped in it, and it lay in darkness, save for an occasional glimmer in a window. It was not difficult to find the house to which I had been directed, between the wine-shop and the cobbler's. There was no light within, and the door was shut. Cautiously I pressed the latch, and I felt that it had yielded. Who was within I could not tell, and yet I must take the risk. I pushed the door open and entered.

It was pitch-dark within—the more so as I had closed the door behind me. I felt round and came upon the edge of a table. Then I stood still and wondered what I should do next, and how I could gain some news of this Hubert, in whose house I found myself. Any mistake would cost me not only my life, but the failure of my mission. Perhaps he did not live alone. Perhaps he was only a lodger in a Spanish family, and my visit might bring ruin to him as well as to myself. Seldom in my life have I been more perplexed. And then, suddenly, something turned my blood cold in my veins. It was a voice, a whispering voice, in my very ear. "Mon Dieu!" cried the voice in a tone of agony. "Oh, mon Dieu! mon Dieu!" Then there was a dry sob in the darkness, and all was still once more.

It thrilled me with horror, that terrible voice; but it thrilled me also with hope, for it was the voice of a Frenchman.

"Who is there?" I asked.

There was a groaning, but no reply.

"Is that you, Monsieur Hubert?"

"Yes, yes," sighed the voice, so low that I could hardly hear it. "Water, water, for Heaven's sake, water!"

I advanced in the direction of the sound, but only to come in contact with the wall. Again I heard a groan, but this time there could be no doubt that it was above my head. I put up my hands, but they felt only empty air.

"Where are you?" I cried.

"Here! Here!" whispered the strange, tremulous voice. I stretched my hand along the wall, and I came upon a man's naked foot. It was as high as my face, and yet, so far as I could feel, it had nothing to support it. I staggered back in amazement. Then I took a tinder-box from my pocket and struck a light. At the first flash a man seemed to be floating in the air in front of me, and I dropped the box in my amazement. Again, with tremulous fingers, I struck the flint against the steel, and this time I lit not only the tinder, but the wax taper. I held it up, and if my amazement was lessened, my horror was increased by that which it revealed.

The man had been chained to the wall. The poor wretch was in his last agony, his head sunk upon his shoulder and his blackened tongue protruded from his lips. He was dying as much from thirst as from his wounds, and these inhuman wretches had placed a beaker of wine upon the table in front of him to add a fresh pang to his tortures. I raised it to his lips. He had still strength enough to swallow, and the light came back a little to his dim eyes.

"Are you a Frenchman?" he whispered.

"Yes. They have sent me to learn what had befallen you."

"They discovered me. They have killed me for it. But before I die let me tell you what I know. A little more of that wine, please! Quick! Quick! I am very near the end. My strength is going. Listen to me! The powder is stored in the Mother Superior's room. The wall is pierced, and the end of the train is in Sister Angela's cell, next the chapel. All was ready two days ago. But they discovered a letter, and they tortured me."

"Good Heavens! have you been hanging here for two days?"

"It seems like two years. Comrade, I have served France, have I not? Then do one little service for me. Stab me to the heart, dear friend! I implore you, I entreat you, to put an end to my sufferings."

The man was indeed in a hopeless plight, and the kindest action would have been that for which he begged. And yet I could not in cold blood drive my knife into his body, although I knew how I should have prayed for such a mercy had I been in his place. But a sudden thought crossed my mind. In my pocket I held that which would give an instant and painless death. It was my own safeguard against torture, and yet this poor soul was in very pressing need of it, and he had deserved well of France.

I took out my phial and emptied it into the cup of wine. I

was in the act of handing it to him when I heard a sudden clash of arms outside the door. In an instant I put out my light and slipped behind the window-curtains. Next moment the door was flung open, and two Spaniards strode into the room—fierce, swarthy men in the dress of citizens, but with muskets slung over their shoulders. I looked through the chink in the curtains in an agony of fear lest they had come upon my traces, but it was evident that their visit was simply in order to feast their eyes upon my unfortunate compatriot. One of them held the lantern which he carried up in front of the dying man, and both of them burst into a shout of mocking laughter. Then the eyes of the man with the lantern fell upon the flagon of wine upon the table. He picked it up, held it, with a devilish grin, to the lips of Hubert, and then, as the poor wretch involuntarily inclined his head forward to reach it, snatched it back and took a long gulp himself. At the same instant he uttered a loud cry, clutched wildly at his own throat, and fell stone-dead upon the floor. His comrade stared at him in horror and amazement. Then, overcome by his own superstitious fears, he gave a yell of terror and rushed madly from the room. I heard his feet clattering wildly on the cobblestones until the sound died away in the distance.

The lantern had been left burning upon the table, and by its light I saw, as I came out from behind my curtain, that the unfortunate Hubert's head had fallen forward upon his chest and that he also was dead. That motion to reach the wine with his lips had been his last. A clock ticked loudly in the house, but otherwise all was absolutely still. On the wall hung the twisted form of the Frenchman, on the floor lay the motionless body of the Spaniard, all dimly lit by the horn lantern. For the first time in my life a frantic spasm of terror came over me. I had seen ten thousand men in every conceivable degree of mutilation stretched upon the ground, but the sight had never affected me like those two silent figures who were my companions in that shadowy room. I rushed into the street as the Spaniard had done, eager only to leave that house of gloom behind me, and I had run as far as the cathedral before my wits came back to me. There I stopped, panting, in the shadow, and, my hand pressed to my side, I tried to collect my scattered senses and to plan out what I should do. As I stood there, breathless, the great brass bells roared twice above my head. It was two o'clock. Four was the hour when the storming party would be in its place. I had still two hours in which to act.

The cathedral was brilliantly lit within, and a number of people were passing in and out; so I entered, thinking that I was less likely to be accosted there and that I might have quiet to form my plans. It was certainly a singular sight, for the place had been turned into a hospital, a refuge, and a storehouse. One aisle was crammed with provisions, another was littered with sick and wounded, while in the centre a great number of helpless people had taken up their abode and had even lit their cooking fires upon the mosaic floors. There were many at prayer, so I knelt in the shadow of a pillar and I prayed with all my heart that I might have the good luck to get out of this scrape alive, and that I might do such a deed that night as would make my name as famous in Spain as it had become in Germany. I waited until the clock struck three and then I left the cathedral and made my way towards the Convent of the Madonna, where the assault was to be delivered. You will understand, you who know me so well, that I was not the man to return tamely to the French camp with the report that our agent was dead and that other means must be found of entering the city. Either I should find some means to finish his uncompleted task or there would be a vacancy for a senior captain in the Hussars of Conflans.

I passed unquestioned down the broad boulevard, which I have already described, until I came to the great stone convent which formed the outwork of the defence. It was built in a square with a garden in the centre. In this garden some hundreds of men were assembled, all armed and ready, for it was known, of course, within the town that this was the point against which the French attack was likely to be made. Up to this time our fighting all over Europe had always been done between one army and another. It was only here in Spain that we learned how terrible a thing it is to fight against a people. On the one hand there is no glory, for what glory could be gained by defeating this rabble of elderly shopkeepers, ignorant peasants, fanatical priests, excited women, and all the other creatures who made up the garrison? On the other hand there were extreme discomfort and danger, for these people would give you no rest, would observe no rules of war, and were desperately earnest in their desire by hook or by crook to do you an injury. I began to realize how odious was our task as I looked upon the motley but ferocious groups who were gathered round the watch fires in the garden of the Convent of the Madonna. It was not for us soldiers to think about politics, but from the beginning there always seemed to be a curse upon this war in Spain.

However, at the moment I had no time to brood over such matters as these. There was, as I have said, no difficulty in getting as far as the convent garden, but to pass inside the convent unquestioned was not so easy. The first thing which I did was to walk round the garden, and I was soon able to pick out one large stained-glass window which must belong to the chapel. I had understood from Hubert that the Mother Superior's room in which the powder was stored was near to this, and that the train had been laid through a hole in the wall from some neighboring cell. I must at all costs get into the convent. There was a guard at the door, and how could I get in without explanations? But a sudden inspiration showed me how the thing might be done. In the garden was a well, and beside the well were a number of empty buckets. I filled two of these and approached the door. The errand of a man who carries a bucket of water in each hand does not need to be explained. The guard opened to let me through. I found myself in a long stone-flagged corridor lit with lanterns, with the cells of the nuns leading out from one side of it. Now at last I was on the high road to success. I walked on without hesitation, for I knew by my observations in the garden which way to go for the chapel.

A number of Spanish soldiers were lounging and smoking in the corridor, several of whom addressed me as I passed. I fancy it was for my blessing that they asked, and my "*Ora pro nobis*" seemed to entirely satisfy them. Soon I had got as far as the chapel, and it was easy to see that the cell next door was used as a magazine, for the floor was all black with powder in front of it. The door was shut, and two fierce-looking fellows stood on guard outside it, one of them with a key stuck in his belt. Had we been alone it would not have been long before it would have been in my hand, but with his comrade there it was impossible for me to hope to take it by force. The cell next door to the magazine on the far side from the chapel must be the one which belonged to Sister Angela. It was half open. I took my courage in both hands, and leav-

ing my buckets in the corridor, I walked unchallenged into
the room.

I was prepared to find half a dozen fierce Spanish des-
peradoes within, but what actually met my eyes was even
more embarrassing. The room had apparently been set aside
for the use of some of the nuns, who for some reason had
refused to quit their home. Three of them were within, one
an elderly, stern-faced dame who was evidently the Mother
Superior, the others young ladies of charming appearance.
They were seated together at the far side of the room, and
I saw with some amazement, by their manner and expressions,
that my coming was both welcome and expected. In a moment my presence of mind had returned, and I saw exactly
how the matter lay. Naturally, since an attack was about to
be made upon the convent, these sisters had been expecting to
be directed to some place of safety. Probably they were under
vow not to quit the walls, and they had been told to remain
in this cell until they had received further orders. In any
case I adapted my conduct to this supposition, since it was
clear that I must get them out of the room, and this would
give me a ready excuse to do so. I first cast a glance at the
door and observed that the key was within. I then made a
gesture to the nuns to follow me. The Mother Superior asked
me some question, but I shook my head impatiently and beckoned to her again. She hesitated, but I stamped my foot and
called them forth in so imperious a manner that they came at
once. They would be safer in the chapel, and thither I led
them, placing them at the end which was farthest from the
magazine. As the three nuns took their places before the altar
my heart bounded with joy and pride within me, for I felt
that the last obstacle had been lifted from my path.

And yet how often have I not found that this is the very
moment of danger? I took a last glance at the Mother Superior, and to my dismay I saw that her piercing dark eyes
were fixed, with an expression in which surprise was deepen-
ing into suspicion, upon my right hand. There were two
points which might well have attracted her attention. One
was that it was red with the blood of the sentinel whom I had
stabbed in the tree. That alone might count for little, as the
knife is as familiar as the breviary to the monks of Saragossa.
But on my forefinger I wore a heavy gold ring—the gift of a

German baroness whose name I may not mention. It shone brightly in the light of the altar lamp. Now, a ring upon a friar's hand is an impossibility, since they are vowed to absolute poverty. I turned quickly and made for the door of the chapel, but the mischief was done. As I glanced back I saw that the Mother Superior was already hurrying after me. I ran through the chapel door and along the corridor, but she called out some shrill warning to the two guards in front. Fortunately I had the presence of mind to call out also, and to point down the passage as if we were both pursuing the same object. Next instant I had dashed past them, sprung into the cell, slammed the heavy door, and fastened it upon the inside. With a bolt above and below and a huge lock in the center it was a piece of timber that would take some forcing.

Even now if they had had the wit to put a barrel of gunpowder against the door I should have been ruined. It was their only chance, for I had come to the final stage of my adventure. Here at last, after such a string of dangers as few men have ever lived to talk of I was at one end of the powder train, with the Saragossa magazine at the other. They were howling like wolves out in the passage, and muskets were crashing against the door. I paid no heed to their clamor, but I looked eagerly round for that train of which Hubert had spoken. Of course, it must be at the side of the room next to the magazine. I crawled along it on my hands and knees, looking into every crevice, but no sign could I see. Two bullets flew through the door and flattened themselves against the wall. The thudding and smashing grew ever louder. I saw a grey pile in a corner, flew to it with a cry of joy, and found that it was only dust. Then I got back to the side of the door where no bullets could ever reach me—they were streaming freely into the room—and I tried to forget this fiendish howling in my ear and to think out where this train could be. It must have been carefully laid by Hubert lest these nuns should see it. I tried to imagine how I should myself have arranged it had I been in his place. My eye was attracted by a statue of St. Joseph which stood in the corner. There was a wreath of leaves along the edge of the pedestal, with a lamp burning amidst them. I rushed across to it and tore the leaves aside. Yes, yes, there was a thin black line, which disappeared through a small hole in the wall. I tilted over the lamp, and threw myself on the ground. Next instant came a roar like thunder, the walls wavered and tottered around me, the ceiling clattered down from above, and over the yell of the terrified Spaniards was heard the terrific shout of the storming column of the Grenadiers. As in a dream—a happy dream—I heard it, and then I heard no more.

When I came to my senses two French soldiers were propping me up, and my head was singing like a kettle. I staggered to my feet and looked around me. The plaster had fallen, the furniture was scattered, and there were rents in the bricks, but no signs of a breach. In fact, the walls of the convent had been so solid that the explosion of the magazine had been insufficient to throw them down. On the other hand, it had caused such a panic among the defenders that our stormers had been able to carry the windows and throw open the doors almost without resistance. As I ran out into the corridor I found it full of troops, and I met Marshal Lannes himself, who was entering with his staff. He stopped and listened eagerly to my story.

"Splendid, Captain Gerard, splendid!" he cried. "These facts will certainly be reported to the Emperor."

"I would suggest to your Excellency," said I, "that I have only finished the work that was planned and carried out by Monsieur Hubert, who gave his life for the cause."

"His services will not be forgotten," said the Marshal. "Meanwhile, Captain Gerard, it is half-past four, and you must be starving after such a night of exertion. My staff and I will breakfast inside the city. I assure you that you will be an honored guest."

"I will follow your Excellency," said I. "There is a small engagement which detains me."

He opened his eyes.

"At this hour?"

"Yes, sir," I answered. "My fellow-officers, whom I never saw until last night, will not be content unless they catch another glimpse of me the first thing this morning."

"*Au revoir*, then," said Marshal Lannes, as he passed upon his way.

I hurried through the shattered door of the convent. When I reached the roofless house in which we had held the consultation the night before, I threw off my gown, and I put on the busby and sabre which I had left there. Then, a Hussar once more, I hurried onwards to the grove which was our rendezvous. My brain was still reeling from the concussion of the powder, and I was exhausted by the many emotions which had shaken me during that terrible night. It is like a dream, all that walk in the first dim grey light of dawn, with the smouldering camp-fires around me and the buzz of the waking army. Bugles and drums in every direction were mustering the infantry, for the explosion and the shouting had told their own tale. I strode onwards until, as I entered the little clump of cork oaks behind the horse lines, I saw my twelve comrades waiting in a group, their sabres at their sides. They looked at me curiously as I approached. Perhaps with my powder-blackened face and my blood-stained hands I seemed a different Gerard from the young captain whom they had made game of the night before.

"Good-morning, gentlemen," said I. "I regret exceedingly if I have kept you waiting, but I have not been master of my own time."

They said nothing, but they still scanned me with curious eyes. I can see them now, standing in a line before me, tall men and short men, stout men and thin men; Olivier, with his warlike mustache; the thin, eager face of Pelletan; young Oudin, flushed by his first duel; Mortier, with the sword-cut across his wrinkled brow. I laid aside my busby and drew my sword.

"I have one favor to ask you, gentlemen," said I. "Marshal Lannes has invited me to breakfast, and I cannot keep him waiting."

"What do you suggest?" asked Major Olivier.

"That you release me from my promise to give you five minutes each, and that you will permit me to attack you all together." I stood upon my guard as I spoke.

But their answer was truly beautiful and truly French. With one impulse the twelve swords flew from their scabbards and were raised in salute. There they stood, the twelve of them, motionless, their heels together, each with his sword upright before his face.

I staggered back from them. I looked from one to the other. For an instant I could not believe my own eyes. They were paying me homage, these, the men who had jeered me! Then I understood it all. I saw the effect that I had made upon them and their desire to make reparation. When a man is weak he can steel himself against danger, but not against emotion. "Comrades," I cried, "comrades——!" but I could say no more. Something seemed to take me by the throat and choke me. And then in an instant Olivier's arms were round me, Pelletan had seized me by the right hand, Mortier by the left, some were patting me on the shoulder, some were clapping me on the back, on every side smiling faces were looking into mine; and so it was that I knew that I had won my footing in the Hussars of Conflans.

1810

IV. How the Brigadier Slew the Fox

*I*N ALL *the great hosts of France there was only one officer towards whom the English of Wellington's army retained a deep, steady, and unchangeable hatred. There were plunderers among the French, and men of violence, gamblers, duellists, and roués. All these could be forgiven, for others of their kidney were to be found among the ranks of the English. But one officer of Massena's force had committed a crime which was unspeakable, unheard of, abominable; only to be alluded to with curses late in the evening, when a second bottle had loosened the tongues of men. The news of it was carried back to England, and country gentlemen who knew little of the details of the war grew crimson with passion when they heard of it, and yeomen of the shires raised freckled fists to Heaven and swore. And yet who should be the doer of this dreadful deed but our friend the brigadier, Etienne Gerard, of the Hussars of Conflans, gay-riding, plume-tossing, debonair, the darling of the ladies and of the six brigades of light cavalry.*

But the strange part of it is that this gallant gentleman did this hateful thing, and made himself the most unpopular man in the Peninsula, without ever knowing that he had done a crime for which there is hardly a name amid all the resources of our language. He died of old age, and never once in that imperturbable self-confidence which adorned or disfigured his character knew that so many thousand Englishmen would gladly have hanged him with their own hands. On the contrary, he numbered this adventure among those other exploits

64

which he has given to the world, and many a time he chuckled
and hugged himself as he narrated it to the eager circle who
gathered round him in that humble café where, between his
dinner and his dominoes, he would tell, amid tears and laugh-
ter, of that inconceivable Napoleonic past when France, like
an angel of wrath, rose up, splendid and terrible, before a
cowering continent. Let us listen to him as he tells the story
in his own way and from his own point of view.

You must know, my friends, that it was toward the end
of the year eighteen hundred and ten that I and Massena and
the others pushed Wellington backwards until we had hoped
to drive him and his army into the Tagus. But when we were
still twenty-five miles from Lisbon we found that we were
betrayed, for what had this Englishman done but build an
enormous line of works and forts at a place called Torres
Vedras, so that even we were unable to get through them!
They lay across the whole peninsula, and our army was so
far from home that we did not dare to risk a reverse, and we
had already learned at Busaco that it was no child's play to
fight against these people. What could we do, then, but sit
down in front of these lines and blockade them to the best
of our power? There we remained for six months, amid such
anxieties that Massena said afterwards that he had not one hair
which was not white upon his body. For my own part, I did
not worry much about our situation, but I looked after our
horses, who were in great need of rest and green fodder. For
the rest, we drank the wine of the country and passed the time
as best we might. There was a lady at Santarem—but my
lips are sealed. It is the part of a gallant man to say nothing,
though he may indicate that he could say a great deal.

One day Massena sent for me, and I found him in his tent
with a great plan pinned upon the table. He looked at me in
silence with that single piercing eye of his, and I felt by his
expression that the matter was serious. He was nervous and ill
at ease, but my bearing seemed to reassure him. It is good to
be in contact with brave men.

"Colonel Etienne Gerard," said he, "I have always heard
that you are a very gallant and enterprising officer."

It was not for me to confirm such a report, and yet it would
be folly to deny it, so I clinked my spurs together and
saluted.

"You are also an excellent rider."

I admitted it.

"And the best swordsman in the six brigades of light cavalry."

Massena was famous for the accuracy of his information.

"Now," said he, "if you will look at this plan you will have no difficulty in understanding what it is that I wish you to do. These are the lines of Torres Vedras. You will perceive that they cover a vast space, and you will realize that the English can only hold a position here and there. Once through the lines, you have twenty-five miles of open country which lie between them and Lisbon. It is very important to me to learn how Wellington's troops are distributed throughout that space, and it is my wish that you should go and ascertain."

His words turned me cold.

"Sir," said I, "it is impossible that a colonel of light cavalry should condescend to act as a spy."

He laughed and clapped me on the shoulder. "You would not be a Hussar if you were not a hot-head," said he. "If you will listen you will understand that I have not asked you to act as a spy. What do you think of that horse?"

He had conducted me to the opening of his tent, and there was a Chasseur who led up and down a most admirable creature. He was a dapple grey, not very tall—a little over fifteen hands perhaps—but with the short head and splendid arch of the neck which comes with the Arab blood. His shoulders and haunches were so muscular, and yet his legs so fine, that it thrilled me with joy just to gaze upon him. A fine horse or a beautiful woman, I cannot look at them unmoved, even now when seventy winters have chilled my blood. You can think how it was in the year '10.

"This," said Massena, "is Voltigeur, the swiftest horse in our army. What I desire is that you should start tonight, ride round the lines upon the flank, make your way across the enemy's rear, and return upon the other flank, bringing me news of his dispositions. You will wear a uniform, and will, therefore, if captured, be safe from the death of a spy. It is probable that you will get through the lines unchallenged, for the posts are very scattered. Once through, in daylight you can outride anything which you meet, and if you keep off the roads you may escape entirely unnoticed. If you have not reported yourself by tomorrow night I will understand that you are taken, and I will offer them Colonel Petrie in exchange."

Ah, how my heart swelled with pride and joy as I sprang into the saddle and galloped this grand horse up and down to show the marshal the mastery which I had of him! He was magnificent—we were both magnificent, for Massena clapped his hands and cried out in his delight. It was not I, but he, who said that a gallant beast deserves a gallant rider. Then, when for the third time, with my panache flying and my dolman streaming behind me, I thundered past him, I saw upon his hard old face that he had no longer any doubt that he had chosen the man for his purpose. I drew my sabre, raised the hilt to my lips in salute, and galloped on to my own quarters. Already the news had spread that I had been chosen for a mission, and my little rascals came swarming out of their tents to cheer me. Ah! it brings the tears to my old eyes when I think how proud they were of their colonel. And I was proud of them also. They deserved a dashing leader.

The night promised to be a stormy one, which was very much to my liking. It was my desire to keep my departure most secret, for it was evident that if the English heard that I had been detached from the army they would naturally conclude that something important was about to happen. My horse was taken, therefore, beyond the picket line, as if for watering, and I followed and mounted him there. I had a map, a compass, and a paper of instructions from the marshal, and with these in the bosom of my tunic, and a sabre at my side, I set out upon my adventure. A thin rain was falling, and there was no moon, so you may imagine that it was not very cheerful. But my heart was light at the thought of the honor which had been done me, and the glory which awaited me. This exploit should be one more in that brilliant series which was to change my sabre into a baton. Ah, how we dreamed, we foolish fellows, young, and drunk with success! Could I have foreseen that night as I rode, the chosen man of sixty thousand, that I should spend my life planting cabbages on a hundred francs a month! Oh, my youth, my hopes, my comrades! But the wheel turns and never stops. Forgive me, my friends, for an old man has his weakness.

My route, then, lay across the face of the high ground of Torres Vedras, then over a streamlet, past a farmhouse which had been burned down and was now only a landmark, then through a forest of young cork oaks, and so to the monastery of San Antonio, which marked the left of the English position. Here I turned south and rode quietly over the downs, for it was at this point that Massena thought that it would be most easy for me to find my way unobserved through the position. I went very slowly, for it was so dark that I could not see my hand in front of me. In such cases I leave my bridle loose, and let my horse pick its own way. Voltigeur went confidently forward, and I was very content to sit upon his back, and to peer about me, avoiding every light. For three hours we advanced in this cautious way, until it seemed to me that I must have left all danger behind me. I then pushed on more briskly, for I wished to be in the rear of the whole army by daybreak. There are many vineyards in these parts which in winter become open plains, and a horseman finds few difficulties in his way.

But Massena had underrated the cunning of these English, for it appears that there was not one line of defence, but three, and it was the third which was the most formidable, through which I was at that instant passing. As I rode, elated at my own success, a lantern flashed suddenly before me, and I saw the glint of polished gun-barrels and the gleam of a red coat.

"Who goes there?" cried a voice—such a voice! I swerved to the right and rode like a madman, but a dozen squirts of fire came out of the darkness, and the bullets whizzed all round my ears. That was no new sound to me, my friends, though I will not talk like a foolish conscript and say that I have ever liked it. But at least it had never kept me from thinking clearly, and so I knew that there was nothing for it but to gallop hard and try my luck elsewhere. I rode round the English picket, and then, as I heard nothing more of them, I concluded rightly that I had at last come through their defences. For five miles I rode south, striking a tinder from time to time to look at my pocket compass. And then in an instant—I feel the pang once more as my memory brings back the moment—my horse, without a sob or stagger, fell stone dead beneath me!

I had not known it, but one of the bullets from that infernal picket had passed through his body. The gallant creature had never winced nor weakened, but had gone while life was in him. One instant I was secure on the swiftest, most graceful horse in Massena's army. The next he lay upon his side, worth only the price of his hide, and I stood there that most helpless, most ungainly of creatures, a dismounted Hussar. What could I do with my boots, my spurs, my trailing sabre? I was far inside the enemy's lines. How could I hope to get back again? I am not ashamed to say that I, Etienne Gerard, sat upon my dead horse and sank my face in my hands in my despair. Already the first streaks were whitening in the east. In half an hour it would be light. That I should have won my way past every obstacle, and then at this last instant be left at the mercy of my enemies, my mission ruined, and myself a prisoner—was it not enough to break a soldier's heart?

But courage, my friends! We have these moments of weakness, the bravest of us; but I have a spirit like a slip of steel, for the more you bend it the higher it springs. One spasm of despair, and then a brain of ice and a heart of fire. All was not yet lost. I, who had come through so many hazards, would come through this one also. I rose from my horse and considered what had best be done.

And first of all it was certain that I could not get back. Long before I could pass the lines it would be broad daylight. I must hide myself for the day, and devote the next night to my escape. I took the saddle, holsters, and bridle from my poor Voltigeur, and I concealed them among some bushes, so that no one finding him could know that he was a French horse. Then, leaving him lying there, I wandered on in search of some place where I might be safe for the day. In every direction I could see camp fires upon the sides of the hills, and already figures had begun to move around them. I must hide quickly or I was lost. But where was I to hide? It was a vineyard in which I found myself, the poles of the vines still standing, but the plants gone. There was no cover there. Besides, I should want some food and water before another night had come. I hurried wildly onwards through the waning darkness, trusting that chance would be my friend. And I was not disappointed. Chance is a woman, my friends, and she has her eye always upon a gallant Hussar.

Well, then, I stumbled through the vineyard, something loomed in front of me, and I came upon a great square house with another long, low building upon one side of it. Three roads met there, and it was easy to see that this was the *posada*, or wine-shop. There was no light in the windows, and everything was dark and silent, but, of course, I knew that such comfortable quarters were certainly occupied, and probably by someone of importance. I have learned, however, that the nearer the danger may really be the safer the place, and so I was by no means inclined to trust myself away from this shelter. The low building was evidently the stable, and into this I crept, for the door was unlatched. The place was full of bullocks and sheep, gathered there, no doubt, to be out of the clutches of marauders. A ladder led to a loft, and up this I climbed, and concealed myself very snugly among some bales of hay upon the top. This loft had a small open window, and I was able to look down upon the front of the inn and also upon the road. Then I crouched and waited to see what would happen.

It was soon evident that I had not been mistaken when I had thought that this might be the quarters of some person of importance. Shortly after daybreak an English light dragoon arrived with a despatch, and from then onwards the place was in a turmoil, officers continually riding up and away. Always the same name was upon their lips: "Sir Stapleton—Sir Stapleton." It was hard for me to lie there with a dry moustache and watch the great flagons which were brought out by the landlord to these English officers. But it amused me to look at their fresh-colored, clean-shaven, careless faces, and to wonder what they would think if they knew that so celebrated a person was lying so near to them. And then, as I lay and watched, I saw a sight which filled me with surprise.

It is incredible, the insolence of these English! What do you suppose Milord Wellington had done when he found that Massena had blockaded him and that he could not move his army? I might give you many guesses. You might say that he had raged, that he had despaired, that he had brought his troops together and spoken to them about glory and the fatherland before leading them to one last battle. No, Milord did none of these things. But he sent a fleet ship to England to bring him a number of fox-dogs, and he with his officers settled himself down to chase the fox. It is true what I tell you. Behind the lines of Torres Vedras these mad Englishmen made the fox-chase three days in the week. We had heard of it in the camp, and now I myself was to see that it was true.

For, along the road which I have described, there came

these very dogs, thirty or forty of them, white and brown, each with its tail at the same angle, like the bayonets of the Old Guard. My faith, but it was a pretty sight! And behind and amidst them there rode three men with peaked caps and red coats, whom I understood to be the hunters. After them came many horsemen with uniforms of various kinds, stringing along the road in twos and threes, talking together and laughing. They did not seem to be going above a trot, and it appeared to me that it must indeed be a slow fox which they hoped to catch. However, it was their affair, not mine, and soon they had all passed my window and were out of sight. I waited and I watched, ready for any chance which might offer.

Presently an officer, in a blue uniform not unlike that of our flying artillery, came cantering down the road—an elderly, stout man he was, with grey side-whiskers. He stopped and began to talk with an orderly officer of dragoons, who waited outside the inn, and it was then that I learned the advantage of the English which had been taught me. I could hear and understand all that was said.

"Where is the meet?" said the officer, and I thought that he was hungering for his *biftek*. But the other answered him that it was near Altara, so I saw that it was a place of which he spoke.

"You are late, Sir George," said the orderly.

"Yes, I had a court-martial. Has Sir Stapleton Cotton gone?"

At this moment a window opened, and a handsome young man in a very splendid uniform looked out of it.

"Halloa, Murray!" said he. "These cursed papers keep me, but I will be at your heels."

"Very good, Cotton. I am late already, so I will ride on."

"You might order my groom to bring round my horse," said the young general at the window to the orderly below, while the other went on down the road.

The orderly rode away to some outlying stable, and then in a few minutes there came a smart English groom with a cockade in his hat, leading by the bridle a horse—and, oh, my friends, you have never known the perfection to which a horse can attain until you have seen a first-class English hunter. He was superb: tall, broad, strong, and yet as graceful and agile as a deer. Coal black he was in color, and his neck, and his shoulder, and his quarters, and his fetlocks—how can I describe him all to you? The sun shone upon him as on polished ebony, and he raised his hoofs in a little playful dance so lightly and prettily, while he tossed his mane and whinnied with impatience. Never have I seen such a mixture of strength and beauty and grace. I have often wondered how the English Hussars had managed to ride over the Chasseurs of the Guards in the affair at Astorga, but I wondered no longer when I saw the English horses.

There was a ring for fastening bridles at the door of the inn, and the groom tied the horse there while he entered the house. In an instant I had seen the chance which Fate had brought to me. Were I in that saddle I should be better off than when I started. Even Voltigeur could not compare with this magnificent creature. To think is to act with me. In one instant I was down the ladder and at the door of the stable. The next I was out and the bridle was in my hand. I bounded into the saddle. Somebody, the master or the man, shouted wildly behind me. What cared I for his shouts! I touched the horse with my spurs, and he bounded forward with such a spring that only a rider like myself could have sat him. I gave him his head and let him go—it did not matter to me where, so long as we left this inn far behind us. He thundered away across the vineyards, and in a very few minutes I had placed miles between myself and my pursuers. They could no longer tell, in that wild country, in which direction I had gone. I knew that I was safe, and so, riding to the top of a small hill, I drew my pencil and note-book from my pocket, and proceeded to make plans of those camps which I could see, and to draw the outline of the country.

He was a dear creature upon whom I sat, but it was not easy to draw upon his back, for every now and then his two ears would cock, and he would start and quiver with impatience. At first I could not understand this trick of his, but soon I observed that he only did it when a peculiar noise— "Yoy, yoy, yoy"—came from somewhere among the oak woods beneath us. And then suddenly this strange cry changed into a most terrible screaming, with the frantic blowing of a horn. Instantly he went mad—this horse. His eyes blazed. His mane bristled. He bounded from the earth and bounded again, twisting and turning in a frenzy. My pencil flew one way and my note-book another. And then, as I looked down into the

valley, an extraordinary sight met my eyes. The hunt was
streaming down it. The fox I could not see, but the dogs were
in full cry, their noses down, their tails up, so close together
that they might have been one great yellow and white moving
carpet. And behind them rode the horsemen—my faith, what
a sight! Consider every type which a great army could show:
some in hunting dress, but the most in uniforms; blue dragoons, red dragoons, red-trousered hussars, green riflemen,
artillerymen, gold slashed lancers, and most of all red, red,
red, for the infantry officers ride as hard as the cavalry. Such
a crowd, some well mounted, some ill, but all flying along as
best they might, the subaltern as good as the general, jostling
and pushing, spurring and driving, with every thought thrown
to the winds save that they should have the blood of this
absurd fox! Truly, they are an extraordinary people, the English! But I had little time to watch the hunt or to marvel at
these islanders, for of all these mad creatures the very horse
upon which I sat was the maddest. You understand that he
was himself a hunter, and that the crying of these dogs was
to him what the call of a cavalry trumpet in the street yonder
would be to me. It thrilled him. It drove him wild. Again and
again he bounded into the air, and then, seizing the bit between his teeth, he plunged down the slope, and galloped after
the dogs. I swore, and tugged, and pulled, but I was power-
less. This English general rode his horse with a snaffle only,
and the beast had a mouth of iron. It was useless to pull him
back. One might as well try to keep a Grenadier from a wine
bottle. I gave it up in despair, and, settling down in the saddle,
I prepared for the worst which could befall.

What a creature he was! Never have I felt such a horse
between my knees. His great haunches gathered under him
with every stride, and he shot forward ever faster and faster,
stretched like a greyhound, while the wind beat in my face
and whistled past my ears. I was wearing our undress jacket,
a uniform simple and dark in itself—though some figures give
distinction to any uniform—and I had taken the precaution to
remove the long panache from my busby. The result was that,
amidst the mixture of costumes in the hunt, there was no
reason why mine should attract attention, or why these men,
whose thoughts were all with the chase, should give any heed
to me. The idea that a French officer might be riding with
them was too absurd to enter their minds. I laughed as I rode,

for, indeed, amid all the danger, there was something of comic in the situation.

I have said that the hunters were very unequally mounted, and so, at the end of a few miles, instead of being one body of men, like a charging regiment, they were scattered over a considerable space, the better riders well up to the dogs, and the others trailing away behind. Now, I was as good a rider as any, and my horse was the best of them all, and so you can imagine that it was not long before he carried me to the front. And when I saw the dogs streaming over the open, and the red-coated huntsmen behind them, and only seven or eight horsemen between us, then it was that the strangest thing of all happened, for I, too, went mad—I, Etienne Gerard! In a moment it came upon me, this spirit of sport, this desire to excel, this hatred of the fox. Accursed animal, should he then defy us? Vile robber, his hour was come! Ah, it is a great feeling, this feeling of sport, my friends, this desire to trample the fox under the hoofs of your horse. I have made the fox-chase with the English. I have also, as I may tell you some day, fought the box-fight with the Bustler, of Bristol. And I say to you that this sport is a wonderful thing—full of interest as well as madness.

The farther we went the faster galloped my horse, and soon there were but three men as near the dogs as I was. All thought of fear of discovery had vanished. My brain throbbed, my blood ran hot—only one thing upon earth seemed worth living for, and that was to overtake this infernal fox. I passed one of the horsemen—a Hussar like myself. There were only two in front of me now—the one in a black coat, the other the blue artilleryman whom I had seen at the inn. His grey whiskers streamed in the wind, but he rode magnificently. For a mile or more we kept in this order, and then, as we galloped up a steep slope, my lighter weight brought me to the front. I passed them both, and when I reached the crown I was riding level with the little, hard-faced English huntsman. In front of us were the dogs, and then, a hundred paces beyond them, was a brown wisp of a thing, the fox itself, stretched to the uttermost. The sight of him fired my blood. "Aha, we have you then, assassin!" I cried, and shouted my encouragement to the huntsman. I waved my hand to show him that there was one upon whom he could rely.

And now there were only the dogs between me and my

prey. These dogs, whose duty it is to point out the game, were now rather a hindrance than a help to us, for it was hard to know how to pass them. The huntsman felt the difficulty as much as I, for he rode behind them and could make no progress towards the fox. He was a swift rider, but wanting in enterprise. For my part, I felt that it would be unworthy of the Hussars of Conflans if I could not overcome such a difficulty as this. Was Etienne Gerard to be stopped by a herd of fox-dogs? It was absurd. I gave a shout and spurred my horse.

"Hold hard, sir! Hold hard!" cried the huntsman.

He was uneasy for me, this good old man, but I reassured him by a wave and a smile. The dogs opened in front of me. One or two may have been hurt, but what would you have? The egg must be broken for the omelette. I could hear the huntsman shouting his congratulations behind me. One more effort, and the dogs were all behind me. Only the fox was in front.

Ah, the joy and pride of that moment! To know that I had beaten the English at their own sport. Here were three hundred all thirsting for the life of this animal, and yet it was I who was about to take it. I thought of my comrades of the light cavalry brigade, of my mother, of the Emperor, of France. I had brought honor to each and all. Every instant brought me nearer to the fox. The moment for action had arrived, so I unsheathed my sabre. I waved it in the air, and the brave English all shouted behind me.

Only then did I understand how difficult is this fox-chase, for one may cut again and again at the creature and never strike him once. He is small, and turns quickly from a blow. At every cut I heard those shouts of encouragement behind me, and they spurred me to yet another effort. And then at last the supreme moment of my triumph arrived. In the very act of turning I caught him fair with such another back-handed cut as that with which I killed the aide-de-camp of the Emperor of Russia. He flew into two pieces, his head one way and his tail another. I looked back and waved the blood-stained sabre in the air. For the moment I was exalted—superb!

Ah! how I should have loved to have waited to have received the congratulations of these generous enemies. There were fifty of them in sight, and not one of them who was not waving his hand and shouting. They are not really such a phlegmatic race, the English. A gallant deed in war or in sport will always warm their hearts. As to the old huntsman, he was the nearest to me, and I could see with my own eyes how overcome he was by what he had seen. He was like a man paralyzed—his mouth open, his hand, with outspread fingers, raised in the air. For a moment my inclination was to return and embrace him. But already the call of duty was sounding in my ears, and these English, in spite of all the fraternity which exists among sportsmen, would certainly have made me prisoner. There was no hope for my mission now, and I had done all that I could do. I could see the lines of Massena's camp no very great distance off, for, by a lucky chance, the chase had taken us in that direction. I turned from the dead fox, saluted with my sabre, and galloped away.

But they would not leave me so easily, these gallant huntsmen. I was the fox now, and the chase swept bravely over the plain. It was only at the moment when I started for the camp that they could have known that I was a Frenchman, and now the whole swarm of them were at my heels. We were within gunshot of our pickets before they would halt, and then they stood in knots and would not go away, but shouted and waved their hands at me. No, I will not think that it was in enmity. Rather would I fancy that a glow of admiration filled their breasts, and that their one desire was to embrace the stranger who had carried himself so gallantly and well.

1811

V. How the Brigadier Took the Field Against the Marshal Millefleurs

MASSENA was a thin, sour little fellow, and after his hunting accident he had only one eye, but when it looked out from under his cocked hat there was not much upon a field of battle which escaped it. He could stand in front of a battalion, and with a single sweep tell you if a buckle or a gaiter button were out of place. Neither the officers nor the men were very fond of him, for he was, as you know, a miser, and soldiers love that their leaders should be free-handed. At the same time, when it came to work they had a very high respect for him, and they would rather fight under him than under anyone except the Emperor himself, and Lannes, when he was alive. After all, if he had a tight grasp upon his money-bags, there was a day also, you must remember, when that same grip was upon Zurich and Genoa. He clutched on to his positions as he did to his strong box, and it took a very clever man to loosen him from either.

When I received his summons I went gladly to his head-quarters, for I was always a great favorite of his, and there was no officer of whom he thought more highly. That was the best of serving with those good old generals, that they knew enough to be able to pick out a fine soldier when they saw one. He was seated alone in his tent, with his chin upon his hand, and his brow as wrinkled as if he had been asked for a subscription. He smiled, however, when he saw me before him.

"Good-day, Colonel Gerard."

"Good-day, Marshal."

"How is the Third of Hussars?"

"Seven hundred incomparable men upon seven hundred excellent horses."

"And your wounds—are they healed?"

"My wounds never heal, Marshal," I answered.

"And why?"

"Because I have always new ones."

"General Rapp must look to his laurels," said he, his face all breaking into wrinkles as he laughed. "He has had twenty-one from the enemy's bullets, and as many from Larrey's knives and probes. Knowing that you were hurt, Colonel, I have spared you of late."

"Which hurt me most of all."

"Tut, tut! Since the English got behind these accursed lines of Torres Vedras, there has been little for us to do. But now we are on the eve of action."

"We advance?"

"No, retire."

My face must have shown my dismay. What, retire before this sacred dog of a Wellington—he who had listened unmoved to my words, and had sent me to his land of fogs? I could have sobbed as I thought of it.

"What would you have?" cried Massena, impatiently. "When one is in check, it is necessary to move the king."

"Forwards," I suggested.

He shook his grizzled head.

"The lines are not to be forced," said he. "I have already lost General St. Croix and more men than I can replace. On the other hand, we have been here at Santarem for nearly six months. There is not a pound of flour nor a jug of wine on the country-side. We must retire."

"There are flour and wine in Lisbon," I persisted.

"Tut, you speak as if an army could charge in and charge out again like your regiment of hussars. If Soult were here with thirty thousand men—but he will not come. I sent for you, however, Colonel Gerard, to say that I have a very singular and important expedition which I intend to place under your direction."

I pricked up my ears, as you can imagine. The Marshal unrolled a great map of the country and spread it upon the table. He flattened it out with his little, hairy hands.

"This is Santarem," he said, pointing.

I nodded.

"And here, twenty-five miles to the east, is Almeixal, celebrated for its vintages and for its enormous Abbey."

Again I nodded; I could not think what was coming.

"Have you heard of the Marshal Millefleurs?" asked Massena.

"I have served with all the Marshals," said I, "but there is none of that name."

"It is but the nickname which the soldiers have given him," said Massena. "If you had not been away from us for some months, it would not be necessary for me to tell you about him. He is an Englishman, and a man of good breeding. It is on account of his manners that they have given him his title. I wish you to go to this polite Englishman at Almeixal."

"Yes, Marshal."

"And to hang him to the nearest tree."

"Certainly, Marshal."

I turned briskly upon my heels, but Massena recalled me before I could reach the opening of his tent.

"One moment, Colonel," said he; "you had best learn how matters stand before you start. You must know, then, that this Marshal Millefleurs, whose real name is Alexis Morgan, is a man of very great ingenuity and bravery. He was an officer in the English Guards, but having been broken for cheating at cards, he left the army. In some manner he gathered a number of English deserters round him and took to the mountains. French stragglers and Portuguese brigands joined him, and he found himself at the head of five hundred men. With these he took possession of the Abbey of Almeixal, sent the monks about their business, fortified the place, and gathered in the plunder of all the country round."

"For which it is high time he was hanged," said I, making once more for the door.

"One instant!" cried the Marshal, smiling at my impatience. "The worst remains behind. Only last week the Dowager Countess of La Ronda, the richest woman in Spain, was taken by these ruffians in the passes as she was journeying from King Joseph's Court to visit her grandson. She is now a prisoner in the Abbey, and is only protected by her——"

"Grandmotherhood," I suggested.

"Her power of paying a ransom," said Massena. "You have three missions, then: To rescue this unfortunate lady; to punish this villain; and, if possible, to break up this nest of brigands. It will be a proof of the confidence which I have in you when I say that I can only spare you half a squadron with which to accomplish all this."

My word, I could hardly believe my ears! I thought that I should have had my regiment at the least.

"I would give you more," said he, "but I commence my retreat today, and Wellington is so strong in horse that every trooper becomes of importance. I cannot spare you another man. You will see what you can do, and you will report yourself to me at Abrantes not later than tomorrow night."

It was very complimentary that he should rate my powers so high, but it was also a little embarrassing. I was to rescue an old lady, to hang an Englishman, and to break up a band of five hundred assassins—all with fifty men. But after all, the fifty men were Hussàrs of Conflans, and they had an Etienne Gerard to lead them. As I came out into the warm Portuguese sunshine my confidence had returned to me, and I had already begun to wonder whether the medal which I had so often deserved might not be waiting for me at Almeixal.

You may be sure that I did not take my fifty men at haphazard. They were all old soldiers of the German wars, some of them with three stripes, and most of them with two. Oudet and Papilette, two of the best sub-officers in the regiment, were at their head. When I had them formed up in fours, all in silver grey and upon chestnut horses, with their leopard skin shabracks and their little red panaches, my heart beat high at the sight. I could not look at their weather-stained faces, with the great moustaches which bristled over their chin-straps, without feeling a glow of confidence, and, between ourselves, I have no doubt that that was exactly how they felt when they saw their young Colonel on his great black war-horse riding at their head.

Well, when we got free of the camp and over the Tagus, I threw out my advance and my flankers, keeping my own place at the head of the main body. Looking back from the hills above Santarem, we could see the dark lines of Massena's army, with the flash and twinkle of the sabres and bayonets as he moved his regiments into position for their retreat. To the south lay the scattered red patches of the English outposts, and behind the grey smoke-cloud which rose from Wellington's camp—thick, oily smoke, which seemed to our poor starving fellows to bear with it the rich smell of seething camp-kettles. Away to the west lay a curve of blue sea flecked with the white sails of the English ships.

You will understand that as we were riding to the east, our road lay away from both armies. Our own marauders, however, and the scouting parties of the English, covered the country, and it was necessary with my small troop that I should take every precaution. During the whole day we rode over desolate hill-sides, the lower portions covered by the budding vines, but the upper turning from green to grey, and jagged along the skyline like the back of a starved horse. Mountain streams crossed our path, running west to the Tagus, and once we came to a deep, strong river, which might have checked us had I not found the ford by observing where houses had been built opposite each other upon either bank. Between them, as every scout should know, you will find your ford. There was none to give us information, for neither man nor beast, nor any living thing except great clouds of crows, was to be seen during our journey.

The sun was beginning to sink when we came to a valley clear in the center, but shrouded by huge oak trees upon either side. We could not be more than a few miles from Almeixal, so it seemed to me to be best to keep among the groves, for the spring had been an early one and the leaves were already thick enough to conceal us. We were riding then in open order among the great trunks, when one of my flankers came galloping up.

"There are English across the valley, Colonel," he cried, as he saluted.

"Cavalry or infantry?"

"Dragoons, Colonel," said he; "I saw the gleam of their helmets, and heard the neigh of a horse."

Halting my men I hastened to the edge of the wood. There could be no doubt about it. A party of English cavalry was traveling in a line with us, and in the same direction. I caught a glimpse of their red coats and of their flashing arms glowing and twinkling among the tree-trunks. Once, as they passed through a small clearing, I could see their whole force, and I judged that they were of about the same strength as my own —a half squadron at the most.

You who have heard some of my little adventures will give me credit for being quick in my decisions, and prompt in carrying them out. But here I must confess that I was in two minds. On the one hand there was the chance of a fine cavalry skirmish with the English. On the other hand, there was my mission at the Abbey of Almeixal, which seemed already to be so much above my power. If I were to lose any of my men, it was certain that I should be unable to carry out my orders. I was sitting my horse, with my chin in my gauntlet, looking across at the rippling gleams of light from the further wood, when suddenly one of these red-coated Englishmen rode out from the cover, pointing at me and breaking into a shrill whoop and halloa as if I had been a fox. Three others joined him, and one who was a bugler sounded a call, which brought the whole of them into the open. They were, as I had thought, a half squadron, and they formed a double line with a front of twenty-five, their officer—the one who had whooped at me —at their head.

For my own part, I had instantly brought my own troopers into the same formation, so that there we were, hussars and dragoons, with only two hundred yards of grassy sward between us. They carried themselves well, those red-coated troopers, with their silver helmets, their high white plumes, and their long, gleaming swords; while, on the other hand, I am sure they would acknowledge that they had never looked upon finer light horsemen than the fifty hussars of Conflans who were facing them. They were heavier, it is true, and they may have seemed the smarter, for Wellington used to make them burnish their metal work, which was not usual among us. On the other hand, it is well known that the English tunics were too tight for the sword-arm, which gave our men an advantage. As to bravery, foolish, inexperienced people of every nation always think that their own soldiers are braver than any others. There is no nation in the world which does not entertain this idea. But when one has seen as much as I have done, one understands that there is no very marked difference, and that although nations differ very much in discipline, they are all equally brave—except that the French have rather more courage than the rest.

Well, the cork was drawn and the glasses ready, when suddenly the English officer raised his sword to me as if in a challenge, and cantered his horse across the grassland. My word, there is no finer sight upon earth than that of a gallant man upon a gallant steed! I could have halted there just to watch him as he came with such careless grace, his sabre down by his horse's shoulder, his head thrown back, his white plume tossing—youth and strength and courage, with the violet evening sky above and the oak trees behind. But it was not for me to stand and stare. Etienne Gerard may have his faults, but, my faith, he was never accused of being backward in taking his own part. The old horse, Rataplan, knew me so well that he had started off before ever I gave the first shake to the bridle.

There are two things in this world that I am very slow to forget: the face of a pretty woman, and the legs of a fine horse. Well, as we drew together, I kept on saying, "Where have I seen those great roan shoulders? Where have I seen that dainty fetlock?" Then suddenly I remembered, and as I looked up at the reckless eyes and the challenging smile, whom should I recognize but the man who had saved me from the brigands and played me for my freedom—he whose correct title was Milor the Hon. Sir Russell Bart!*

"Bart!" I shouted.

He had his arm raised for a cut, and three parts of his body open to my point, for he did not know very much about the use of the sword. As I brought my hilt to the salute he dropped his hand and stared at me.

"Halloa!" said he. "It's Gerard!" You would have thought by his manner that I had met him by appointment. For my own part, I would have embraced him had he but come an inch of the way to meet me.

"I thought we were in for some sport," said he. "I never dreamed that it was you."

I found this tone of disappointment somewhat irritating. Instead of being glad at having met a friend, he was sorry at having missed an enemy.

"I should have been happy to join in your sport, my dear Bart," said I. "But I really cannot turn my sword upon a man who saved my life."

"Tut, never mind about that."

* Young Lord Russell, whose name and title Gerard always got hopelessly confused, first appeared in a story entitled "How the Brigadier Held the King," not included in this collection. In this story, Gerard, having been taken prisoner by the English, had induced the sport-loving Lord Russell to stake Gerard's freedom on the outcome of a card game. Gerard won, but before he could escape, he was captured by other English troops. He spent a few adventurous months as a prisoner of war in England before being returned to France in a prisoners exchange.

"No, it is impossible. I should never forgive myself."

"You make too much of a trifle."

"My mother's one desire is to embrace you. If ever you should be in Gascony——"

"Lord Wellington is coming there with sixty thousand men."

"Then one of them will have a chance of surviving," said I, laughing. "In the meantime, put your sword in your sheath!"

Our horses were standing head to tail, and the Bart put out his hand and patted me on the thigh.

"You're a good chap, Gerard," said he. "I only wish you had been born on the right side of the Channel."

"I was," said I.

"Poor devil!" he cried, with such an earnestness of pity that he set me laughing again. "But look here, Gerard," he continued; "this is all very well, but it is not business, you know. I don't know what Massena would say to it, but our Chief would jump out of his riding-boots if he saw us. We weren't sent out here for a picnic—either of us."

"What would you have?"

"Well, we had a little argument about our hussars and dragoons, if you remember. I've got fifty of the Sixteenth all chewing their carbine bullets behind me. You've got as many fine-looking boys over yonder, who seem to be fidgeting in their saddles. If you and I took the right flanks we should not spoil each other's beauty—though a little blood-letting is a friendly thing in this climate."

There seemed to me to be a good deal of sense in what he said. For the moment Mr. Alexis Morgan and the Countess of La Ronda and the Abbey of Almeixal went right out of my head, and I could only think of the fine level turf and of the beautiful skirmish which we might have.

"Very good, Bart," said I. "We have seen the front of your dragoons. We shall now have a look at their backs."

"Any betting?" he asked.

"The stake," said I, "is nothing less than the honor of the Hussars of Conflans."

"Well, come on!" he answered. "If we break you, well and good—if you break us, it will be all the better for Marshal Millefleurs."

When he said that I could only stare at him in astonishment.

"Why for Marshal Millefleurs?" I asked.

"It is the name of a rascal who lives out this way. My dragoons have been sent by Lord Wellington to see him safely hanged."

"Name of a name!" I cried. "Why, my hussars have been sent by Massena for that very object."

We burst out laughing at that, and sheathed our swords. There was a whirr of steel from behind us as our troopers followed our example.

"We are allies!" he cried.

"For a day."

"We must join forces."

"There is no doubt of it."

And so, instead of fighting, we wheeled our half squadrons round and moved in two little columns down the valley, the shakos and the helmets turned inwards, and the men looking their neighbors up and down, like old fighting dogs with tattered ears who have learned to respect each other's teeth. The most were on the broad grin, but there were some on either side who looked black and challenging, especially the English sergeant and my own sub-officer Papilette. They were men of habit, you see, who could not change all their ways of thinking in a moment. Besides, Papilette had lost his only brother at Busaco. As for the Bart and me, we rode together at the head and chatted about all that had occurred to us since that famous game of écarté of which I have told you.

For my own part, I spoke to him of my adventures in England. They are a very singular people, these English. Although he knew that I had been engaged in twelve campaigns, yet I am sure that the Bart thought more highly of me because I had had an affair with the Bristol Bustler. He told me, too, that the Colonel who presided over his court-martial for playing cards with a prisoner acquitted him of neglect of duty, but nearly broke him because he thought that he had not cleared his trumps before leading his suit. Yes, indeed, they are a singular people.

At the end of the valley the road curved over some rising ground before winding down into another wider valley beyond. We called a halt when we came to the top; for there, right in front of us, at the distance of about three miles, was a scattered, grey town, with a single enormous building upon the flank of the mountain which overlooked it. We could not doubt that we were at last in sight of the Abbey that held the gang of rascals whom we had come to disperse. It was only now, I think, that we fully understood what a task lay in front of us, for the place was a veritable fortress, and it was evident that cavalry should never have been sent out upon such an errand.

"That's got nothing to do with us," said the Bart; "Wellington and Massena can settle that between them."

"Courage!" I answered. "Piré took Leipzig with fifty hussars."

"Had they been dragoons," said the Bart, laughing, "he would have had Berlin. But you are senior officer; give us a lead, and we'll see who will be the first to flinch."

"Well," said I, "whatever we do must be done at once, for my orders are to be on my way to Abrantes by tomorrow night. But we must have some information first, and here is someone who should be able to give it to us."

There was a square, whitewashed house standing by the roadside, which appeared, from the bush hanging over the door, to be one of those wayside tabernas which are provided for the muleteers. A lantern was hung in the porch, and by its light we saw two men, the one in the brown habit of a Capuchin monk, and the other girt with an apron, which showed him to be the landlord. They were conversing together so earnestly that we were upon them before they were aware of us. The innkeeper turned to fly, but one of the Englishmen seized him by the hair, and held him tight.

"For mercy's sake, spare me," he yelled. "My house has been gutted by the French and harried by the English, and my feet have been burned by the brigands. I swear by the Virgin that I have neither money nor food in my inn, and the good Father Abbot, who is starving upon my doorstep, will be witness to it."

"Indeed, sir," said the Capuchin, in excellent French, "what this worthy man says is very true. He is one of the many victims to these cruel wars, although his loss is but a feather-weight compared to mine. Let him go," he added, in English, to the trooper, "he is too weak to fly, even if he desired to."

In the light of the lantern I saw that this monk was a magnificent man, dark and bearded, with the eyes of a hawk, and so tall that his cowl came up to Rataplan's ears. He wore the look of one who had been through much suffering, but he carried himself like a king, and we could form some opinion of his learning when we each heard him talk our own language as fluently as if he were born to it.

"You have nothing to fear," said I, to the trembling innkeeper. "As to you, father, you are, if I am not mistaken, the very man who can give us the information which we require."

"All that I have is at your service, my son. But," he added, with a wan smile, "my Lenten fare is always somewhat meagre, and this year it has been such that I must ask you for a crust of bread if I am to have the strength to answer your questions."

We bore two days' rations in our haversacks, so that he soon had the little he asked for. It was dreadful to see the wolfish way in which he seized the piece of dried goat's flesh which I was able to offer him.

"Time presses, and we must come to the point," said I. "We want your advice as to the weak points of yonder Abbey, and concerning the habits of the rascals who infest it."

He cried out something which I took to be Latin, with his hands clasped and his eyes upturned. "The prayer of the just availeth much," said he, "and yet I had not dared to hope that mine would have been so speedily answered. In me you see the unfortunate Abbot of Almeixal, who has been cast out by this rabble of three armies with their heretical leader. Oh! to think of what I have lost!" His voice broke, and the tears hung upon his lashes.

"Cheer up, sir," said the Bart. "I'll lay nine to four that we have you back again by tomorrow night."

"It is not of my own welfare that I think," said he, "nor even of that of my poor, scattered flock. But it is of the holy relics which are left in the sacrilegious hands of these robbers."

"It's even betting whether they would ever bother their heads about them," said the Bart. "But show us the way inside the gates, and we'll soon clear the place out for you."

In a few short words the good Abbot gave us the very points that we wished to know. But all that he said only made our task more formidable. The walls of the Abbey were forty feet high. The lower windows were barricaded, and the whole building loopholed for musketry fire. The gang preserved military discipline, and their sentries were too numerous for us to hope to take them by surprise. It was more than ever evident that a battalion of grenadiers and a couple of breaching pieces were what was needed. I raised my eyebrows, and the Bart began to whistle.

"We must have a shot at it, come what may," said he.

The men had already dismounted, and, having watered their horses, were eating their suppers. For my own part I went into the sitting-room of the inn with the Abbot and the Bart, that we might talk about our plans.

I had a little cognac in my *sauve vie*, and I divided it among us—just enough to wet our mustaches.

"It is unlikely," said I, "that those rascals know anything about our coming. I have seen no signs of scouts along the road. My own plan is that we should conceal ourselves in some neighboring wood, and then, when they open their gates, charge down upon them and take them by surprise."

The Bart was of opinion that this was the best that we could do, but, when we came to talk it over, the Abbot made us see that there were difficulties in the way.

"Save on the side of the town, there is no place within a mile of the Abbey where you could shelter man or horse," said he. "As to the townsfolk, they are not to be trusted. I fear, my son, that your excellent plan would have little chance of success in the face of the vigilant guard which these men keep."

"I see no other way," answered I. "Hussars of Conflans are not so plentiful that I can afford to run half a squadron of them against a forty-foot wall with five hundred infantry behind it."

"I am a man of peace," said the Abbot, "and yet I may, perhaps, give a word of counsel. I know these villains and their ways. Who should do so better, seeing that I have stayed for a month in this lonely spot, looking down in weariness of heart at the Abbey which was my own? I will tell you now what I should myself do if I were in your place."

"Pray tell us, father," we cried, both together.

"You must know that bodies of deserters, both French and English, are continually coming in to them, carrying their weapons with them. Now, what is there to prevent you and your men from pretending to be such a body, and so making your way into the Abbey?"

I was amazed at the simplicity of the thing, and I embraced

the good Abbot. The Bart, however, had some objections to offer.

"That is all very well," said he, "but if these fellows are as sharp as you say, it is not very likely that they are going to let a hundred armed strangers into their crib. From all I have heard of Mr. Morgan, or Marshal Millefleurs, or whatever the rascal's name is, I give him credit for more sense than that."

"Well, then," I cried, "let us send fifty in, and let them at daybreak throw open the gates to the other fifty, who will be waiting outside."

We discussed the question at great length and with much foresight and discretion. If it had been Massena and Wellington instead of two young officers of light cavalry, we could not have weighed it all with more judgment. At last we agreed, the Bart and I, that one of us should indeed go with fifty men, under pretense of being deserters, and that in the early morning he should gain command of the gate and admit the others. The Abbot, it is true, was still of opinion that it was dangerous to divide our force, but finding that we were both of the same mind, he shrugged his shoulders and gave in.

"There is only one thing that I would ask," said he. "If you lay hands upon this Marshal Millefleurs—this dog of a brigand —what will you do with him?"

"Hang him," I answered.

"It is too easy a death," cried the Capuchin, with a vindictive glow in his dark eyes. "Had I my way with him—but oh, what thoughts are these for a servant of God to harbor!" He clapped his hands to his forehead like one who is half demented by his troubles, and rushed out of the room.

There was an important point which we had still to settle, and that was whether the French or the English party should have the honor of entering the Abbey first. My faith, it was asking a great deal of Etienne Gerard that he should give place to any man at such a time! But the poor Bart pleaded so hard, urging the few skirmishes which he had seen against my four-and-seventy engagements, that at last I consented that he should go. We had just clasped hands over the matter when there broke out such a shouting and cursing and yelling from the front of the inn, that out we rushed with our drawn sabres in our hands, convinced that the brigands were upon us.

You may imagine our feelings when, by the light of the

lantern which hung from the porch, we saw a score of our
hussars and dragoons all mixed in one wild heap, red coats and
blue, helmets and busbies, pommelling each other to their
hearts' content. We flung ourselves upon them, imploring,
threatening, tugging at a lace collar, or at a spurred heel, until,
at last, we had dragged them all apart. There they stood,
flushed and bleeding, glaring at each other, and all panting
together like a line of troop horses after a ten-mile chase. It
was only with our drawn swords that we could keep them
from each other's throats. The poor Capuchin stood in the
porch in his long brown habit, wringing his hands and calling
upon all the saints for mercy.

He was, indeed, as I found upon inquiry, the innocent
cause of all the turmoil, for, not understanding how soldiers
look upon such things, he had made some remark to the English sergeant that it was a pity that his squadron was not as
good as the French. The words were not out of his mouth
before a dragoon knocked down the nearest hussar, and then,
in a moment, they all flew at each other like tigers. We would
trust them no more after that, but the Bart moved his men to
the front of the inn, and I mine to the back, the English all
scowling and silent, and our fellows shaking their fists and
chattering, each after the fashion of their own people.

Well, as our plans were made, we thought it best to carry
them out at once, lest some fresh cause of quarrel should break
out between our followers. The Bart and his men rode off,
therefore, he having first torn the lace from his sleeves, and
the gorget and sash from his uniform, so that he might pass as
a simple trooper. He explained to his men what it was that
was expected of them, and though they did not raise a cry
or wave their weapons as mine might have done, there was
an expression upon their stolid and clean-shaven faces which
filled me with confidence. Their tunics were left unbuttoned,
their scabbards and helmets stained with dirt, and their harness
badly fastened, so that they might look the part of deserters,
without order or discipline. At six o'clock next morning they
were to gain command of the main gate of the Abbey, while
at that same hour my hussars were to gallop up to it from outside. The Bart and I pledged our words to it before he trotted
off with his detachment. My sergeant, Papilette, with two
troopers, followed the English at a distance, and returned in
half an hour to say that, after some parley, and the flashing

of lanterns upon them from the grille, they had been admitted into the Abbey.

So far, then, all had gone well. It was a cloudy night with a sprinkling of rain, which was in our favor, as there was the less chance of our presence being discovered. My vedettes I placed two hundred yards in every direction, to guard against a surprise, and also to prevent any peasant who might stumble upon us from carrying the news to the Abbey. Oudin and Papilette were to take turns of duty, while the others with their horses had snug quarters in a great wooden granary. Having walked round and seen that all was as it should be, I flung myself upon the bed which the innkeeper had set apart for me, and fell into a dreamless sleep.

No doubt you have heard my name mentioned as being the beau-ideal of a soldier, and that not only by friends and admirers like our fellow-townsfolk, but also by old officers of the great wars who have shared the fortunes of those famous campaigns with me. Truth and modesty compel me to say, however, that this is not so. There are some gifts which I lack —very few, no doubt—but, still, amid the vast armies of the Emperor there may have been some who were free from those blemishes which stood between me and perfection. Of bravery I say nothing. Those who have seen me in the field are best fitted to speak about that. I have often heard the soldiers discussing around the camp-fires as to who was the bravest man in the Grand Army. Some said Murat, and some said Lasalle, and some Ney; but for my own part, when they asked me, I merely shrugged my shoulders and smiled. It would have seemed mere conceit if I had answered that there was no man braver than Brigadier Gerard. At the same time, facts are facts, and a man knows best what his own feelings are. But there are other gifts besides bravery which are necessary for a soldier, and one of them is that he should be a light sleeper. Now, from my boyhood onwards, I have been hard to wake, and it was this which brought me to ruin upon that night.

It may have been about two o'clock in the morning that I was suddenly conscious of a feeling of suffocation. I tried to call out, but there was something which prevented me from uttering a sound. I struggled to rise, but I could only flounder like a hamstrung horse. I was strapped at the ankles, strapped at the knees, and strapped again at the wrists. Only my eyes were free to move, and there at the foot of my couch, by the light of a Portuguese lamp, whom should I see but the Abbot and the innkeeper!

The latter's heavy, white face had appeared to me when I looked upon it the evening before to express nothing but stupidity and terror. Now, on the contrary, every feature bespoke brutality and ferocity. Never have I seen a more dreadful-looking villain. In his hand he held a long, dull-colored knife. The Abbot, on the other hand, was as polished and as dignified as ever. His Capuchin gown had been thrown open, however, and I saw beneath it a black, frogged coat, such as I have seen among the English officers. As our eyes met he leaned over the wooden end of the bed and laughed silently until it creaked again.

"You will, I am sure, excuse my mirth, my dear Colonel Gerard," said he. "The fact is, that the expression upon your face when you grasped the situation was just a little funny. I have no doubt that you are an excellent soldier, but I hardly think that you are fit to measure wits with the Marshal Mille-fleurs, as your fellows have been good enough to call me. You appear to have given me credit for singularly little intelligence, which argues, if I may be allowed to say so, a want of acute-ness upon your own part. Indeed, with the single exception of my thick-headed compatriot, the British dragoon, I have never met anyone who was less competent to carry out such a mission."

You can imagine how I felt and how I looked, as I listened to this insolent harangue, which was all delivered in that flowery and condescending manner which had gained this rascal his nickname. I could say nothing, but they must have read my threat in my eyes, for the fellow who had played the part of the innkeeper whispered something to his companion.

"No, no, my dear Chenier, he will be infinitely more valu-able alive," said he. "By the way, Colonel, it is just as well that you are a sound sleeper, for my friend here, who is a little rough in his ways, would certainly have cut your throat if you had raised any alarm. I should recommend you to keep in his good graces, for Sergeant Chenier, late of the Seventh Imperial Light Infantry, is a much more dangerous person than Captain Alexis Morgan, of His Majesty's foot-guards."

Chenier grinned and shook his knife at me, while I tried to

look the loathing which I felt at the thought that a soldier of
the Emperor could fall so low.

"It may amuse you to know," said the Marshal, in that soft,
suave voice of his, "that both your expeditions were watched
from the time that you left your respective camps. I think
that you will allow that Chenier and I played our parts with
some subtlety. We had made every arrangement for your reception at the Abbey, though we had hoped to receive the
whole squadron instead of half. When the gates were secured
behind them, our visitors find themselves in a very charming
mediæval quadrangle, with no possible exit, commanded by
musketry fire from a hundred windows. They may choose
to be shot down; or they may choose to surrender. Between
ourselves, I have not the slightest doubt that they have been
wise enough to do the latter. But since you are naturally interested in the matter, we thought that you would care to
come with us and to see for yourself. I think I can promise
you that you will find your titled friend waiting for you at
the Abbey with a face as long as your own."

The two villains began whispering together, debating, as
far as I could hear, which was the best way of avoiding my
vedettes.

"I will make sure that it is all clear upon the other side of
the barn," said the Marshal at last. "You will stay here, my
good Chenier, and if the prisoner gives any trouble you will
know what to do."

So we were left together, this murderous renegade and I—
he sitting at the end of the bed, sharpening his knife upon his
boot in the light of the single smoky little oil-lamp. As to me,
I only wonder now, as I look back upon it, that I did not go
mad with vexation and self-reproach as I lay helplessly upon
the couch, unable to utter a word or move a finger, with the
knowledge that my fifty gallant lads were so close to me, and
yet with no means of letting them know the straits to which
I was reduced. It was no new thing for me to be a prisoner;
but to be taken by these renegades, and to be led into their
Abbey in the midst of their jeers, befooled and outwitted by
their insolent leaders—that was indeed more than I could endure. The knife of the butcher beside me would cut less deeply
than that.

I twitched softly at my wrists, and then at my ankles, but
whichever of the two had secured me was no bungler at his

work. I could not move either of them an inch. Then I tried
to work the handkerchief down over my mouth, but the
ruffian beside me raised his knife with such a threatening snarl
that I had to desist. I was lying still looking at his bull neck,
and wondering whether it would ever be my good fortune to
fit it for a cravat, when I heard returning steps coming down
the inn passage and up the stair. What word would the villain
bring back? If he found it impossible to kidnap me, he would
probably murder me where I lay. For my own part, I was
indifferent which it might be, and I looked at the doorway
with the contempt and defiance which I longed to put into
words. But you can imagine my feelings, my dear friends,
when, instead of the tall figure and dark, sneering face of the
Capuchin, my eyes fell upon the grey pelisse and huge mustaches of my good little sub-officer, Papilette!

The French soldier of those days had seen too much to be
ever taken by surprise. His eyes had hardly rested upon my
bound figure and the sinister face beside me before he had
seen how the matter lay.

"Sacred name of a dog!" he growled, and out flashed his
great sabre. Chenier sprang forward at him with his knife, and
then, thinking better of it, he darted back and stabbed frantically at my heart. For my own part, I had hurled myself off
the bed on the side opposite to him, and the blade grazed my
side before ripping its way through blanket and sheet. An
instant later I heard the thud of a heavy fall, and then almost
simultaneously a second object struck the floor—something
lighter but harder, which rolled under the bed. I will not
horrify you with details, my friends. Suffice it that Papilette
was one of the strongest swordsmen in the regiment, and that
his sabre was heavy and sharp. It left a red blotch upon my
wrists and my ankles, as it cut the thongs which bound me.

When I had thrown off my gag, the first use which I made
of my lips was to kiss the sergeant's scarred cheeks. The next
was to ask him if all was well with the command. Yes, they
had had no alarms. Oudin had just relieved him, and he had
come to report. Had he seen the Abbot? No, he had seen
nothing of him. Then we must form a cordon and prevent
his escape. I was hurrying out to give the orders, when I heard
a slow and measured step enter the door below, and come
creaking up the stairs.

Papilette understood it all in an instant. "You are not to

kill him," I whispered, and thrust him into the shadow on one side of the door; I crouched on the other. Up he came, up and up, and every footfall seemed to be upon my heart. The brown skirt of his gown was not over the threshold before we were both on him, like two wolves on a buck. Down we crashed, the three of us, he fighting like a tiger, and with such amazing strength that he might have broken away from the two of us. Thrice he got to his feet, and thrice we had him over again, until Papilette made him feel that there was a point to his sabre. He had sense enough then to know that the game was up, and to lie still while I lashed him with the very cords which had been round my own limbs.

"There has been a fresh deal, my fine fellow," said I, "and you will find that I have some of the trumps in *my* hand this time."

"Luck always comes to the aid of a fool," he answered. "Perhaps it is as well, otherwise the world would fall too completely into the power of the astute. So, you have killed Chenier, I see. He was an insubordinate dog, and always smelt abominably of garlic. Might I trouble you to lay me upon the bed? The floor of these Portuguese tabernas is hardly a fitting couch for anyone who has prejudices in favor of cleanliness."

I could not but admire the coolness of the man, and the way in which he preserved the same insolent air of condescension in spite of this sudden turning of the tables. I dispatched Papilette to summon a guard, whilst I stood over our prisoner with my drawn sword, never taking my eyes off him for an instant, for I must confess that I had conceived a great respect for his audacity and resource.

"I trust," said he, "that your men will treat me in a becoming manner."

"You will get your deserts—you may depend upon that."

"I ask nothing more. You may not be aware of my exalted birth, but I am so placed that I cannot name my father without treason, nor my mother without a scandal. I cannot *claim* Royal honors, but these things are so much more graceful when they are conceded without a claim. The thongs are cutting my skin. Might I beg you to loosen them?"

"You do not give me credit for much intelligence," I remarked, repeating his own words.

"*Touché*," he cried, like a pinked fencer. "But here come your men, so it matters little whether you loosen them or not."

I ordered the gown to be stripped from him and placed him under a strong guard. Then, as morning was already breaking, I had to consider what my next step was to be. The poor Bart and his Englishmen had fallen victims of the deep scheme which might, had we adopted all the crafty suggestions of our adviser, have ended in the capture of the whole instead of the half of our force. I must extricate them if it were still possible. Then there was the old lady, the Countess of La Ronda, to be thought of. As to the Abbey, since its garrison was on the alert it was hopeless to think of capturing that. All turned now upon the value which they placed upon their leader. The game depended upon my playing that one card. I will tell you how boldly and how skillfully I played it.

It was hardly light before my bugler blew the assembly, and out we trotted on to the plain. My prisoner was placed on horseback in the very center of the troops. It chanced that there was a large tree just out of musket-shot from the main gate of the Abbey, and under this we halted. Had they opened the great doors in order to attack us, I should have charged home upon them; but, as I had expected, they stood upon the defensive, lining the long wall and pouring down a torrent of hootings and taunts and derisive laughter upon us. A few fired their muskets, but finding that we were out of reach they soon ceased to waste their powder. It was the strangest sight to see that mixture of uniforms, French, English, and Portuguese, cavalry, infantry, and artillery, all wagging their heads and shaking their fists at us.

My word, their hubbub soon died away when we opened our ranks, and showed whom we had got in the midst of us! There was silence for a few seconds, and then such a howl of rage and grief! I could see some of them dancing like madmen upon the wall. He must have been a singular person, this prisoner of ours, to have gained the affection of such a gang.

I had brought a rope from the inn, and we slung it over the lower bough of the tree.

"You will permit me, monsieur, to undo your collar," said Papilette, with mock politeness.

"If your hands are perfectly clean," answered our prisoner, and set the whole half-squadron laughing.

There was another yell from the wall, followed by a profound hush as the noose was tightened round Marshal Mille-fleurs' neck. Then came a shriek from a bugle, the Abbey gates flew open, and three men rushed out waving white cloths in their hands. Ah, how my heart bounded with joy at the sight of them. And yet I would not advance an inch to meet them, so that all the eagerness might seem to be upon their side. I allowed my trumpeter, however, to wave a handkerchief in reply, upon which the three envoys came running towards us. The Marshal, still pinioned, and with the rope round his neck, sat his horse with a half smile, as one who is slightly bored and yet strives out of courtesy not to show it. If I were in such a situation I could not wish to carry myself better, and surely I can say no more than that.

They were a singular trio, these ambassadors. The one was a Portuguese caçadore in his dark uniform, the second a French chasseur in the lightest green, and the third a big English artilleryman in blue and gold. They saluted, all three, and the Frenchman did the talking.

"We have thirty-seven English dragoons in our hands," said he. "We give you our most solemn oath that they shall all hang from the Abbey wall within five minutes of the death of our Marshal."

"Thirty-seven!" I cried. "You have fifty-one."

"Fourteen were cut down before they could be secured."

"And the officer?"

"He would not surrender his sword save with his life. It was not our fault. We would have saved him if we could."

Alas for my poor Bart! I had met him but twice, and yet he was a man very much after my heart. I have always had a regard for the English for the sake of that one friend. A braver man and a worse swordsman I have never met.

I did not, as you may think, take these rascals' word for anything. Papilette was dispatched with one of them, and returned to say that it was too true. I had now to think of the living.

"You will release the thirty-seven dragoons if I free your leader?"

"We will give you ten of them."

"Up with him!" I cried.

"Twenty," shouted the chasseur.

"No more words," said I. "Pull on the rope!"

"All of them," cried the envoy, as the cord tightened round the Marshal's neck.

"With horses and arms?"

They could see that I was not a man to jest with.

"All complete," said the chasseur, sulkily.

"And the Countess of La Ronda as well?" said I.

But here I met with firmer opposition. No threats of mine could induce them to give up the Countess. We tightened the cord. We moved the horse. We did all but leave the Marshal suspended. If once I broke his neck the dragoons were dead men. It was as precious to me as to them.

"Allow me to remark," said the Marshal, blandly, "that you are exposing me to a risk of a quinsy. Do you not think, since there is a difference of opinion upon this point, that it would be an excellent idea to consult the lady herself? We would neither of us, I am sure, wish to override her own inclinations."

Nothing could be more satisfactory. You can imagine how quickly I grasped at so simple a solution. In ten minutes she was before us, a most stately dame, with her grey curls peeping out from under her mantilla. Her face was as yellow as though it reflected the countless doubloons of her treasury.

"This gentleman," said the Marshal, "is exceedingly anxious to convey you to a place where you will never see us more. It is for you to decide whether you would wish to go with him, or whether you prefer to remain with me."

She was at his horse's side in an instant. "My own Alexis," she cried, "nothing can ever part us."

He looked at me with a sneer upon his handsome face.

"By the way, you made a small slip of the tongue, my dear Colonel," said he. "Except by courtesy, no such person exists as the Dowager Countess of La Ronda. The lady whom I have the honor to present to you is my very dear wife, Mrs. Alexis Morgan—or shall I say Madame la Marèchale Millefleurs?"

It was at this moment that I came to the conclusion that I was dealing with the cleverest, and also the most unscrupulous, man whom I had ever met. As I looked upon this unfortunate old woman my soul was filled with wonder and disgust. As for her, her eyes were raised to his face with such a look as a young recruit might give to the Emperor.

"So be it," said I at last; "give me the dragoons and let me go."

They were brought out with their horses and weapons, and the rope was taken from the Marshal's neck.

"Good-bye, my dear Colonel," said he. "I am afraid that

you will have rather a lame account to give of your mission, when you find your way back to Massena, though, from all I hear, he will probably be too busy to think of you. I am free to confess that you have extricated yourself from your difficulties with greater ability than I had given you credit for. I presume that there is nothing which I can do for you before you go?"

"There is one thing."

"And that is?"

"To give fitting burial to this young officer and his men."

"I pledge my word to it."

"And there is one other."

"Name it."

"To give me five minutes in the open with a sword in your hand and a horse between your legs."

"Tut, tut!" said he. "I should either have to cut short your promising career, or else to bid adieu to my own bonny bride. It is unreasonable to ask such a request of a man in the first joys of matrimony."

I gathered my horsemen together and wheeled them into column.

"Au revoir," I cried, shaking my sword at him. "The next time you may not escape so easily."

"Au revoir," he answered. "When you are weary of the Emperor, you will always find a commission waiting for you in the service of the Marshal Millefleurs."

1812

VI. How the Brigadier Rode to Minsk

I WOULD have a stronger wine tonight, my friends, a wine of Burgundy rather than of Bordeaux. It is that my heart, my old soldier heart, is heavy within me. It is a strange thing, this age which creeps upon one. One does not know, one does not understand; the spirit is ever the same, and one does not remember how the poor body crumbles. But there comes a moment when it is brought home, when quick as the sparkle of a whirling sabre it is clear to us, and we see the men we were and the men we are. Yes, yes, it was so today, and I would have a wine of Burgundy tonight, White Burgundy—Montrachet—— Sir, I am your debtor!

It was this morning in the Champ de Mars. Your pardon, friends, while an old man tells his trouble. You saw the review. Was it not splendid? I was in the enclosure for veteran officers who have been decorated. This ribbon on my breast was my passport. The cross itself I keep at home in a leathern pouch. They did us honor, for we were placed at the saluting point, with the Emperor and the carriages of the Court upon our right.

It is years since I have been to a review, for I cannot approve of many things which I have seen. I do not approve of the red breeches of the infantry. It was in white breeches that the infantry used to fight. Red is for the cavalry. A little more, and they would ask our busbies and our spurs! Had I been seen at a review they might well have said that I, Etienne Gerard, had condoned it. So I have stayed at home. But this war of the Crimea is different. The men go to battle. It is not for me to be absent when brave men gather.

My faith, they march well, those little infantrymen! They are not large, but they are very solid and they carry themselves well. I took off my hat to them as they passed. Then there came the guns. They were good guns, well horsed, and well manned. I took off my hat to them. Then came the Engineers, and to them also I took off my hat. There are no braver men than the Engineers. Then came the cavalry, Lancers, Cuirassiers, Chasseurs, and Spahis. To all of them in turn I was able to take off my hat, save only to the Spahis. The Emperor had no Spahis. But when all of the others had passed, what think you came at the close? A brigade of Hussars, and at the charge! Oh, my friends, the pride and the glory and the beauty, the flash and the sparkle, the roar of the hoofs, and the jingle of chains, the tossing manes, the noble heads, the rolling cloud, and the dancing waves of steel! My heart drummed to them as they passed. And the last of all, was it not my own old regiment? My eyes fell upon the gray and silver dolmans, with the leopard skin shabracks, and at that instant the years fell away from me and I saw my own beautiful men and horses, even as they had swept behind their young colonel, in the pride of our youth and our strength, just forty years ago. Up flew my cane. "*Chargez! En avant! Vive l'Empereur!*" It was the past calling to the present. But, oh, what a thin, piping voice! Was this the voice that had once thundered from wing to wing of a strong brigade? And the arm that could scarce wave a cane, were these the muscles of fire and steel which had no match in all Napoleon's mighty host? They smiled at me. They cheered me. The Emperor laughed and bowed. But to me the present was a dim dream, and what was real were my eight hundred dead Hussars and the Etienne of long ago. Enough—a brave man can face age and fate as he faced Cossacks and Uhlans. But there are times when Montrachet is better than the wine of Bordeaux.

It is to Russia that they go, and so I will tell you a story of Russia. Ah, what an evil dream of the night it seems! Blood and ice. Ice and blood. Fierce faces with snow upon the whiskers. Blue hands held out for succor. And across the great white plain the one long black line of moving figures, trudging, trudging, a hundred miles, another hundred, and still always the same white plain. Sometimes there were fir-woods to limit it, sometimes it stretched away to the cold blue sky, but the black line stumbled on and on. Those weary, ragged, starving men, the spirit frozen out of them, looked neither to right nor left, but with sunken faces and rounded backs trailed onwards and ever onwards, making for France as wounded beasts make for their lair. There was no speaking, and you could scarce hear the shuffle of feet in the snow. Once only I heard them laugh. It was outside Vilna, when an aide-de-camp rode up to the head of that dreadful column and asked if that were the Grand Army. All who were within hearing lookèd round, and when they saw those broken men, those ruined regiments, those fur-capped skeletons who were once the Guard, they laughed, and the laugh crackled down the column like a *feu de joie*. I have heard many a groan and cry and scream in my life, but nothing so terrible as the laugh of the Grand Army.

But why was it that these helpless men were not destroyed by the Russians? Why was it that they were not speared by the Cossacks or herded into droves, and driven as prisoners into the heart of Russia? On every side as you watched the black snake winding over the snow you saw also the dark, moving shadows which came and went like cloud drifts on either flank and behind. They were the Cossacks, who hung round us like wolves round the flock. But the reason why they did not ride in upon us was that all the ice of Russia could not cool the hot hearts of some of our soldiers. To the end there were always those who were ready to throw themselves between these savages and their prey. One man above all rose greater as the danger thickened, and won a higher name amid disaster than he had done when he led our van to victory. To him I drink this glass—to Ney, the red-maned Lion, glaring back over his shoulder at the enemy who feared to tread too closely on his heels. I can see him now, his broad white face convulsed with fury, his light blue eyes sparkling like flints, his great voice roaring and crashing amid the roll of the musketry. His glazed and featherless cocked hat was the ensign upon which France rallied during those dreadful days.

It is well known that neither I nor the regiment of Hussars of Conflans were at Moscow. We were left behind on the lines of communication at Borodino. How the Emperor could have advanced without us is incomprehensible to me, and, indeed, it was only then that I understood that his judgment was weakening, and that he was no longer the man that he had been. However, a soldier has to obey orders, and so I remained at this village, which was poisoned by the bodies of thirty thousand men who had lost their lives in the great battle. I spent the late autumn in getting my horses into condition and reclothing my men, so that when the army fell back on Borodino my Hussars were the best of the cavalry, and were placed under Ney in the rear-guard. What could he have done without us during those dreadful days? "Ah, Gerard," said he one evening—but it is not for me to repeat the words. Suffice it that he spoke what the whole army felt. The rear-guard covered the army, and the Hussars of Conflans covered the rear-guard. There was the whole truth in a sentence. Always the Cossacks were on us. Always we held them off. Never a day passed that we had not to wipe our sabres. That was soldiering indeed.

But there came a time between Vilna and Smolensk when the situation became impossible. Cossacks and even cold we could fight, but we could not fight hunger as well. Food must be got at all costs. That night Ney sent for me to the wagon in which he slept. His great head was sunk on his hands. Mind and body, he was wearied to death.

"Colonel Gerard," said he, "things are going very badly with us. The men are starving. We must have food at all costs."

"The horses," I suggested.

"Save your handful of cavalry, there are none left."

"The band," said I.

He laughed, even in his despair.

"Why the band?" he asked.

"Fighting men are of value."

"Good!" said he. "You would play the game down to the last card, and so would I. Good, Gerard, good!" He clasped my hand in his. "But there is one chance for us yet, Gerard." He unhooked a lantern from the roof of the wagon, and he laid it on a map which was stretched before him. "To the south of us," said he, "there lies the town of Minsk. I have word from a Russian deserter that much corn has been stored in the town-hall. I wish you to take as many men as you think best, set forth for Minsk, seize the corn, load any carts which you may collect in the town, and bring them to me between here and Smolensk. If you fail, it is but a detachment cut off. If you succeed, it is new life to the army."

He had not expressed himself well, for it was evident that if we failed it was not merely the loss of a detachment. It is quality as well as quantity which counts. And yet how honorable a mission, and how glorious a risk! If mortal men could bring it, then the corn should come from Minsk. I said so, and spoke a few burning words about a brave man's duty until the Marshal was so moved that he rose and, taking me affectionately by the shoulders, pushed me out of the wagon.

It was clear to me that in order to succeed in my enterprise I should take a small force and depend rather upon surprise than upon numbers. A large body could not conceal itself, would have great difficulty in getting food, and would cause all the Russians around us to concentrate for its certain destruction. On the other hand, if a small body of cavalry could get past the Cossacks unseen it was probable that they would find no troops to oppose them, for we knew that the main Russian army was several days' march behind us. This corn was meant, no doubt, for their consumption. A squadron of Hussars and thirty Polish Lancers were all whom I chose for the venture. That very night we rode out of the camp, and struck south in the direction of Minsk.

Fortunately there was but half a moon, and we were able to pass without being attacked by the enemy. Twice we saw great fires burning amid the snow, and around them a thick bristle of long poles. These were the lances of Cossacks, which they had stood upright while they slept. It would have been a great joy to us to have charged in amongst them, for we had much to revenge, and the eyes of my comrades looked longingly from me to those red flickering patches in the darkness. My faith, I was sorely tempted to do it, for it would have been a good lesson to teach them that they must keep a few miles between themselves and a French army. It is the essence of good generalship, however, to keep one thing before one at a time, and so we rode silently on through the snow, leaving these Cossack bivouacs to right and left. Behind us the black sky was all mottled with a line of flame, which showed where our own poor wretches were trying to keep themselves alive for another day of misery and starvation.

All night we rode slowly onwards, keeping our horses'
tails to the Pole Star. There were many tracks in the snow,
and we kept to the line of these, that no one might remark
that a body of cavalry had passed that way. These are the
little precautions which mark the experienced officer. Besides,
by keeping to the tracks we were most likely to find the villages, and only in the villages could we hope to get food. The
dawn of day found us in a thick fir-wood, the trees so loaded
with snow that the light could hardly reach us. When we had
found our way out of it it was full daylight, the rim of the
rising sun peeping over the edge of the great snow-plain and
turning it crimson from end to end. I halted my Hussars and
Lancers under the shadow of the wood, and I studied the
country. Close to us there was a small farmhouse. Beyond, at a
distance of several miles, was a village. Far away on the skyline rose a considerable town all bristling with church towers.
This was Minsk. In no direction could I see any signs of
troops. It was evident that we had passed through the Cossacks, and that there was nothing between us and our goal. A
joyous shout burst from my men when I told them our position, and we advanced rapidly towards the village.

I have said, however, that there was a small farmhouse im-
mediately in front of us. As we rode up to it I observed that a
fine gray horse with a military saddle was tethered by the
door. Instantly I galloped forward, but before I could reach
it a man dashed out of the door, flung himself on to the horse,
and rode furiously away, the crisp, dry snow flying up in a
cloud behind him. The sunlight gleamed upon his gold epaulettes, and I knew that he was a Russian officer. He would
raise the whole country-side if we did not catch him. I put
spurs to Violette and flew after him. My troopers followed;
but there was no horse among them to compare with Violette,
and I knew well that if I could not catch the Russian I need
expect no help from them.

But it is a swift horse indeed and a skilful rider who can
hope to escape from Violette with Etienne Gerard in the saddle. He rode well, this young Russian, and his mount was a
good one, but gradually we wore him down. His face glanced
continually over his shoulder—a dark, handsome face, with
eyes like an eagle—and I saw as I closed with him that he was
measuring the distance between us. Suddenly he half turned;

there were a flash and a crack as his pistol bullet hummed past my ear. Before he could draw his sword I was upon him; but he still spurred his horse, and the two galloped together over the plain, I with my leg against the Russian's and my left hand upon his right shoulder. I saw his hand fly up to his mouth. Instantly I dragged him across my pommel and seized him by the throat, so that he could not swallow. His horse shot from under him, but I held him fast, and Violette came to a stand. Sergeant Oudin of the Hussars was the first to join us. He was an old soldier, and he saw at a glance what I was after.

"Hold tight, Colonel," said he; "I'll do the rest."

He slipped out his knife, thrust the blade between the clenched teeth of the Russian, and turned it so as to force his mouth open. There, on his tongue, was the little wad of wet paper which he had been so anxious to swallow. Oudin picked it out, and I let go of the man's throat. From the way in which, half strangled as he was, he glanced at the paper I was sure that it was a message of extreme importance. His hands twitched as if he longed to snatch it from me. He shrugged his shoulders, however, and smiled good-humoredly when I apologized for my roughness.

"And now to business," said I, when he had done coughing and hawking. "What is your name?"

"Alexis Barakoff."

"Your rank and regiment?"

"Captain of the Dragoons of Grodno."

"What is this note which you were carrying?"

"It is a line which I had written to my sweetheart."

"Whose name," said I, examining the address, "is the Hetman Platoff. Come, come, sir, this is an important military document, which you are carrying from one general to another. Tell me this instant what it is."

"Read it, and then you will know." He spoke perfect French, as do most of the educated Russians. But he knew well that there is not one French officer in a thousand who knows a word of Russian. The inside of the note contained one single line which ran like this:—

"Pustj Franzuzy pridutt v Minsk. Min gotovy."

I stared at it, and I had to shake my head. Then I showed it to my Hussars, but they could make nothing of it. The Poles were all rough fellows who could not read or write, save only the sergeant, who came from Memel, in East Prussia, and knew no Russian. It was maddening, for I felt that I had possession of some important secret upon which the safety of the army might depend, and yet I could make no sense of it. Again I entreated our prisoner to translate it, and offered him his freedom if he would do so. He only smiled at my request. I could not but admire him, for it was the very smile which I should have myself smiled had I been in his position.

"At least," said I, "tell us the name of this village."

"It is Dobrova."

"And that is Minsk over yonder I suppose?"

"Yes, that is Minsk."

"Then we shall go to the village and we shall very soon find some one who will translate this dispatch."

So we rode onward together, a trooper with his carbine on either side of our prisoner. The village was but a little place, and I set a guard at the ends of the single street, so that no one could escape from it. It was necessary to call a halt and to find some food for the men and horses, since they had travelled all night and had a long journey still before them.

There was one large stone house in the center of the village, and to this I rode. It was the house of the priest—a snuffy and ill-favored old man who had not a civil answer to any of our questions. An uglier fellow I never met, but, my faith, it was very different with his only daughter, who kept house for him. She was a brunette, a rare thing in Russia, with creamy skin, raven hair, and a pair of the most glorious dark eyes that ever kindled at the sight of a Hussar. From the first glance I saw that she was mine. It was no time for love-making when a soldier's duty had to be done, but still, as I took the simple meal which they laid before me, I chatted lightly with the lady, and we were the best of friends before an hour had passed. Sophie was her first name, her second I never knew. I taught her to call me Etienne, and I tried to cheer her up, for her sweet face was sad and there were tears in her beautiful dark eyes. I pressed her to tell me what it was which was grieving her.

"How can I be otherwise," said she, speaking French with a most adorable lisp, "when one of my poor countrymen is a prisoner in your hands? I saw him between two of your Hussars as you rode into the village."

"It is the fortune of war," said I. "His turn today; mine, perhaps, tomorrow."

"But consider, Monsieur——" said she.

"Etienne," said I.

"Well, then," she cried, beautifully flushed and desperate, "consider, Etienne, that this young officer will be taken back to your army and will be starved or frozen, for if, as I h..he your own soldiers have a hard march, what will be the l..uad-a prisoner?"

I shrugged my shoulders.

"You have a kind face, Etienne," said she; "you w.. often he condemn this poor man to certain death. I entreat y.. onvoy of him go."

Her delicate hand rested upon my sleeve, her the future looked imploringly into mine.

A sudden thought passed through my mind. I w..tm-grant her request, but I would demand a favor in return. At.. my order the prisoner was brought up into the room.

"Captain Barakoff," said I, "this young lady has begged me to release you, and I am inclined to do so. I would ask you to give your parole that you will remain in this dwelling for twenty-four hours, and take no steps to inform any one of our movements."

"I will do so," said he.

"Then I trust in your honor. One man more or less can make no difference in a struggle between great armies, and to take you back as a prisoner would be to condemn you to death. Depart, sir, and show your gratitude not to me, but to the first French officer who falls into your hands."

When he was gone I drew my paper from my pocket.

"Now, Sophie," said I, "I have done what you asked me, and all that I ask in return is that you will give me a lesson in Russian."

"With all my heart," said she.

"Let us begin on this," said I spreading out the paper before her. "Let us take it word for word and see what it means."

She looked at the writing with some surprise. "It means," said she, "if the French come to Minsk all is lost." Suddenly a look of consternation passed over her beautiful face. "Great heavens!" she cried, "what is it that I have done? I have be-trayed my country! Oh, Etienne, your eyes are the last for

whom this message is meant. How could you be so cunning as
to make a poor, simpleminded, and unsuspecting girl betray
the cause of her country?"

I consoled my poor Sophie as best I might, and I assured
her that it was no reproach to her that she should be outwitted by so old a campaigner and so shrewd a man as myself.
But it was no time now for talk. This message made it clear
the corn was indeed at Minsk, and that there were no
there to defend it. I gave a hurried order from the
the trumpeter blew the assembly, and in ten minutes
left the village behind us and were riding hard for
the gilded domes and minarets of which glimmered
now of the horizon. Higher they rose and higher,
as the sun sank towards the west, we were in the
street, and galloped up it amid the shouts of the
the cries of frightened women until we found
front of the great town-hall. My cavalry I drew
square, and I, with my two sergeants, Oudin and
ette, rushed into the building.

Heavens! shall I ever forget the sight which greeted us?
Right in front of us was drawn up a triple line of Russian
Grenadiers. Their muskets rose as we entered, and a crashing
volley burst into our very faces, Oudin and Papilette dropped
upon the floor, riddled with bullets. For myself, my busby was
shot away and I had two holes through my dolman. The
Grenadiers ran at me with their bayonets. "Treason!" I cried.
"We are betrayed! Stand to your horses!" I rushed out of the
hall, but the whole square was swarming with troops. From
every side street Dragoons and Cossacks were riding down
upon us, and such a rolling fire had burst from the surround-
ing houses that half my men and horses were on the ground.
"Follow me!" I yelled, and sprang upon Violette, but a giant
of a Russian Dragoon officer threw his arms round me, and
we rolled on the ground together. He shortened his sword to
kill me, but, changing his mind, he seized me by the throat
and banged my head against the stones until I was unconscious.
So it was that I became the prisoner of the Russians.

When I came to myself my only regret was that my captor
had not beaten out my brains. There in the grand square of
Minsk lay half my troopers dead or wounded, with exultant
crowds of Russians gathered round them. The rest, in a melan-

choly group, were herded into the porch of the town-hall, a *sotnia* of Cossacks keeping guard over them. Alas! what could I say, what could I do? It was evident that I had led my men into a carefully baited trap. They had heard of our mission, and they had prepared for us. And yet there was that dispatch which had caused me to neglect all precautions and to ride straight into the town. How was I to account for that? The tears ran down my cheeks as I surveyed the ruin of my squadron, and as I thought of the plight of my comrades of the Great Army who awaited the food which I was to have brought them. Ney had trusted me, and I had failed him. How often would strain his eyes over the snowfields for that convoy of grain which should never gladden his sight! My own fate was hard enough. An exile in Siberia was the best which I could bring me. But you will believe me, my friend, it was not for his own sake, but for that of his starving comrades, that Etienne Gerard's cheeks were lined by hot tears, frozen even as they were shed.

"What's this?" said a gruff voice at my elbow; and I turned to face the huge, black-bearded Dragoon who had dragged me from my saddle. "Look at the Frenchman crying! I thought that the Corsican was followed by brave men, and not by children."

"If you and I were face to face and alone, I should let you see which is the better man," said I.

For answer the brute struck me across the face with his open hand. I seized him by the throat, but a dozen of his soldiers tore me away from him, and he struck me again while they held my hands.

"You base hound," I cried, "is this the way to treat an officer and a gentleman?"

"We never asked you to come to Russia," said he. "If you do you must take such treatment as you can get. I would shoot you off-hand if I had my way."

"You will answer for this some day," I cried, as I wiped the blood from my moustache.

"If the Hetman Platoff is of my way of thinking you will not be alive this time tomorrow," he answered, with a ferocious scowl. He added some words in Russian to his troops, and instantly they all sprang to their saddles. Poor Violette, looking as miserable as her master, was led round and I was told to mount her. My left arm was tied with a thong which was fastened to the stirrup-iron of a sergeant of Dragoons. So in most sorry plight I and the remnant of my men set forth from Minsk.

Never have I met such a brute as this man Sergine, who commanded the escort. The Russian army contains the best and the worst in the world, but a worse than Major Sergine of the Dragoons of Kieff I have never seen in any force outside of the guerillas of the Peninsula. He was a man of great stature, with a fierce, hard face and a bristling black beard, which fell over his cuirass. I have been told since that he was noted for his strength and his bravery, and I could answer for it that he had the grip of a bear, for I had felt it when he tore me from my saddle. He was a wit, too, in his way, and made continual remarks in Russian at our expense which set all his Dragoons and Cossacks laughing. Twice he beat my comrades with his riding-whip, and once he approached me with the lash swung over his shoulder, but there was something in my eyes which prevented it from falling. So in misery and humiliation, cold and starving, we rode in a disconsolate column across the vast snow-plain. The sun had sunk, but still in the long northern twilight we pursued our weary journey: Numbed and frozen, with my head aching from the blows it had received, I was borne onwards by Violette, hardly conscious of where I was or whither I was going. The little mare walked with a sunken head, only raising it to snort her contempt for the mangy Cossack ponies who were round her.

But suddenly the escort stopped, and I found that we had halted in the single street of a small Russian village. There was a church on one side, and on the other was a large stone house, the outline of which seemed to me to be familiar. I looked around me in the twilight, and then I saw that we had been led back to Dobrova, and that this house at the door of which we were waiting was the same house of the priest at which we had stopped in the morning. Here it was that my charming Sophie in her innocence had translated the unlucky message which had in some strange way led us to our ruin. To think that only a few hours before we had left this very spot with such high hopes and all fair prospects for our mission, and now the remnants of us waited as beaten and humiliated men for whatever lot a brutal enemy might ordain! But such is the fate of the soldier, my friends—kisses today, blows tomorrow. Tokay in a palace, ditch-water in a hovel, furs or rags, a full purse or an empty pocket, ever swaying from the best to the worst, with only his courage and his honor unchanging.

The Russian horsemen dismounted, and my poor fellows were ordered to do the same. It was already late, and it was clearly their intention to spend the night in this village. There were great cheering and joy amongst the peasants when they understood that we had all been taken, and they flocked out of their houses with flaming torches, the women carrying out tea and brandy for the Cossacks. Amongst others, the old priest came forth—the same whom we had seen in the morning. He was all smiles now, and he bore with him some hot punch on a salver, the reek of which I can remember still. Behind her father was Sophie. With horror I saw her clasp Major Sergine's hand as she congratulated him upon the victory he had won and the prisoners he had made. The old priest, her father, looked at me with an insolent face, and made insulting remarks at my expense, pointing at me with his lean and grimy hand. His fair daughter Sophie looked at me also, but she said nothing, and I could read her tender pity in her dark eyes. At last she turned to Major Sergine and said something to him in Russian, on which he frowned and shook his head impatiently. She appeared to plead with him, standing there in the flood of light which shone from the open door of her father's house. My eyes were fixed upon the two faces, that of the beautiful girl and of the dark, fierce man, for my instinct told me that it was my own fate which was under debate. For a long time the soldier shook his head, and then, at last softening before her pleadings, he appeared to give way. He turned to where I stood with my guardian sergeant beside me.

"These good people offer you the shelter of their roof for the night," said he to me, looking me up and down with vindictive eyes. "I find it hard to refuse them, but I tell you straight that for my part I had rather see you on the snow. It would cool your hot blood, you rascal of a Frenchman!"

I looked at him with the contempt that I felt.

"You were born a savage, and you will die one," said I.

My words stung him, for he broke into an oath, raising his whip as if he would strike me.

"Silence, you crop-eared dog!" he cried. "Had I my way

some of the insolence would be frozen out of you before morning." Mastering his passion, he turned upon Sophie with what he meant to be a gallant manner. "If you have a cellar with a good lock," said he, "the fellow may lie in it for the night, since you have done him the honor to take an interest in his comfort. I must have his parole that he will not attempt to play us any tricks, as I am answerable for him until I hand him over to the Hetman Platoff tomorrow."

His supercilious manner was more than I could endure. He had evidently spoken French to the lady in order that I might understand the humiliating way in which he referred to me.

"I will take no favor from you," said I. "You may do what you like, but I will never give you my parole."

The Russian shrugged his great shoulders, and turned away as if the matter were ended.

"Very well, my fine fellow, so much the worse for your fingers and toes. We shall see how you are in the morning after a night in the snow."

"One moment, Major Sergine," cried Sophie. "You must not be so hard upon this prisoner. There are some special reasons why he has a claim upon our kindness and mercy."

The Russian looked with suspicion upon his face from her to me.

"What are the special reasons? You certainly seem to take a remarkable interest in this Frenchman," said he.

"The chief reason is that he has this very morning of his own accord released Captain Alexis Barakoff, of the Dragoons of Grodno."

"It is true," said Barakoff, who had come out of the house. "He captured me this morning, and he released me upon parole rather than take me back to the French army, where I should have been starved."

"Since Colonel Gerard has acted so generously you will surely, now that fortune has changed, allow us to offer him the poor shelter of our cellar upon this bitter night," said Sophie. "It is a small return for his generosity."

But the Dragoon was still in the sulks.

"Let him give me his parole first that he will not attempt to escape," said he. "Do you hear, sir? Do you give me your parole?"

"I give you nothing," said I.

"Colonel Gerard," cried Sophie, turning to me with a coaxing smile, "you will give *me* your parole, will you not?"

"To you, mademoiselle, I can refuse nothing. I will give you my parole, with pleasure."

"There, Major Sergine," cried Sophie, in triumph, "that is surely sufficient. You have heard him say that he gives me his parole. I will be answerable for his safety."

In an ungracious fashion my Russian bear grunted his consent, and so I was led into the house, followed by the scowling father and by the big, black-bearded Dragoon. In the basement there was a large and roomy chamber, where the winter logs were stored. Thither it was that I was led, and I was given to understand that this was to be my lodging for the night. One side of this bleak apartment was heaped up to the ceiling with faggots of firewood. The rest of the room was stone-flagged and bare-walled, with a single, deep-set window upon one side, which was safely guarded with iron bars. For light I had a large stable lantern, which swung from a beam of the low ceiling. Major Sergine smiled as he took this down, and swung it round so as to throw its light into every corner of that dreary chamber.

"How do you like our Russian hotels, monsieur?" he asked, with his hateful sneer. "They are not very grand, but they are the best that we can give you. Perhaps the next time that you Frenchmen take a fancy to travel you will choose some other country where they will make you more comfortable." He stood laughing at me, his white teeth gleaming through his beard. Then he left me, and I heard the great key creak in the lock.

For an hour of utter misery, chilled in body and soul, I sat upon a pile of faggots, my face sunk upon my hands and my mind full of the saddest thoughts. It was cold enough within those four walls, but I thought of the sufferings of my poor troopers outside, and I sorrowed with their sorrow. Then I paced up and down, and I clapped my hands together and kicked my feet against the walls to keep them from being frozen. The lamp gave out some warmth, but still it was bitterly cold, and I had had no food since morning. It seemed to me that every one had forgotten me, but at last I heard the key turn in the lock, and who should enter but my prisoner of the morning, Captain Alexis Barakoff. A bottle of wine projected from under his arm, and he carried a great plate of hot stew in front of him.

"Hush!" said he; "not a word! Keep up your heart! I cannot stop to explain, for Sergine is still with us. Keep awake and ready!" With these hurried words he laid down the welcome food and ran out of the room.

"Keep awake and ready!" The words rang in my ears. I ate my food and I drank my wine, but it was neither food nor wine which had warmed the heart within me. What could those words of Barakoff mean? Why was I to remain awake? For what was I to be ready? Was it possible that there was a chance yet of escape? I have never respected the man who neglects his prayers at all other times and yet prays when he is in peril. It is like a bad soldier who pays no respect to the colonel save when he would demand a favor of him. And yet when I thought of the salt-mines of Siberia on the one side and of my mother in France upon the other, I could not help a prayer rising not from my lips, but from my heart, that the words of Barakoff might mean all that I hoped. But hour after hour struck upon the village clock, and still I heard nothing save the call of the Russian sentries in the street outside.

Then at last my heart leaped within me, for I heard a light step in the passage. An instant later the key turned, the door opened, and Sophie was in the room.

"Monsieur——" she cried.

"Etienne," said I.

"Nothing will change you," said she. "But is it possible that you do not hate me? Have you forgiven me the trick which I played you?"

"What trick?" I asked.

"Good heavens! Is it possible that even now you have not understood it? You asked me to translate the despatch. I have told you that it meant, 'If the French come to Minsk all is lost.' "

"What did it mean, then?"

"It means, 'Let the French come to Minsk. We are awaiting them.' "

I sprang back from her.

"You betrayed me!" I cried. "You lured me into this trap. It is to you that I owe the death and capture of my men. Fool that I was to trust a woman!"

"Do not be unjust, Colonel Gerard. I am a Russian woman, and my first duty is to my country. Would you not wish a French girl to have acted as I have done? Had I translated the message correctly you would not have gone to Minsk and your squadron would have escaped. Tell me that you forgive me!"

She looked bewitching as she stood pleading her cause in front of me. And yet, as I thought of my dead men, I could not take the hand which she held out to me.

"Very good," said she, as she dropped it by her side. "You feel for your own people and I feel for mine, and so we are equal. But you have said one wise and kindly thing within these walls, Colonel Gerard. You have said, 'One man more or less can make no difference in a struggle between two great armies.' Your lesson of nobility is not wasted. Behind these faggots is an unguarded door. Here is the key to it. Go forth, Colonel Gerard, and I trust that we may never look upon each other's faces again."

I stood for an instant with the key in my hand and my head in a whirl. Then I handed it back to her.

"I cannot do it," I said.

"Why not?"

"I have given my parole."

"To whom?" she asked.

"Why, to you."

"And I release you from it."

My heart bounded with joy. Of course, it was true what she said. I had refused to give my parole to Sergine. I owed him no duty. If she relieved me from my promise my honor was clear. I took the key from her hand.

"You will find Captain Barakoff at the end of the village street," she said. "We of the North never forget either an injury or a kindness. He has your mare and your sword waiting for you. Do not delay an instant, for in two hours it will be dawn."

So I passed out into the starlit Russian night, and had that last glimpse of Sophie as she peered after me through the open door. She looked wistfully at me as if she expected something more than the cold thanks which I gave her, but even the humblest man has his pride, and I will not deny that mine was hurt by the deception which she had played upon me. I could not have brought myself to kiss her hand, far less her lips. The door led into a narrow alley, and at the end of it stood a muffled figure who held Violette by the birdle.

"You told me to be kind to the next French officer whom I found in distress," said he. "Good luck! Bon voyage!" he whispered, as I bounded into the saddle. "Remember 'Poltava' is the watchword."

It was well that he had given it to me, for twice I had to pass Cossack pickets before I was clear of the lines. I had just ridden past the last vedettes and hoped that I was a free man again when there was a soft thudding in the snow behind me, and a heavy man upon a great black horse came swiftly after me. My first impulse was to put spurs to Violette. My second, as I saw a long black beard against a steel cuirass, was to halt and await him.

"I thought that it was you, you dog of a Frenchman," he cried, shaking his drawn sword at me. "So you have broken your parole, you rascal?"

"I gave no parole."

"You lie, you hound!"

I looked around and no one was coming. The vedettes were motionless and distant. We were all alone, with the moon above and the snow beneath. Fortune has ever been my friend.

"I gave you no parole."

"You gave it to the lady."

"Then I will answer for it to the lady."

"That would suit you better, no doubt. But, unfortunately, you will have to answer for it to me."

"I am ready."

"Your sword, too! There is treason in this! Ah, I see it all! The woman has helped you. She shall see Siberia for this night's work."

The words were his death-warrant. For Sophie's sake I could not let him go back alive. Our blades crossed, and an instant later mine was through his black beard and deep in his throat. I was on the ground almost as soon as he, but the one thrust was enough. He died, snapping his teeth at my ankles like a savage wolf.

Two days later I had rejoined the army at Smolensk, and was a part once more of that dreary procession which tramped onwards through the snow, leaving a long weal of blood to show the path which it had taken.

Enough, my friends; I would not reawaken the memory of those days of misery and death. They still come to haunt me in my dreams. When we halted at last in Warsaw, we had left behind us our guns, our transport, three-fourths of our comrades. But we did not leave behind us the honor of Etienne Gerard. They have said that I broke my parole. Let them beware how they say it to my face, for the story is as I tell it, and old as I am my forefinger is not too weak to press a trigger when my honor is in question.

1814

VII. How the Brigadier Won His Medal

THE Duke of Tarentum, or Macdonald, as his old comrades prefer to call him, was, as I could perceive, in the vilest of tempers. His grim, Scotch face was like one of those grotesque door-knockers which one sees in the Faubourg St. Germain. We heard afterwards that the Emperor had said in jest that he would have sent him against Wellington in the South, but that he was afraid to trust him within the sound of the pipes. Major Charpentier and I could plainly see that he was smouldering with anger.

"Brigadier Gerard of the Hussars," said he, with the air of the corporal with the recruit.

I saluted.

"Major Charpentier of the Horse Grenadiers."

My companion answered to his name.

"The Emperor has a mission for you."

Without more ado he flung open the door and announced us.

I have seen Napoleon ten times on horseback to one on foot, and I think that he does wisely to show himself to the troops in this fashion, for he cuts a very good figure in the saddle. As we saw him now he was the shortest man out of six by a good hand's breadth, and yet I am no very big man myself, though I ride quite heavy enough for a hussar. It is evident, too, that his body is too long for his legs. With his big, round head, his curved shoulders, and his clean-shaven face, he is more like a Professor at the Sorbonne than the first soldier in France. Every man to his taste, but it seems to me that, if I could clap a pair of fine light cavalry whiskers, like my own, on to him, it would do him no harm. He has a firm mouth, however, and his eyes are remarkable. I have seen them once turned on me in anger, and I had rather ride at a square on a spent horse than face them again. I am not a man who is easily daunted, either.

He was standing at the side of the room, away from the window, looking up at a great map of the country which was hung upon the wall. Berthier stood beside him, trying to look wise, and just as we entered, Napoleon snatched his sword impatiently from him and pointed with it on the map. He was talking fast and low, but I heard him say, "The valley of the Meuse," and twice he repeated "Berlin." As we entered, his aide-de-camp advanced to us, but the Emperor stopped him and beckoned us to his side.

"You have not yet received the cross of honor, Brigadier Gerard?" he asked.

I replied that I had not, and was about to add that it was not for want of having deserved it, when he cut me short in his decided fashion.

"And you, Major?" he asked.

"No, sir."

"Then you shall both have your opportunity now."

He led us to the great map upon the wall and placed the tip of Berthier's sword on Rheims.

"I will be frank with you, gentlemen, as with two comrades. You have both been with me since Marengo, I believe?" He had a strangely pleasant smile, which used to light up his pale face with a kind of cold sunshine. "Here at Rheims are our present headquarters on this the 14th of March. Very good. Here is Paris, distant by road a good twenty-five leagues. Blucher lies to the north, Schwarzenburg to the south." He prodded at the map with the sword as he spoke.

"Now," said he, "the further into the country these people march, the more completely I shall crush them. They are about to advance upon Paris. Very good. Let them do so. My brother, the King of Spain, will be there with a hundred thousand men. It is to him that I send you. You will hand him this letter, a copy of which I confide to each of you. It is to tell him that I am coming at once, in two days' time, with every man and horse and gun to his relief. I must give them forty-eight hours to recover. Then straight to Paris! You understand me, gentlemen?"

Ah, if I could tell you the glow of pride which it gave me to be taken into the great man's confidence in this way. As he handed our letters to us I clicked my spurs and threw out my chest, smiling and nodding to let him know that I saw what he would be after. He smiled also, and rested his hand for a moment upon the cape of my dolman. I would have given half my arrears of pay if my mother could have seen me at that instant.

"I will show you your route," said he, turning back to the map. "Your orders are to ride together as far as Bazoches. You will then separate, the one making for Paris by Oulchy and Neuilly, and the other to the north by Braine, Soissons, and Senlis. Have you anything to say, Brigadier Gerard?"

I am a rough soldier, but I have words and ideas. I had begun to speak about glory and the peril of France when he cut me short.

"And you, Major Charpentier?"

"If we find our route unsafe, are we at liberty to choose another?" said he.

"Soldiers do not choose, they obey." He inclined his head to show that we were dismissed, and turned round to Berthier. I do not know what he said, but I heard them both laughing.

Well, as you may think, we lost little time in getting upon our way. In half an hour we were riding down the High Street of Rheims, and it struck twelve o'clock as we passed the Cathedral. I had my little gray mare, Violette, the one which Sebastiani had wished to buy after Dresden. It is the fastest horse in the six brigades of light cavalry, and was only beaten by the Duke of Rovigo's racer from England. As to Charpentier, he had the kind of horse which a horse grenadier or a cuirassier would be likely to ride: a back like a bedstead, you understand, and legs like the posts. He is a hulking fellow himself, so that they looked a singular pair. And yet in his insane conceit he ogled the girls as they waved their handkerchiefs to me from the windows, and he twirled his ugly red moustache up into his eyes, just as if it were to him that their attention was addressed.

When we came out of the town we passed through the French camp, and then across the battlefield of yesterday,

which was still covered both by our own poor fellows and by
the Russians. But of the two the camp was the sadder sight.
Our army was thawing away. The Guards were all right,
though the young guard was full of conscripts. The artillery
and the heavy cavalry were also good if there were more of
them, but the infantry privates with their under officers
looked like schoolboys with their masters. And we had no
reserves. When one considered that there were 80,000 Prussians to the north and 150,000 Russians and Austrians to the
south, it might make even the bravest man grave.

For my own part, I confess that I shed a tear until the
thought came that the Emperor was still with us, and that on
that very morning he had placed his hand upon my dolman
and had promised me a medal of honor. This set me singing,
and I spurred Violette on, until Charpentier had to beg me to
have mercy on his great, snorting, panting camel. The road
was beaten into paste and rutted two feet deep by the artillery,
so that he was right in saying that it was not the place for a
gallop.

I have never been very friendly with this Charpentier; and
now for twenty miles of the way I could not draw a word
from him. He rode with his brows puckered and his chin upon
his breast, like a man who is heavy with thought. More than
once I asked him what was on his mind, thinking that, perhaps,
with my quicker intelligence I might set the matter straight.
His answer always was that it was his mission of which he was
thinking, which surprised me, because, although I had never
thought much of his intelligence, still it seemed to me to be
impossible that anyone could be puzzled by so simple and
soldierly a task.

Well, we came at last to Bazoches, where he was to take
the southern road and I the northern. He half turned in his
saddle before he left me, and he looked at me with a singular
expression of inquiry in his face.

"What do you make of it, Brigadier?" he asked.

"Of what?"

"Of our mission."

"Surely it is plain enough."

"You think so? Why should the Emperor tell us his plans?"

"Because he recognized our intelligence."

My companion laughed in a manner which I found an-
noying.

"May I ask what you intend to do if you find these villages full of Prussians?" he asked.

"I shall obey my orders."

"But you will be killed."

"Very possibly."

He laughed again, and so offensively that I clapped my hand to my sword. But before I could tell him what I thought of his stupidity and rudeness he had wheeled his horse, and was lumbering away down the other road. I saw his big fur cap vanish over the brow of the hill, and then I rode upon my way, wondering at his conduct. From time to time I put my hand to the breast of my tunic, and felt the paper crackle beneath my fingers. Ah, my precious paper, which should be turned into the little silver medal for which I had yearned so long. All the way from Braine to Sermoise I was thinking of what my mother would say when she saw it.

I stopped to give Violette a meal at a wayside auberge on the side of a hill not far from Soissons—a place surrounded by old oaks, and with so many crows that one could scarce hear one's own voice. It was from the innkeeper that I learned that Marmont had fallen back two days before, and that the Prussians were over the Aisne. An hour later, in the fading light, I saw two of their vedettes upon the hill to the right, and then, as darkness gathered, the heavens to the north were all glimmering from the lights of a bivouac.

When I heard that Blucher had been there for two days, I was much surprised that the Emperor should not have known that the country through which he had ordered me to carry my precious letter was already occupied by the enemy. Still, I thought of the tone of his voice when he said to Charpentier that a soldier must not choose, but must obey. I should follow the route he had laid down for me as long as Violette could move a hoof or I a finger upon her bridle. All the way from Sermoise to Soissons, where the road dips up and down, curving among fir-woods, I kept my pistol ready and my sword-belt braced, pushing on swiftly where the path was straight, and then coming slowly round the corners in the way we learned in Spain.

When I came to the farmhouse which lies to the right of the road just after you cross the wooden bridge over the Crise, near where the great statue of the Virgin stands, a woman cried to me from the field, saying that the Prussians were in

Soissons. A small party of their lancers, she said, had come in that very afternoon, and a whole division was expected before midnight. I did not wait to hear the end of her tale, but clapped spurs into Violette, and in five minutes was galloping her into the town.

Three Uhlans were at the mouth of the main street, their horses tethered, and they gossiping together, each with a pipe as long as my sabre. I saw them well in the light of an open door, but of me they could have seen only the flash of Violette's gray side and the black flutter of my cloak. A moment later I flew through a stream of them rushing from an open gateway. Violette's shoulder sent one of them reeling, and I stabbed at another but missed him. Pang, pang, went two carbines, but I had flown round the curve of the street, and never so much as heard the hiss of the balls. Ah, we were great, both Violette and I. She lay down to it like a coursed hare, the fire flying from her hoofs. I stood in my stirrups and brandished my sword. Someone sprang for my bridle. I sliced him through the arm, and I heard him howling behind me. Two horsemen closed upon me. I cut one down and outpaced the other. A minute later I was clear of the town, and flying down a broad white road with the black poplars on either side. For a time I heard the rattle of hoofs behind me, but they died and died until I could not tell them from the throbbing of my own heart. Soon I pulled up and listened, but all was silent. They had given up the chase.

Well, the first thing that I did was to dismount and to lead my mare into a small wood through which a stream ran. There I watered her and rubbed her down, giving her two pieces of sugar soaked in cognac from my flask. She was spent from the sharp chase, but it was wonderful to see how she came round with a half-hour's rest. When my thighs closed upon her again, I could tell by the spring and the swing of her that it would not be her fault if I did not win my way safe to Paris.

I must have been well within the enemy's lines now, for I heard a number of them shouting one of their rough drinking songs out of a house by the roadside, and I went round by the fields to avoid it. At another time two men came out into the moonlight (for by this time it was a cloudless night) and shouted something in German, but I galloped on without heeding them, and they were afraid to fire, for their own hussars are dressed exactly as I was. It is best to take no notice at these times, and then they put you down as a deaf man.

It was a lovely moon, and every tree threw a black bar across the road. I could see the countryside just as if it were daytime, and very peaceful it looked, save that there was a great fire raging somewhere in the north. In the silence of the nighttime, and with the knowledge that danger was in front and behind me, the sight of that great distant fire was very striking and awesome. But I am not easily clouded, for I have seen too many singular things, so I hummed a tune between my teeth and thought of little Lisette, whom I might see in Paris. My mind was full of her when, trotting round a corner, I came straight upon half-a-dozen German dragoons, who were sitting round a brushwood fire by the roadside.

I am an excellent soldier. I do not say this because I am prejudiced in my own favor, but because I really am so. I can weigh every chance in a moment, and decide with as much certainty as though I had brooded for a week. Now I saw like a flash that, come what might, I should be chased, and on a horse which had already done a long twelve leagues. But it was better to be chased onwards than to be chased back. On this moonlit night, with fresh horses behind me, I must take my risk in either case; but if I were to shake them off, I preferred that it should be near Senlis than near Soissons.

All this flashed on me as if by instinct, you understand. My eyes had hardly rested on the bearded faces under the brass helmets before my rowels had touched Violette, and she was off with a rattle like a *pas-de-charge*. Oh, the shouting and rushing and stamping from behind us! Three of them fired and three swung themselves on to their horses. A bullet rapped on the crupper of my saddle with a noise like a stick on a door. Violette sprang madly forward, and I thought she had been wounded, but it was only a graze above the near forefetlock. Ah, the dear little mare, how I loved her when I felt her settle down into that long, easy gallop of hers, her hoofs going like a Spanish girl's castanets. I could not hold myself. I turned on my saddle and shouted and raved, "Vive l'Empereur!" I screamed and laughed at the gust of oaths that came back to me.

But it was not over yet. If she had been fresh she might have gained a mile in five. Now she could only hold her own with a very little over. There was one of them, a young boy of an officer, who was better mounted than the others. He drew ahead with every stride. Two hundred yards behind him were two troopers, but I saw every time that I glanced round that the distance between them was increasing. The other three who had waited to shoot were a long way in the rear.

The officer's mount was a bay—a fine horse, though not to be spoken of with Violette; yet it was a powerful brute, and it seemed to me that in a few miles its freshness might tell. I waited until the lad was a long way in front of his comrades, and then I eased my mare down a little—a very, very little, so that he might think he was really catching me. When he came within pistol-shot of me I drew and cocked my own pistol, and laid my chin upon my shoulder to see what he would do. He did not offer to fire, and I soon discerned the cause. The silly boy had taken his pistols from his holsters when he had camped for the night. He wagged his sword at me now and roared some threat or other. He did not seem to understand that he was at my mercy. I eased Violette down until there was not the length of a long lance between the gray tail and the bay muzzle.

"*Rendez-vous!*" he yelled.

"I must compliment monsieur upon his French," said I, resting the barrel of my pistol upon my bridle-arm, which I have always found best when shooting from the saddle. I aimed at his face, and could see, even in the moonlight, how white he grew when he understood that it was all up with him. But even as my finger pressed the trigger I thought of his mother, and I put my ball through his horse's shoulder. I fear he hurt himself in the fall, for it was a fearful crash, but I had my letter to think of, so I stretched the mare into a gallop once more.

But they were not so easily shaken off, these brigands. The two troopers thought no more of their young officer than if he had been a recruit thrown in the riding-school. They left him to the others and thundered on after me. I had pulled up on the brow of a hill, thinking that I had heard the last of them; but, my faith, I soon saw there was no time for loitering, so away we went, the mare tossing her head and I my shako, to show what we thought of two dragoons who tried to catch a hussar. But at this moment, even while I laughed at the thought, my heart stood still within me, for there at the end of the long white road was a black patch of cavalry waiting to receive me. To a young soldier it might have seemed the shadow of the trees, but to me it was a troop of hussars, and, turn where I could, death seemed to be waiting for me.

Well, I had the dragoons behind me, and the hussars in front. Never since Moscow have I seemed to be in such peril. But for the honor of the brigade I had rather be cut down by a light cavalryman than by a heavy. I never drew bridle, therefore, or hesitated for an instant, but I let Violette have her head. I remembered that I tried to pray as I rode, but I am a little out of practice at such things, and the only words I could remember were the prayer for fine weather which we used at the school on the evening before holidays. Even this seemed better than nothing, and I was pattering it out, when suddenly I heard French voices in front of me. Ah, *mon Dieu*, but the joy went through my heart like a musket-ball. They were ours—our own dear little rascals from the corps of Marmont. Round whisked my two dragoons and galloped for their lives, with the moon gleaming on their brass helmets, while I trotted up to my friends with no undue haste, for I would have them understand that though a hussar may fly, it is not in his nature to fly very fast. Yet I fear that Violette's heaving flanks and foam-spattered muzzle gave the lie to my careless bearing.

Who should be at the head of the troop but old Bouvet, whom I saved at Leipzig! When he saw me his little pink eyes filled with tears, and, indeed, I could not but shed a few myself at the sight of his joy. I told him of my mission, but he laughed when I said that I must pass through Senlis.

"The enemy is there," said he. "You cannot go."

"I prefer to go where the enemy is," I answered.

"But why not go straight to Paris with your dispatch? Why should you choose to pass through the one place where you are almost sure to be taken or killed?"

"A soldier does not choose—he obeys," said I, just as I had heard Napoleon say it.

Old Bouvet laughed in his wheezy way, until I had to give my moustachios a twirl and look him up and down in a manner which brought him to reason.

"Well," said he, "you had best come along with us, for we are all bound for Senlis. Our orders are to reconnoitre the place. A squadron of Poniatowski's Polish Lancers are in front of us. If you must ride through it, it is possible that we may be able to go with you."

So away we went, jingling and clanking through the quiet night until we came up with the Poles—fine old soldiers all of them, though a trifle heavy for their horses. It was a treat to see them, for they could not have carried themselves better if they had belonged to my own brigade. We rode together, until in the early morning we saw the lights of Senlis. A peasant was coming along with a cart, and from him we learned how things were going there.

His information was certain, for his brother was the Mayor's coachman, and he had spoken with him late the night before. There was a single squadron of Cossacks—or a polk, as they call it in their frightful language—quartered upon the Mayor's house, which stands at the corner of the market-place, and is the largest building in the town. A whole division of Prussian infantry was encamped in the woods to the north, but only the Cossacks were in Senlis. Ah, what a chance to avenge ourselves upon these barbarians, whose cruelty to our poor countryfolk was the talk at every camp fire.

We were into the town like a torrent, hacked down the vedettes, rode over the guard, and were smashing in the doors of the Mayor's house before they understood that there was a Frenchman within twenty miles of them. We saw horrid heads at the windows—heads bearded to the temples, with tangled hair and sheepskin caps, and silly, gaping mouths. "Hourra! Hourra!" they shrieked, and fired with their carbines, but our fellows were into the house and at their throats before they had wiped the sleep out of their eyes. It was dreadful to see how the Poles flung themselves upon them, like starving wolves upon a herd of fat bucks—for, as you know, the Poles have a blood feud against the Cossacks. The most were killed in the upper rooms, whither they had fled for shelter, and the blood was pouring down into the hall like rain from a roof. They are terrible soldiers, these Poles, though I think they are a trifle heavy for their horses. Man for man, they are as big as Kellermann's cuirassiers. Their equipment is, of course, much lighter, since they are without the cuirass, back-plate, and helmet.

Well, it was at this point that I made an error—a very serious error it must be admitted. Up to this moment I had carried out my mission in a manner which only my modesty prevents me from describing as remarkable. But now I did that which an official would condemn and a soldier excuse.

There is no doubt that the mare was spent, but still it is true that I might have galloped on through Senlis and reached the country, where I should have had no enemy between me and Paris. But what hussar can ride past a fight and never draw rein? It is to ask too much of him. Besides, I thought that if Violette had an hour of rest I might have three hours the better at the other end. Then on top of it came those heads at the windows, with their sheepskin hats and their barbarous cries. I sprang from my saddle, threw Violette's bridle over a rail-post, and ran into the house with the rest. It is true that I was too late to be of service, and that I was nearly wounded by a lance-thrust from one of these dying savages. Still, it is a pity to miss even the smallest affair, for one never knows what opportunity for advancement may present itself. I have seen more soldierly work in outpost skirmishes and little gallop-and-hack affairs of the kind than in any of the Emperor's big battles.

When the house was cleared I took a bucket of water out for Violette, and our peasant guide showed me where the good Mayor kept his fodder. My faith, but the little sweet-heart was ready for it. Then I sponged down her legs, and leaving her still tethered I went back into the house to find a mouthful for myself, so that I should not need to halt again until I was in Paris.

And now I come to the part of my story which may seem singular to you, although I could tell you at least ten things every bit as queer which have happened to me in my life-time. You can understand that, to a man who spends his life in scouting and vedette duties on the bloody ground which lies between two great armies, there are many chances of strange experiences. I'll tell you, however, exactly what occurred.

Old Bouvet was waiting in the passage when I entered, and he asked me whether we might not crack a bottle of wine together. "My faith, we must not be long," said he. "There are ten thousand of Theilmann's Prussians in the woods up yonder."

"Where is the wine?" I asked.

"Ah, you may trust two hussars to find where the wine is," said he, and taking a candle in his hand, he led the way down the stone stairs into the kitchen.

When we got there we found another door, which opened on to a winding stair with the cellar at the bottom. The Cos-

sacks had been there before us, as was easily seen by the broken bottles littered all over it. However, the Mayor was a *bon-vivant*, and I do not wish to have a better set of bins to pick from. Chambertin, Graves, Alicant, white wine and red, sparkling and still, they lay in pyramids peeping coyly out of sawdust. Old Bouvet stood with his candle looking here and peeping there, purring in his throat like a cat before a milk-pail. He had picked up a Burgundy at last, and had his hand outstretched to the bottle when there came a roar of musketry from above us, a rush of feet, and such a yelping and scream-ing as I have never listened to. The Prussians were upon us!

Bouvet is a brave man: I will say that for him. He flashed out his sword and away he clattered up the stone steps, his spurs clinking as he ran. I followed him, but just as we came out into the kitchen passage a tremendous shout told us that the house had been recaptured.

"It's all over," I cried, grasping at Bouvet's sleeve.

"There is one more to die," he shouted, and away he went like a madman up the second stair. In effect, I should have gone to my death also had I been in his place, for he had done very wrong in not throwing out his scouts to warn him if the Germans advanced upon him. For an instant I was about to rush up with him, and then I bethought myself that, after all, I had my own mission to think of, and that if I were taken the important letter of the Emperor would be sacrificed. I let Bouvet die alone, therefore, and I went down into the cellar again, closing the door behind me.

Well, it was not a very rosy prospect down there either. Bouvet had dropped the candle when the alarm came, and I, pawing about in the darkness, could find nothing but broken bottles. At last I came upon the candle, which had rolled under the curve of a cask, but, try as I would with my tinder-box, I could not light it. The reason was that the wick had been wet in a puddle of wine, so suspecting that this might be the case, I cut the end off with my sword. Then I found that it lighted easily enough. But what to do I could not imagine. The scoundrels upstairs were shouting themselves hoarse, several hundred of them from the sound, and it was clear that some of them would soon want to moisten their throats. There would be an end to a dashing soldier, and of the mission and of the medal. I thought of my mother and I thought of the Emperor. It made me weep to think that the one would lose so excellent a son and the other the best light cavalry officer he ever had since Lasalle's time. But presently I dashed the tears from my eyes. "Courage!" I cried, striking myself upon the chest. "Courage, my brave boy! Is it possible that one who has come safely from Moscow without so much as a frost-bite will die in a French wine-cellar?" At the thought I was up on my feet and clutching at the letter in my tunic, for the crackle of it gave me courage.

My first plan was to set fire to the house, in the hope of escaping in the confusion. My second to get into an empty wine-cask. I was looking round to see if I could find one, when suddenly, in the corner, I espied a little low door, painted of the same gray color as the wall, so that it was only a man with quick sight who would have noticed it. I pushed against it, and at first I imagined that it was locked. Presently, however, it gave a little, and then I understood that it was held by the pressure of something on the other side. I put my feet against a hogshead of wine, and I gave such a push that the door flew open and I came down with a crash upon my back, the candle flying out of my hands, so that I found myself in darkness once more. I picked myself up and stared through the black archway into the gloom beyond.

There was a slight ray of light coming from some slit or grating. The dawn had broken outside, and I could dimly see the long, curving sides of several huge casks, which made me think that perhaps this was where the Mayor kept his reserves of wine while they were maturing. At any rate, it seemed to be a safer hiding-place than the outer cellar, so gathering up my candle, I was just closing the door behind me, when I suddenly saw something which filled me with amazement, and even, I confess, with the smallest little touch of fear.

I have said that at the further end of the cellar there was a dim gray fan of light striking downwards from somewhere near the roof. Well, as I peered through the darkness, I suddenly saw a great, tall man skip into this belt of daylight, and then out again into the darkness at the further end. My word, I gave such a start that my shako nearly broke its chin-strap! It was only a glance, but, none the less, I had time to see that the fellow had a hairy Cossack cap on his head, and that he was a great, long-legged, broad-shouldered brigand, with a sabre at his waist. My faith, even Etienne Gerard was a little staggered at being left alone with such a creature in the dark.

But only for a moment. "Courage!" I thought. "Am I not a hussar, a brigadier, too, at the age of thirty-one, and the chosen messenger of the Emperor?" After all, this skulker had more cause to be afraid of me than I of him. And then suddenly I understood that he was afraid—horribly afraid. I could read it from his quick step and his bent shoulders as he ran among the barrels, like a rat making for its hole. And, of course, it must have been he who had held the door against me, and not some packing-case or wine-cask as I had imagined. He was the pursued then, and I the pursuer. Aha, I felt my whiskers bristle as I advanced upon him through the darkness! He would find that he had no chicken to deal with, this robber from the North. For the moment I was magnificent.

At first I had feared to light my candle lest I should make a mark of myself, but now, after cracking my shin over a box, and catching my spurs in some canvas, I thought the bolder course the wiser. I lit it, therefore, and then I advanced with long strides, my sword in my hand. "Come out, you rascal!" I cried. "Nothing can save you. You will at last meet with your deserts."

I held my candle high, and presently I caught a glimpse of the man's head staring at me over a barrel. He had a gold chevron on his black cap, and the expression of his face told me in an instant that he was an officer and a man of refinement.

"Monsieur," he cried, in excellent French, "I surrender myself on a promise of quarter. But if I do not have your promise, I will then sell my life as dearly as I can."

"Sir," said I, "a Frenchman knows how to treat an unfortunate enemy. Your life is safe." With that he handed his sword over the top of the barrel, and I bowed with the candle on my heart. "Whom have I the honor of capturing?" I asked.

"I am the Count Boutkine, of the Emperor's own Don Cossacks," said he. "I came out with my troops to reconnoiter Senlis, and as we found no sign of your people we determined to spend the night here."

"And would it be an indiscretion," I asked, "if I were to inquire how you came into the back cellar?"

"Nothing more simple," said he. "It was our intention to start at early dawn. Feeling chilled after dressing, I thought that a cup of wine would do me no harm, so I came down to see what I could find. As I was rummaging about, the house was suddenly carried by assault so rapidly that by the time I had climbed the stairs it was all over. It only remained for me to save myself, so I came down here and hid myself in the back cellar, where you have found me."

I thought of how old Bouvet had behaved under the same conditions, and the tears sprang to my eyes as I contemplated the glory of France. Then I had to consider what I should do next. It was clear that this Russian Count, being in the back cellar while we were in the front one, had not heard the sounds which would have told him that the house was once again in the hands of his own allies. If he should once understand this the tables would be turned, and I should be his prisoner instead of he being mine. What was I to do? I was at my wits' end, when suddenly there came to me an idea so brilliant that I could not but be amazed at my own invention.

"Count Boutkine," said I, "I find myself in a most difficult position."

"And why?" he asked.

"Because I have promised you your life."

His jaw dropped a little.

"You would not withdraw your promise?" he cried.

"If the worst comes to the worst I can die in your defence," said I; "but the difficulties are great."

"What is it, then?" he asked.

"I will be frank with you," said I. "You must know that our fellows, and especially the Poles, are so incensed against the Cossacks that the mere sight of the uniform drives them mad. They precipitate themselves instantly upon the wearer and tear him limb from limb. Even their officers cannot restrain them."

The Russian grew pale at my words and the way in which I said them.

"But this is terrible," said he.

"Horrible!" said I. "If we were to go up together at this moment I cannot promise how far I could protect you."

"I am in your hands," he cried. "What would you suggest that we should do? Would it not be best that I should remain here?"

"That worst of all."

"And why?"

"Because our fellows will ransack the house presently, and

then you would be cut to pieces. No, no, I must go and break it to them. But even then, when once they see that accursed uniform, I do not know what may happen."

"Should I then take the uniform off?"

"Excellent!" I cried. "Hold, we have it! You will take your uniform off and put on mine. That will make you sacred to every French soldier."

"It is not the French I fear so much as the Poles."

"But my uniform will be a safeguard against either."

"How can I thank you?" he cried. "But you—what are you to wear?"

"I will wear 'yours."

"And perhaps fall a victim to your generosity?"

"It is my duty to take the risk," I answered; "but I have no fears. I will ascend in your uniform. A hundred swords will be turned upon me. "Hold!" I will shout, "I am the Brigadier Gerard!" Then they will see my face. They will know me. And I will tell them about you. Under the shield of these clothes you will be sacred."

His fingers trembled with eagerness as he tore off his tunic. His boots and breeches were much like my own, so there was no need to change them, but I gave him my hussar jacket, my dolman, my shako, my sword-belt, and my sabretasche, while I took in exchange his high sheep-skin cap with the gold chevron, his fur-trimmed coat, and his crooked sword. Be it well understood that in changing the tunics I did not forget to change my thrice-precious letter also from my old one to my new.

"With your leave," said I, "I shall now bind you to a barrel."

He made a great fuss over this, but I have learned in my soldiering never to throw away chances, and how could I tell that he might not, when my back was turned, see how the matter really stood, and break in upon my plans? He was leaning against a barrel at the time, so I ran six times round it with a rope, and then tied it with a big knot behind. If he wished to come upstairs he would, at least, have to carry a thousand litres of good French wine for a knapsack. I then shut the door of the back cellar behind me, so that he might not hear what was going forward, and tossing the candle away I ascended the kitchen stair.

There were only about twenty steps, and yet, while I came

up them, I seemed to have time to think of everything that I had ever hoped to do. It was the same feeling that I had at Eylau when I lay with my broken leg and saw the horse artillery galloping down upon me. Of course, I knew that if I were taken I should be shot instantly as being disguised within the enemy's lines. Still, it was a glorious death—in the direct service of the Emperor—and I reflected that there could not be less than five lines, and perhaps seven, in the *Moniteur* about me. Palaret had eight lines, and I am sure that he had not so fine a career.

When I made my way out into the hall, with all the nonchalance in my face and manner that I could assume, the very first thing that I saw was Bouvet's dead body, with his legs drawn up and a broken sword in his hand. I could see by the black smudge that he had been shot at close quarters. I should have wished to salute as I went by, for he was a gallant man, but I feared lest I should be seen, and so I passed on.

The front of the hall was full of Prussian infantry, who were knocking loopholes in the wall, as though they expected that there might be yet another attack. Their officer, a little man, was running about giving directions. They were all too busy to take much notice of me, but another officer, who was standing by the door with a long pipe in his mouth, strode across and clapped me on the shoulder, pointing to the dead bodies of our poor hussars, and saying something which was meant for a jest, for his long beard opened and showed every fang in his head. I laughed heartily also, and said the only Russian words that I knew. I learned them from little Sophie, at Vilna, and they meant: "If the night is fine we shall meet under the oak tree, but if it rains we shall meet in the byre." It was all the same to this German, however, and I have no doubt that he gave me credit for saying something very witty indeed, for he roared laughing, and slapped me on my shoulder again. I nodded to him and marched out of the hall-door as coolly as if I were the commandant of the garrison.

There were a hundred horses tethered about outside, most of them belonging to the Poles and hussars. Good little Violette was waiting with the others, and she whinnied when she saw me coming towards her. But I would not mount her. No. I was much too cunning for that. On the contrary, I chose the most shaggy little Cossack horse that I could see, and I sprang upon it with as much assurance as though it had belonged to my father before me. It had a great bag of plunder slung over its neck, and this I laid upon Violette's back, and led her along beside me. Never have you seen such a picture of the Cossack returning from the foray. It was superb.

Well, the town was full of Prussians by this time. They lined the side-walks and pointed me out to each other, saying, as I could judge from their gestures, "There goes one of those devils of Cossacks. They are the boys for foraging and plunder."

One or two officers spoke to me with an air of authority, but I shook my head and smiled, and said, "If the night is fine we shall meet under the oak tree, but if it rains we shall meet in the byre," at which they shrugged their shoulders and gave the matter up. In this way I worked along until I was beyond the northern outskirt of the town. I could see in the roadway two lancer vedettes with their black and white pennons, and I knew that when I was once past these I should be a free man once more. I made my pony trot, therefore, Violette rubbing her nose against my knee all the time, and looking up at me to ask how she had deserved that this hairy doormat of a creature should be preferred to her. I was not more than a hundred yards from the Uhlans when, suddenly, you can imagine my feelings when I saw a real Cossack coming galloping along the road towards me.

Ah, my friend, you who read this, if you have any heart, you will feel for a man like me, who had gone through so many dangers and trials, only at this very last moment to be confronted with one which appeared to put an end to everything. I will confess that for a moment I lost heart, and was inclined to throw myself down in my despair, and to cry out that I had been betrayed. But, no; I was not beaten even now. I opened two buttons of my tunic so that I might get easily at the Emperor's message, for it was my fixed determination when all hope was gone to swallow the letter and then die sword in hand. Then I felt that my little, crooked sword was loose in its sheath, and I trotted on to where the vedettes were waiting. They seemed inclined to stop me, but I pointed to the other Cossack, who was still a couple of hundred yards off, and they, understanding that I merely wished to meet him, let me pass with a salute.

I dug my spurs into my pony then, for if I were only far

enough from the lancers I thought I might manage the Cossack without much difficulty. He was an officer, a large, bearded man, with a gold chevron in his cap, just the same as mine. As I advanced he unconsciously aided me by pulling up his horse, so that I had a fine start of the vedettes. On I came for him, and I could see wonder changing to suspicion in his brown eyes as he looked at me and at my pony, and at my equipment. I do not know what it was that was wrong, but he saw something which was as it should not be. He shouted out a question, and then when I gave no answer he pulled out his sword. I was glad in my heart to see him do so, for I had always rather fight than cut down an unsuspecting enemy. Now I made at him full tilt, and, parrying his cut, I got my point in just under the fourth button of his tunic. Down he went, and the weight of him nearly took me off my horse before I could disengage. I never glanced at him to see if he were living or dead, for I sprang off my pony and on to Violette, with a shake of my bridle and a kiss of my hand to the two Uhlans behind me. They galloped after me, shouting, but Violette had had her rest, and was just as fresh as when she started. I took the first side road to the west and then the first to the south, which would take me away from the enemy's country. On we went and on, every stride taking me further from my foes and nearer to my friends. At last, when I reached the end of a long stretch of road, and looking back from it could see no sign of any pursuers, I understood that my troubles were over.

And it gave me a glow of happiness, as I rode, to think that I had done to the letter what the Emperor had ordered. What would he say when he saw me? What could he say which would do justice to the incredible way in which I had risen above every danger? He had ordered me to go through Sermoise, Soissons, and Senlis, little dreaming that they were all three occupied by the enemy. And yet I had done it. I had borne his letter in safety through each of these towns. Hussars, dragoons, lancers, Cossacks, and infantry—I had run the gauntlet of all of them, and had come out unharmed.

When I had got as far as Dammartin I caught a first glimpse of our own outposts. There was a troop of dragoons in a field, and of course I could see from the horsehair crests that they were French. I galloped towards them in order to ask them if all was safe between there and Paris, and as I rode I felt such a pride at having won my way back to my friends again, that I could not refrain from waving my sword in the air.

At this a young officer galloped out from among the dragoons, also brandishing his sword, and it warmed my heart to think that he should come riding with such ardor and enthusiasm to greet me. I made Violette caracole, and as we came together I brandished my sword more gallantly than ever, but you can imagine my feelings when he suddenly made a cut at me which would certainly have taken my head off if I had not fallen forward with my nose in Violette's mane. My faith, it whistled just over my cap like an east wind. Of course, it came from this accursed Cossack uniform which, in my excitement, I had forgotten all about, and this young dragoon had imagined that I was some Russian champion who was challenging the French cavalry. My word, he was a frightened man when he understood how near he had been to killing the celebrated Brigadier Gerard.

Well, the road was clear, and about three o'clock in the afternoon I was at St. Denis, though it took me a long two hours to get from there to Paris, for the road was blocked with commissariat wagons and guns of the artillery reserve, which was going north to Marmont and Mortier. You cannot conceive the excitement which my appearance in such a costume made in Paris, and when I came to the Rue de Rivoli I should think I had a quarter of a mile of folk riding or running behind me. Word had got about from the dragoons (two of whom had come with me), and everybody knew about my adventures and how I had come by my uniform. It was a triumph—men shouting and women waving their handkerchiefs and blowing kisses from the windows.

Although I am a man singularly free from conceit, still I must confess that, on this one occasion, I could not restrain myself from showing that this reception gratified me. The Russian's coat had hung very loose upon me, but now I threw out my chest until it was as tight as a sausage-skin. And my little sweetheart of a mare tossed her mane and pawed with her front hoofs, frisking her tail about as though she said, "We've done it together this time. It is to us that commissions should be intrusted." When I kissed her between the nostrils as I dismounted at the gate of the Tuileries, there was as much shouting as if a bulletin had been read from the Grand Army.

I was hardly in costume to visit a King; but, after all, if one has a soldierly figure one can do without all that. I was shown up straight away to Joseph, whom I had often seen in Spain. He seemed as stout, as quiet, and as amiable as ever. Talleyrand was in the room with him, or I suppose I should call him the Duke of Benevento, but I confess that I like old names best. He read my letter when Joseph Buonaparte handed it to him, and then he looked at me with the strangest expression in those funny little, twinkling eyes of his.

"Were you the only messenger?" he asked.

"There was one other, sir," said I. "Major Charpentier, of the Horse Grenadiers."

"He has not yet arrived," said the King of Spain.

"If you had seen the legs of his horse, sire, you would not wonder at it," I remarked.

"There may be other reasons," said Talleyrand, and he gave that singular smile of his.

Well, they paid me a compliment or two, though they might have said a good deal more and yet have said too little. I bowed myself out, and very glad I was to get away, for I hate a Court as much as I love a camp. Away I went to my old friend Chaubert, in the Rue Miromesnil, and there I got his hussar uniform, which fitted me very well. He and Lisette and I supped together in his rooms, and all my dangers were forgotten. In the morning I found Violette ready for another twenty-league stretch. It was my intention to return instantly to the Emperor's headquarters, for I was, as you may well imagine, impatient to hear his words of praise, and to receive my reward.

I need not say that I rode back by a safe route, for I had seen quite enough of Uhlans and Cossacks. I passed through Meaux and Château-Thierry, and so in the evening I arrived at Rheims, where Napoleon was still lying. The bodies of our fellows and of St. Prest's Russians had all been buried, and I could see changes in the camp also. The soldiers looked better cared for; some of the cavalry had received remounts, and everything was in excellent order. It was wonderful what a good general can effect in a couple of days.

When I came to the headquarters I was shown straight into the Emperor's room. He was drinking coffee at a writing-table, with a big plan drawn out on paper in front of him. Berthier and Macdonald were leaning, one over each shoulder, and he was talking so quickly that I don't believe that either of them could catch a half of what he was saying. But when his eyes fell upon me he dropped the pen on to the chart, and he sprang up with a look in his pale face which struck me cold.

"What the deuce are you doing here?" he shouted. When he was angry he had a voice like a peacock.

"I have the honor to report to you, sire," said I, "that I have delivered your despatch safely to the King of Spain."

"What!" he yelled, and his two eyes transfixed me like bayonets. Oh, those dreadful eyes, shifting from grey to blue, like steel in the sunshine. I can see them now when I have a bad dream.

"What has become of Charpentier?" he asked.

"He is captured," said Macdonald.

"By whom?"

"The Russians."

"The Cossacks?"

"No, a single Cossack."

"He gave himself up?"

"Without resistance."

"He is an intelligent officer. You will see that the medal of honor is awarded to him."

When I heard those words I had to rub my eyes to make sure that I was awake.

"As to you," cried the Emperor, taking a step forward as if he would have struck me, "you brain of a hare, what do you think that you were sent upon this mission for? Do you conceive that I would send a really important message by such a hand as yours, and through every village which the enemy holds? How you came through them passes my comprehension; but if your fellow-messenger had had but as little sense as you, my whole plan of campaign would have been ruined. Can you not see, *coglione*, that this message contained false news, and that it was intended to deceive the enemy whilst I put a very different scheme into execution?"

When I heard those cruel words and saw the angry, white face which glared at me, I had to hold the back of a chair, for my mind was failing me and my knees would hardly bear me up. But then I took courage as I reflected that I was an honorable gentleman, and that my whole life had been spent in toiling for this man and for my beloved country.

"Sire," said I, and the tears would trickle down my cheeks whilst I spoke, "when you are dealing with a man like me you would find it wiser to deal openly. Had I known that you had wished the despatch to fall into the hands of the enemy, I would have seen that it came there. As I believed that I was to guard it, I was prepared to sacrifice my life for it. I do not believe, sire, that any man in the world ever met with more toils and perils than I have done in trying to carry out what I thought was your will."

I dashed the tears from my eyes as I spoke, and with such fire and spirit as I could command I gave him an account of it all, of my dash through Soissons, my brush with the dragoons, my adventure in Senlis, my rencontre with Count Boutkine in the cellar, my disguise, my meeting with the Cossack officer, my flight, and how at the last moment I was nearly cut down by a French dragoon. The Emperor, Berthier, and Macdonald listened with astonishment on their faces. When I had finished Napoleon stepped forward and he pinched me by the ear.

"There, there!" said he. "Forget anything which I may have said. I would have done better to trust you. You may go."

I turned to the door, and my hand was upon the handle, when the Emperor called upon me to stop.

"You will see," said he, turning to the Duke of Tarentum, "that Brigadier Gerard has the special medal of honor, for I believe that if he has the thickest head he has also the stoutest heart in my army."

1814

VIII. How the Brigadier was Tempted by the Devil

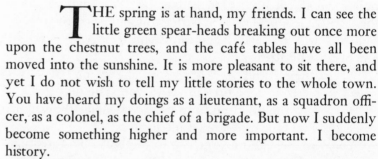

THE spring is at hand, my friends. I can see the little green spear-heads breaking out once more upon the chestnut trees, and the café tables have all been moved into the sunshine. It is more pleasant to sit there, and yet I do not wish to tell my little stories to the whole town. You have heard my doings as a lieutenant, as a squadron officer, as a colonel, as the chief of a brigade. But now I suddenly become something higher and more important. I become history.

If you have read of those closing years of the life of the Emperor which were spent on the Island of St. Helena, you will remember that, again and again, he implored permission to send out one single letter which should be unopened by those who held him. Many times he made this request, and even went so far as to promise that he would provide for his own wants and cease to be an expense to the British Government if it were granted to him. But his guardians knew that he was a terrible man, this pale, fat gentleman in the straw hat, and they dared not grant him what he asked. Many have wondered who it was to whom he could have had anything so secret to say. Some have supposed that it was to his wife, and some that it was to his father-in-law; some that it was to the Emperor Alexander and some to Marshal Soult. What will you think of me, my friends, when I tell you it was to me—to me, the Brigadier Gerard—that the Emperor wished to write? Yes, humble as you see me, with only my hundred francs a month of half-pay between me and hunger, it is none the less true I was always in the Emperor's mind, and that he would have given his left hand for five minutes' talk with me. I will tell you tonight how this came about.

It was after the Battle of Fère-Champenoise, where the conscripts in their blouses and their sabots made such a fine stand, that we, the more long-headed of us, began to understand that it was all over with us. Our reserve ammunition had been taken in the battle, and we were left with silent guns and empty caissons. Our cavalry, too, was in a deplorable condition, and my own brigade had been destroyed in the charge at Craonne. Then came the news that the enemy had taken Paris, that the citizens had mounted the white cockade; and finally, most terrible of all, that Marmont and his corps had gone over to the Bourbons. We looked at each other and asked how many more of our generals were going to turn against us. Already there were Jourdan, Marmont, Murat, Bernadotte, and Jomini—though nobody minded much about Jomini, for his pen was always sharper than his sword. We had been ready to fight Europe, but it looked now as though we were to fight Europe and half France as well.

We had come to Fontainebleau by a long, forced march, and there we were assembled, the poor remnants of us, the corps of Ney, the corps of my cousin Gerard, and the corps of Macdonald: twenty-five thousand in all, with seven thousand of the guard. But we had our prestige, which was worth fifty thousand, and our Emperor, who was worth fifty thousand more. He was always among us, serene, smiling, confident, taking his snuff and playing with his little riding-whip. Never in the days of his greatest victories have I admired him as much as I did during the Campaign of France.

One evening I was with a few of my officers, drinking a glass of wine of Suresnes. I mention that it was wine of Suresnes just to show you that times were not very good with us. Suddenly I was disturbed by a message from Berthier that he wished to see me. When I speak of my old comrades-in-arms, I will, with your permission, leave out all the fine foreign titles which they had picked up during the wars. They are excellent for a Court, but you never heard them in the camp, for we could not afford to do away with our Ney, our Rapp, or our Soult—names which were as stirring to our ears as the blare of our trumpets blowing the reveille. It was Berthier, then, who sent to say that he wished to see me.

He had a suite of rooms at the end of the gallery of Francis the First, not very far from those of the Emperor. In the antechamber were waiting two men whom I knew well: Colonel Despienne, of the Fifty-seventh of the line, and Captain Tremeau, of the Voltigeurs. They were both old soldiers—Tremeau had carried a musket in Egypt—and they were also both famous in the army for their courage and their skill with weapons. Tremeau had become a little stiff in the wrist, but Despienne was capable at his best of making me exert myself. He was a tiny fellow, about three inches short of the proper height for a man—he was exactly three inches shorter than myself—but both with the sabre and with the small-sword he had several times almost held his own against me when we used to exhibit at Verron's Hall of Arms in the Palais Royal. You may think that it made us sniff something in the wind when we found three such men called together into one room. You cannot see the lettuce and dressing without suspecting a salad.

"Name of a pipe!" said Tremeau, in his barrack-room fashion. "Are we then expecting three champions of the Bourbons?"

To all of us the idea appeared not improbable. Certainly in the whole army we were the very three who might have been chosen to meet them.

"The Prince of Neufchâtel desires to speak with the Brigadier Gerard," said a footman, appearing at the door.

In I went, leaving my two companions consumed with impatience behind me. It was a small room, but very gorgeously furnished. Berthier was seated opposite to me at a little table, with a pen in his hand and a note-book open before him. He was looking weary and slovenly—very different from that Berthier who used to give the fashion to the army, and who had so often set us poorer officers tearing our hair by trimming his pelisse with fur one campaign, and with grey astrakhan the next. On his clean-shaven, comely face there was an expression of trouble, and he looked at me as I entered his chamber in a way which had in it something furtive and displeasing.

"Chief of Brigade Gerard!" said he.

"At your service, your Highness!" I answered.

"I must ask you, before I go farther, to promise me, upon your honor as a gentleman and a soldier, that what is about to pass between us shall never be mentioned to any third person."

My word, this was a fine beginning! I had no choice but to give the promise required.

"You must know, then, that it is all over with the Emperor," said he, looking down at the table and speaking very slowly, as if he had a hard task in getting out the words. "Jourdan at Rouen and Marmont at Paris have both mounted the white cockade, and it is rumored that Talleyrand has talked Ney into doing the same. It is evident that further resistance is useless, and that it can only bring misery upon our country. I wish to ask you, therefore, whether you are prepared to join me in laying hands upon the Emperor's person, and bringing the war to a conclusion by delivering him over to the allies?"

I assure you that when I heard this infamous proposition put forward by the man who had been the earliest friend of the Emperor, and who had received greater favors from him than any of his followers, I could only stand and stare at him in amazement. For his part he tapped his pen-handle against his teeth, and looked at me with a slanting head.

"Well?" he asked.

"I am a little deaf on one side," said I, coldly. "There are some things which I cannot hear. I beg that you will permit me to return to my duties."

"Nay, but you must not be headstrong," rising up and laying his hand upon my shoulder. "You are aware that the Senate has declared against Napoleon, and that the Emperor Alexander refuses to treat with him."

"Sir," I cried, with passion, "I would have you know that I do not care the dregs of a wine-glass for the Senate or for the Emperor Alexander either."

"Then for what do you care?"

"For my own honor and for the service of my glorious master, the Emperor Napoleon."

"That is all very well," said Berthier, peevishly, shrugging his shoulders. "Facts are facts, and as men of the world, we must look them in the face. Are we to stand against the will of the nation? Are we to have civil war on the top of all our misfortunes? And, besides, we are thinning away. Every hour comes the news of fresh desertions. We have still time to make our peace, and, indeed, to earn the highest reward, by giving up the Emperor."

I shook so with passion that my sabre clattered against my thigh.

"Sir," I cried, "I never thought to have seen the day when a Marshal of France would have so far degraded himself as to put forward such a proposal. I leave you to your own conscience; but as for me, until I have the Emperor's own order, there shall always be the sword of Etienne Gerard between his enemies and himself."

I was so moved by my own words and by the fine position which I had taken up, that my voice broke, and I could hardly refrain from tears. I should have liked the whole army to have seen me as I stood with my head so proudly erect and my hand upon my heart proclaiming my devotion to the Emperor in his adversity. It was one of the supreme moments of my life.

"Very good," said Berthier, ringing a bell for the lackey. "You will show the Chief of Brigade Gerard into the salon."

The footman led me into an inner room, where he desired me to be seated. For my own part, my only desire was to get away, and I could not understand why they should wish to detain me. When one has had no change of uniform during a whole winter's campaign, one does not feel at home in a palace.

I had been there about a quarter of an hour when the footman opened the door again, and in came Colonel Despienne. Good heavens, what a sight he was! His face was as white as a guardsman's gaiters, his eyes projecting, the veins swollen upon his forehead, and every hair of his moustache bristling like those of an angry cat. He was too angry to speak, and could only shake his hands at the ceiling and make a gurgling in his throat. "Parricide! Viper!" those were the words that I could catch as he stamped up and down the room.

Of course it was evident to me that he had been subjected to the same infamous proposals as I had, and that he had received them in the same spirit. His lips were sealed to me, as mine were to him, by the promise which we had taken, but I contented myself with muttering "Atrocious! Unspeakable!" —so that he might know that I was in agreement with him.

Well, we were still there, he striding furiously up and down, and I seated in the corner, when suddenly a most extraordinary uproar broke out in the room which we had just quitted. There was a snarling, worrying growl, like that of a fierce dog which has got his grip. Then came a crash and a voice calling for help. In we rushed, the two of us, and, my faith, we were none too soon.

Old Tremeau and Berthier were rolling together upon the floor, with the table upon the top of them. The Captain had one of his great, skinny yellow hands upon the Marshal's throat, and already his face was lead-colored, and his eyes were starting from their sockets. As to Tremeau, he was beside himself, with foam upon the corners of his lips, and such a frantic expression upon him that I am convinced, had we not loosened his iron grip, finger by finger, that it would never have relaxed while the Marshal lived. His nails were white with the power of his grasp.

"I have been tempted by the devil!" he cried, as he staggered to his feet. "Yes, I have been tempted by the devil!"

As to Berthier, he could only lean against the wall, and pant for a couple of minutes, putting his hands up to his throat and rolling his head about. Then, with an angry gesture, he turned to the heavy blue curtain which hung behind his chair.

The curtain was torn to one side and the Emperor stepped out into the room. We sprang to the salute, we three old soldiers, but it was all like a scene in a dream to us, and our eyes were as far out as Berthier's had been. Napoleon was dressed in his green-coated chasseur uniform, and he held his little, silver-headed switch in his hand. He looked at us each in turn, with a smile upon his face—that frightful smile in which neither eyes nor brow joined—and each in turn had, I believe, a pringling on his skin, for that was the effect which the Emperor's gaze had upon most of us. Then he walked across to Berthier and put his hand upon his shoulder.

"You must not quarrel with blows, my dear Prince," said he; "they are your title to nobility." He spoke in that soft, caressing manner which he could assume. There was no one who could make the French tongue sound so pretty as the Emperor, and no one who could make it more harsh and terrible.

"I believe he would have killed me," cried Berthier, still rolling his head about.

"Tut, tut! I should have come to your help had these officers not heard your cries. But I trust that you are not really hurt!" He spoke with earnestness, for he was in truth very fond of Berthier—more so than of any man, unless it were of poor Duroc.

Berthier laughed, though not with a very good grace.

"It is new for me to receive my injuries from French hands," said he.

"And yet it was in the cause of France," returned the Emperor. Then, turning to us, he took old Tremeau by the ear. "Ah, old grumbler," said he, "you were one of my Egyptian grenadiers, were you not, and had your musket of honor at Marengo. I remember you very well, my good friend. So the old fires are not yet extinguished! They still burn up when you think that your Emperor is wronged. And you, Colonel Despienne, you would not even listen to the tempter. And you, Gerard, your faithful sword is ever to be between me and my enemies. Well, well, I have had some traitors about me, but now at last we are beginning to see who are the true men."

You can fancy, my friends, the thrill of joy which it gave us when the greatest man in the whole world spoke to us in this fashion. Tremeau shook until I thought he would have fallen, and the tears ran down his gigantic mustache. If you had not seen it, you could never believe the influence which the Emperor had upon those coarse-grained, savage old veterans.

"Well, my faithful friends," said he, "if you will follow me into this room, I will explain to you the meaning of this little farce which we have been acting. I beg, Berthier, that you will remain in this chamber, and so make sure that no one interrupts us."

It was new for us to be doing business, with a Marshal of France as sentry at the door. However, we followed the Emperor as we were ordered, and he led us into the recess of the window, gathering us around him and sinking his voice as he addressed us.

"I have picked you out of the whole army," said he, "as being not only the most formidable but also the most faithful of my soldiers. I was convinced that you were all three men who would never waver in your fidelity to me. If I have ventured to put that fidelity to the proof, and to watch you while attempts were, at my orders, made upon your honor, it was only because, in the days when I have found the blackest treason amongst my own flesh and blood, it is necessary that

I should be doubly circumspect. Suffice it that I am well convinced now that I can rely upon your valour."

"To the death, sire!" cried Tremeau, and we both repeated it after him.

Napoleon drew us all yet a little closer to him, and sank his voice still lower.

"What I say to you now I have said to no one—not to my wife or my brothers; only to you. It is all up with us, my friends. We have come to our last rally. The game is finished, and we must make provision accordingly."

My heart seemed to have changed to a nine-pounder ball as I listened to him. We had hoped against hope, but now when he, the man who was always serene and who always had reserves—when he, in that quiet, impassive voice of his, said that everything was over, we realized that the clouds had shut for ever, and the last gleam gone. Tremeau snarled and gripped at his sabre, Despienne ground his teeth, and for my own part I threw out my chest and clicked my heels to show the Emperor that there were some spirits which could rise to adversity.

"My papers and my fortune must be secured," whispered the Emperor. "The whole course of the future may depend upon my having them safe. They are our base for the next attempt—for I am very sure that these poor Bourbons would find that my footstool is too large to make a throne for them. Where am I to keep these precious things? My belongings will be searched—so will the houses of my supporters. They must be secured and concealed by men whom I can trust with that which is more precious to me than my life. Out of the whole of France, you are those whom I have chosen for this sacred trust.

"In the first place, I will tell you what these papers are. You shall not say that I have made you blind agents in the matter. They are the official proof of my divorce from Josephine, of my legal marriage to Marie Louise, and of the birth of my son and heir, the King of Rome. If we cannot prove each of these, the future claim of my family to the throne of France falls to the ground. Then there are securities to the value of forty millions of francs—an immense sum, my friends, but of no more value than this riding-switch when compared to the other papers of which I have spoken. I tell you these things that you may realize the enormous importance of the task which I am committing to your care. Listen, now, while I inform you where you are to get these papers, and what you are to do with them.

"They were handed over to my trusty friend, the Countess Walewski, at Paris, this morning. At five o'clock she starts for Fontainebleau in her blue berline. She should reach here between half-past nine and ten. The papers will be concealed in the berline, in a hiding-place which none know but herself. She has been warned that her carriage will be stopped outside the town by three mounted officers, and she will hand the packet over to your care. You are the younger man, Gerard, but you are of the senior grade. I confide to your care this amethyst ring, which you will show the lady as a token of your mission, and which you will leave with her as a receipt for her papers.

"Having received the packet, you will ride with it into the forest as far as the ruined dove-house—the Colombier. It is possible that I may meet you there—but if it seems to me to be dangerous, I will send my body-servant, Mustapha, whose directions you may take as being mine. There is no roof to the Colombier, and tonight will be a full moon. At the right of the entrance you will find three spades leaning against the wall. With these you will dig a hole three feet deep in the northeastern corner—that is, in the corner to the left of the door, and nearest to Fontainebleau. Having buried the papers, you will replace the soil with great care, and you will then report to me at the palace."

These were the Emperor's directions, but given with an accuracy and minuteness of detail such as no one but himself could put into an order. When he had finished, he made us swear to keep his secret as long as he lived, and as long as the papers should remain buried. Again and again he made us swear it before he dismissed us from his presence.

Colonel Despienne had quarters at the "Sign of the Pheasant," and it was there that we supped together. We were all three men who had been trained to take the strangest turns of fortune as part of our daily life and business, yet we were all flushed and moved by the extraordinary interview which we had had, and by the thought of the great adventure which lay before us. For my own part, it had been my fate three several times to take my orders from the lips of the Emperor himself, but neither the incident of the Ajaccio murderers nor the famous ride which I made to Paris appeared to offer such opportunities as this new and most intimate commission.

"If things go right with the Emperor," said Despienne, "we shall all live to be marshals yet."

We drank with him to our future cocked hats and our batons.

It was agreed between us that we should make our way separately to our rendezvous, which was to be the first milestone upon the Paris road. In this way we should avoid the gossip which might get about if three men who were so well known were to be seen riding out together. My little Violette had cast a shoe that morning, and the farrier was at work upon her when I returned, so that my comrades were already there when I arrived at the trysting-place. I had taken with me not only my sabre, but also my new pair of English rifled pistols, with a mallet for knocking in the charges. They had cost me a hundred and fifty francs at Trouvel's, in the Rue de Rivoli, but they would carry far farther and straighter than the others. It was with one of them that I had saved old Bouvet's life at Leipzig.

The night was cloudless, and there was a brilliant moon behind us, so that we always had three black horsemen riding down the white road in front of us. The country is so thickly wooded, however, that we could not see very far. The great palace clock had already struck ten, but there was no sign of the Countess. We began to fear that something might have prevented her from starting.

And then suddenly we heard her in the distance. Very faint at first were the birr of wheels and the tat-tat-tat of the horses' feet. Then they grew louder and clearer and louder yet, until a pair of yellow lanterns swung round the curve, and in their light we saw the two big brown horses tearing along with the high, blue carriage at the back of them. The postilion pulled them up panting and foaming within a few yards of us. In a moment we were at the window and had raised our hands in a salute to the beautiful pale face which looked out at us.

"We are the three officers of the Emperor, madame," said I, in a low voice, leaning my face down to the open window. "You have already been warned that we should wait upon you."

The Countess had a very beautiful, cream-tinted complexion of a sort which I particularly admire, but she grew whiter and whiter as she looked up at me. Harsh lines deepened upon her face until she seemed, even as I looked at her, to turn from youth into age.

"It is evident to me," she said, "that you are three impostors."

If she had struck me across the face with her delicate hand she could not have startled me more. It was not her words only, but the bitterness with which she hissed them out.

"Indeed, madame," said I. "You do us less than justice. These are the Colonel Despienne and Captain Tremeau. For myself, my name is Brigadier Gerard, and I have only to mention it to assure anyone who has heard of me that——"

"Oh, you villains!" she interrupted. "You think that because I am only a woman I am very easily to be hoodwinked! You miserable impostors!"

I looked at Despienne, who had turned white with anger, and at Tremeau, who was tugging at his mustache.

"Madame," said I, coldly, "when the Emperor did us the honor to intrust us with this mission, he gave me this amethyst ring as a token. I had not thought that three honorable gentlemen would have needed such corroboration, but I can only confute your unworthy suspicions by placing it in your hands."

She held it up in the light of the carriage lamp, and the most dreadful expression of grief and of horror contorted her face.

"It is his!" she screamed, and then, "Oh, my God, what have I done? What have I done?"

I felt that something terrible had befallen. "Quick, madame, quick!" I cried. "Give us the papers!"

"I have already given them."

"Given them! To whom?"

"To three officers."

"When?"

"Within the half-hour."

"Where are they?"

"God help me, I do not know. They stopped the berline, and I handed them over to them without hesitation, thinking that they had come from the Emperor."

It was a thunder-clap. But those are the moments when I am at my finest.

"You remain here," said I, to my comrades. "If three

horsemen pass you, stop them at any hazard. The lady will describe them to you. I will be with you presently." One shake of the bridle, and I was flying into Fontainebleau as only Violette could have carried me. At the palace I flung myself off, rushed up the stairs, brushed aside the lackeys who would have stopped me, and pushed my way into the Emperor's own cabinet. He and Macdonald were busy with pencil and compasses over a chart. He looked up with an angry frown at my sudden entry, but his face changed color when he saw that it was I.

"You can leave us, Marshal," said he, and then, the instant the door was closed: "What news about the papers?"

"They are gone!" said I, and in a few curt words I told him what had happened. His face was calm, but I saw the compasses quiver in his hand.

"You must recover them, Gerard!" he cried. "The destinies of my dynasty are at stake. Not a moment is to be lost! To horse, sir, to horse!"

"Who are they, sire?"

"I cannot tell. I am surrounded with treason. But they will take them to Paris. To whom should they carry them but to the villain Talleyrand? Yes, yes, they are on the Paris road, and may yet be overtaken. With the three best mounts in my stables and——"

I did not wait to hear the end of the sentence. I was already clattering down the stair. I am sure that five minutes had not passed before I was galloping Violette out of the town with the bridle of one of the Emperor's own Arab chargers in either hand. They wished me to take three, but I should have never dared to look my Violette in the face again. I feel that the spectacle must have been superb when I dashed up to my comrades and pulled the horses on to their haunches in the moonlight.

"No one has passed?"

"No one."

"Then they are on the Paris road. Quick! Up and after them!"

They did not take long, those good soldiers. In a flash they were upon the Emperor's horses, and their own left masterless by the roadside. Then away we went upon our long chase, I in the center, Despienne upon my right, and Tremeau a little behind, for he was the heavier man. Heavens, how we galloped! The twelve flying hoofs roared and roared along the hard, smooth road. Poplars and moon, black bars and silver streaks, for mile after mile our course lay along the same chequered track, with our shadows in front and our dust behind. We could hear the rasping of bolts and the creaking of shutters from the cottages as we thundered past them, but we were only three dark blurs upon the road by the time that the folk could look after us. It was just striking midnight as we raced into Corbeil; but an hostler with a bucket in either hand was throwing his black shadow across the golden fan which was cast from the open door of the inn.

"Three riders!" I gasped. "Have they passed?"

"I have just been watering their horses," said he. "I should think they——"

"On, my friends!" and away we flew, striking fire from the cobblestones of the little town. A gendarme tried to stop us, but his voice was drowned by our rattle and clatter. The houses slid past, and we were out on the country road again, with a clear twenty miles between ourselves and Paris. How could they escape us, with the finest horses in France behind them? Not one of the three had turned a hair, but Violette was always a head and shoulders to the front. She was going within herself too, and I knew by the spring of her that I had only to let her stretch herself, and the Emperor's horses would see the color of her tail.

"There they are!" cried Despienne.

"We have them!" growled Tremeau.

"On, comrades, on!" I shouted, once more.

A long stretch of white road lay before us in the moonlight. Far away down it we could see three cavaliers, lying low upon their horses' necks. Every instant they grew larger and clearer as we gained upon them. I could see quite plainly that the two upon either side were wrapped in mantles and rode upon chestnut horses, whilst the man between them was dressed in a chasseur uniform and mounted upon a grey. They were keeping abreast, but it was easy enough to see from the way in which he gathered his legs for each spring that the center horse was far the fresher of the three. And the rider appeared to be the leader of the party, for we continually saw the glint of his face in the moonshine as he looked back to measure the distance between us. At first it was only a glimmer, then it was cut across with a moustache, and at last when we began to feel their dust in our throats I could give a name to my man.

"Halt, Colonel de Montluc!" I shouted. "Halt, in the Emperor's name!"

I had known him for years as a daring officer and an unprincipled rascal. Indeed, there was a score between us, for he had shot my friend, Treville, at Warsaw, pulling his trigger, as some said, a good second before the drop of the handkerchief.

Well, the words were hardly out of my mouth when his two comrades wheeled round and fired their pistols at us. I heard Despienne give a terrible cry, and at the same instant both Tremeau and I let drive at the same man. He fell forward with his hands swinging on each side of his horse's neck. His comrade spurred on to Tremeau, sabre in hand, and I heard the crash which comes when a strong cut is met by a stronger parry. For my own part I never turned my head, but I touched Violette with the spur for the first time and flew after the leader. That he should leave his comrades and fly was proof enough that I should leave mine and follow.

He had gained a couple of hundred paces, but the good little mare set that right before we could have passed two milestones. It was in vain that he spurred and thrashed like a gunner driver on a soft road. His hat flew off with his exertions, and his bald head gleamed in the moonshine. But do what he might, he still heard the rattle of the hoofs growing louder and louder behind him. I could not have been twenty yards from him, and the shadow head was touching the shadow haunch, when he turned with a curse in his saddle and emptied both his pistols, one after the other, into Violette.

I have been wounded myself so often that I have to stop and think before I can tell you the exact number of times. I have been hit by musket balls, by pistol bullets, and by bursting shells, besides being pierced by bayonet, lance, sabre, and finally by a brad-awl, which was the most painful of any. Yet out of all these injuries I have never known the same deadly sickness as came over me when I felt the poor, silent, patient creature, which I had come to love more than anything in the world except my mother and the Emperor, reel and stagger beneath me. I pulled my second pistol from my holster and fired point-blank between the fellow's broad shoulders. He slashed his horse across the flank with his whip, and for a moment I thought that I had missed him. But then on the

green of his chasseur jacket I saw an ever-widening black
smudge, and he began to sway in his saddle, very slightly at
first, but more and more with every bound, until at last over
he went, with his foot caught in the stirrup and his shoulders
thud-thudding along the road, until the drag was too much
for the tired horse, and I closed my hand upon the foam-
spattered bridle-chain. As I pulled him up it eased the stirrup
leather, and the spurred heel clinked loudly as it fell.

"Your papers!" I cried, springing from my saddle. "This
instant!"

But even as I said it, the huddle of the green body and the
fantastic sprawl of the limbs in the moonlight told me clearly
enough that it was all over with him. My bullet had passed
through his heart, and it was only his iron will which had held
him so long in the saddle. He had lived hard, this Montluc,
and I will do him the justice to say that he died hard also.

But it was the papers—always the papers—of which I
thought. I opened his tunic and I felt in his shirt. Then I
searched his holsters and his sabre-tasche. Finally I dragged
off his boots, and undid his horse's girth so as to hunt under
the saddle. There was not a nook or crevice which I did not
ransack. It was useless. They were not upon him.

When this stunning blow came upon me I could have sat
down by the roadside and wept. Fate seemed to be fighting
against me, and that is an enemy from whom even a gallant
hussar might not be ashamed to flinch. I stood with my arm
over the neck of my poor wounded Violette, and I tried to
think it all out, that I might act in the wisest way. I was aware
that the Emperor had no great respect for my wits, and I
longed to show him that he had done me an injustice. Montluc
had not the papers. And yet Montluc had sacrificed his companions in order to make his escape. I could make nothing of
that. On the other hand, it was clear that, if he had not got
them, one or other of his comrades had. One of them was certainly dead. The other I had left fighting with Tremeau, and
if he escaped from the old swordsman he had still to pass me.
Clearly, my work lay behind me.

I hammered fresh charges into my pistols after I had turned
this over in my head. Then I put them back in the holsters,
and I examined my little mare, she jerking her head and cock-
ing her ears the while, as if to tell me that an old soldier like
herself did not make a fuss about a scratch or two. The first
shot had merely grazed her off-shoulder, leaving a skin-mark,

as if she had brushed a wall. The second was more serious. It had passed through the muscle of her neck, but already it had ceased to bleed. I reflected that if she weakened I could mount Montluc's grey, and meanwhile I led him along beside us, for he was a fine horse, worth fifteen hundred francs at the least, and it seemed to me that no one had a better right to him than I.

Well, I was all impatience now to get back to the others, and I had just given Violette her head, when suddenly I saw something glimmering in a field by the roadside. It was the brass-work upon the chasseur hat which had flown from Montluc's head; and at the sight of it a thought made me jump in the saddle. How could the hat have flown off? With its weight, would it not have simply dropped? And here it lay, fifteen paces from the roadway! Of course, he must have thrown it off when he had made sure that I would overtake him. And if he threw it off—I did not stop to reason any more, but sprang from the mare with my heart beating the *pas-de-charge*. Yes, it was all right this time. There, in the crown of the hat was stuffed a roll of papers in a parchment wrapper bound round with yellow ribbon. I pulled it out with the one hand, and holding the hat in the other, I danced for joy in the moonlight. The Emperor would see that he had not made a mistake when he put his affairs into the charge of Etienne Gerard.

I had a safe pocket on the inside of my tunic just over my heart, where I kept a few little things which were dear to me, and into this I thrust my precious roll. Then I sprang upon Violette, and was pushing forward to see what had become of Tremeau, when I saw a horseman riding across the field in the distance. At the same instant I heard the sound of hoofs approaching me, and there in the moonlight was the Emperor upon his white charger, dressed in his grey overcoat and his three-cornered hat, just as I had seen him so often upon the field of battle.

"Well!" he cried, in the sharp, sergeant-major way of his. "Where are my papers?"

I spurred forward and presented them without a word. He broke the ribbon and ran his eyes rapidly over them. Then, as we sat our horses head to tail, he threw his left arm across me with his hand upon my shoulder. Yes, my friends, simple as you see me, I have been embraced by my great master.

"Gerard," he cried, "you are a marvel!"

I did not wish to contradict him, and it brought a flush of joy upon my cheeks to know that he had done me justice at last.

"Where is the thief, Gerard?" he asked.

"Dead, sire."

"You killed him?"

"He wounded my horse, sire, and would have escaped had I not shot him."

"Did you recognize him?"

"De Montluc is his name, sire—a Colonel of Chasseurs."

"Tut," said the Emperor. "We have got the poor pawn, but the hand which plays the game is still out of reach." He sat in silent thought for a little, with his chin sunk upon his chest. "Ah, Talleyrand, Talleyrand," I heard him mutter, "if I had been in your place and you in mine, you would have crushed a viper when you held it under your heel. For five years I have known you for what you are, and yet I have let you live to sting me. Never mind, my brave," he continued, turning to me, "there will come a day of reckoning for everybody, and when it arrives, I promise you that my friends will be remembered as well as my enemies."

"Sire," said I, for I had had time for thought as well as he, "if your plans about these papers have been carried to the ears of your enemies, I trust you do not think that it was owing to any indiscretion upon the part of myself or of my comrades."

"It would be hardly reasonable for me to do so," he answered, "seeing that this plot was hatched in Paris, and that you only had your orders a few hours ago."

"Then how——?"

"Enough," he cried, sternly. "You take an undue advantage of your position."

That was always the way with the Emperor. He would chat with you as with a friend and a brother, and then when he had wiled you into forgetting the gulf which lay between you, he would suddenly, with a word or with a look, remind you that it was as impassable as ever. When I have fondled my old hound until he has been encouraged to paw my knees, and I have then thrust him down again, it has made me think of the Emperor and his ways.

He reined his horse round, and I followed him in silence and with a heavy heart. But when he spoke again his words were enough to drive all thought of myself out of my mind.

"I could not sleep until I knew how you had fared," said he. "I have paid a price for my papers. There are not so many of my old soldiers left that I can afford to lose two in one night."

When he said "two" it turned me cold.

"Colonel Despienne was shot, sire," I stammered.

"And Captain Tremeau cut down. Had I been a few minutes earlier, I might have saved him. The other escaped across the fields."

I remembered that I had seen a horseman a moment before I had met the Emperor. He had taken to the fields to avoid me, but if I had known, and Violette been unwounded, the old soldier would not have gone unavenged. I was thinking sadly of his sword-play, and wondering whether it was his stiffening wrist which had been fatal to him, when Napoleon spoke again.

"Yes, Brigadier," said he, "you are now the only man who will know where these papers are concealed."

It must have been imagination, my friends, but for an instant I may confess that it seemed to me that there was a tone in the Emperor's voice which was not altogether one of sorrow. But the dark thought had hardly time to form itself in my mind before he let me see that I was doing him an injustice.

"Yes, I have paid a price for my papers," he said, and I heard them crackle as he put his hand up to his bosom. "No man has ever had more faithful servants—no man since the beginning of the world."

As he spoke we came upon the scene of the struggle. Colonel Despienne and the man whom we had shot lay together some distance down the road, while their horses grazed contentedly beneath the poplars. Captain Tremeau lay in front of us upon his back, with his arms and legs stretched out, and his sabre broken short off in his hand. His tunic was open, and a huge blood-clot hung like a dark handkerchief out of a slit in his white shirt. I could see the gleam of his clenched teeth from under his immense moustache.

The Emperor sprang from his horse and bent down over the dead man.

"He was with me since Rivoli," said he, sadly. "He was one of my old grumblers in Egypt."

And the voice brought the man back from the dead. I saw his eyelids shiver. He twitched his arm, and moved the sword-hilt a few inches. He was trying to raise it in salute. Then the mouth opened, and the hilt tinkled down on to the ground.

"May we all die as gallantly," said the Emperor, as he rose, and from my heart I added "Amen."

There was a farm within fifty yards of where we were standing, and the farmer, roused from his sleep by the clatter of hoofs and the cracking of pistols, had rushed out to the roadside. We saw him now, dumb with fear and astonishment, staring open-eyed at the Emperor. It was to him that we committed the care of the four dead men and of the horses also. For my own part, I thought it best to leave Violette with him and to take De Montluc's grey with me, for he could not refuse to give me back my own mare, whilst there might be difficulties about the other. Besides, my little friend's wound had to be considered, and we had a long return ride before us.

The Emperor did not at first talk much upon the way. Perhaps the deaths of Despienne and Tremeau still weighed heavily upon his spirits. He was always a reserved man, and in those times, when every hour brought him the news of some success of his enemies or defection of his friends, one could not expect him to be a merry companion. Nevertheless, when I reflected that he was carrying in his bosom those papers which he valued so highly, and which only a few hours ago appeared to be forever lost, and when I further thought that it was I, Etienne Gerard, who had placed them there, I felt that I had deserved some little consideration. The same idea may have occurred to him, for when we had at last left the Paris high road, and had entered the forest, he began of his own accord to tell me that which I should have most liked to have asked him.

"As to the papers," said he, "I have already told you that there is no one now, except you and me, who knows where they are to be concealed. My Mameluke carried the spades to the pigeon-house, but I have told him nothing. Our plans, however, for bringing the packet from Paris have been formed since Monday. There were three in the secret, a woman and two men. The woman I would trust with my life; which of the two men has betrayed us I do not know, but I think that I may promise to find out."

We were riding in the shadow of the trees at the time, and

I could hear him slapping his riding-whip against his boot, and taking pinch after pinch of snuff, as was his way when he was excited.

"You wonder, no doubt," said he, after a pause, "why these rascals did not stop the carriage at Paris instead of at the entrance to Fontainebleau."

In truth, the objection had not occurred to me, but I did not wish to appear to have less wits than he gave me credit for, so I answered that it was indeed surprising.

"Had they done so they would have made a public scandal, and run a chance of missing their end. Short of taking the berline to pieces, they could not have discovered the hiding-place. He planned it well—he could always plan well—and he chose his agents well also. But mine were the better."

It is not for me to repeat to you, my friends, all that was said to me by the Emperor as we walked our horses amid the black shadows and through the moon-silvered glades of the great forest. Every word of it is impressed upon my memory, and before I pass away it is likely that I will place it all upon paper, so that others may read it in the days to come. He spoke freely of his past, and something also of his future; of the devotion of Macdonald, of the treason of Marmont, of the little King of Rome, concerning whom he talked with as much tenderness as any bourgeois father of a single child; and finally, of his father-in-law, the Emperor of Austria, who would, he thought, stand between his enemies and himself. For myself, I dared not say a word, remembering how I had already brought a rebuke upon myself; but I rode by his side, hardly able to believe that this was indeed the great Emperor, the man whose glance sent a thrill through me, who was now pouring out his thoughts to me in short, eager sentences, the words rattling and racing like the hoofs of a galloping squaddon. It is possible that, after the word-splittings and diplomacy of a Court, it was a relief to him to speak his mind to a plain soldier like myself.

In this way the Emperor and I—even after years it sends a flush of pride into my cheeks to be able to put those words together—the Emperor and I walked our horses through the Forest of Fontainebleau, until we came at last to the Colombier. The three spades were propped against the wall upon the right-hand side of the ruined door, and at the sight of them the tears sprang to my eyes as I thought of the hands for which they were intended. The Emperor seized one and I another.

"Quick!" said he. "The dawn will be upon us before we get back to the palace."

We dug the hole, and placing the papers in one of my pistol holsters to screen them from the damp, we laid them at the bottom and covered them up. We then carefully removed all marks of the ground having been disturbed, and we placed a large stone upon the top. I dare say that since the Emperor was a young gunner, and helped to train his pieces against Toulon, he had not worked so hard with his hands. He was mopping his forehead with his silk handkerchief long before we had come to the end of our task.

The first grey cold light of morning was stealing through the tree trunks when we came out together from the old pigeon-house. The Emperor laid his hand upon my shoulder as I stood ready to help him to mount.

"We have left the papers there," said he, solemnly, "and I desire that you shall leave all thought of them there also. Let the recollection of them pass entirely from your mind, to be revived only when you receive a direct order under my own hand and seal. From this time onwards you forget all that has passed."

"I forget it, sire," said I.

We rode together to the edge of the town, where he desired that I should separate from him. I had saluted, and was turning my horse, when he called me back.

"It is easy to mistake the points of the compass in the forest," said he. "Would you not say that it was in the north-eastern corner that we buried them?"

"Buried what, sire?"

"The papers, of course," he cried, impatiently.

"What papers, sire?"

"Name of a name! Why, the papers that you have recovered for me."

"I am really at a loss to know what your Majesty is talking about."

He flushed with anger for a moment, and then he burst out laughing.

"Very good, Brigadier!" he cried. "I begin to believe that you are as good a diplomatist as you are a soldier, and I cannot say more than that."

So that was my strange adventure in which I found myself the friend and confident agent of the Emperor. When he returned from Elba he refrained from digging up the papers until his position should be secure, and they still remained in the corner of the old pigeon-house after his exile to St. Helena. It was at this time that he was desirous of getting them into the hands of his own supporters, and for that purpose he wrote me, as I afterwards learned, three letters, all of which were intercepted by his guardians. Finally, he offered to support himself and his own establishment—which he might very easily have done out of the gigantic sum which belonged to him—if they would only pass one of his letters unopened. This request was refused, and so, up to his death in '21, the papers still remained where I have told you. How they came to be dug up by Count Bertrand and myself, and who eventually obtained them, is a story which I would tell you, were it not that the end has not yet come.

Some day you will hear of those papers, and you will see how, after he has been so long in his grave, that great man can still set Europe shaking. When that day comes, you will think of Etienne Gerard, and you will tell your children that you have heard the story from the lips of the man who was the only one living of all who took part in that strange history—the man who was tempted by Marshal Berthier, who led that wild pursuit upon the Paris road, who was honored by the embrace of the Emperor, and who rode with him by moonlight in the Forest of Fontainebleau. The buds are bursting and the birds are calling, my friends. You may find better things to do in the sunlight than listening to the stories of an old broken soldier. And yet you may well treasure what I say, for the buds will have burst and the birds sung in many seasons before France will see such another ruler as he whose servants we were proud to be.

1815

IX. How the Brigadier Bore Himself At Waterloo

I—THE STORY OF THE FOREST INN

OF ALL the great battles in which I had the honor of drawing my sword for the Emperor and for France there was not one which was lost. At Waterloo, although, in a sense, I was present, I was unable to fight, and the enemy was victorious. It is not for me to say that there is a connection between these two things. You know me too well, my friends, to imagine that I would make such a claim. But it gives matter for thought, and some have drawn flattering conclusions from it. After all, it was only a matter of breaking a few English squares and the day would have been our own. If the Hussars of Conflans, with Etienne Gerard to lead them, could not do this, then the best judges are mistaken. But let that pass. The Fates had ordained that I should hold my hand and that the Empire should fall. But they had also ordained that this day of gloom and sorrow should bring such honor to me as had never come when I swept on the wings of victory from Boulogne to Vienna. Never had I burned so brilliantly as at that supreme moment when the darkness fell upon all around me. You are aware that I was faithful to the Emperor in his adversity, and that I refused to sell my sword and my honor to the Bourbons. Never again was I to feel my war horse between my knees, never again to hear the kettledrums and silver trumpets behind me as I rode in front of my little rascals. But it comforts my heart, my friends, and

164

it brings the tears to my eyes, to think how great I was upon
that last day of my soldier life, and to remember that of all the
remarkable exploits which have won me the love of so many
beautiful women, and the respect of so many noble men,
there was none which, in splendor, in audacity, and in the
great end which was attained, could compare with my famous
ride upon the night of June 18th, 1815. I am aware that the
story is often told at mess-tables and in barrack-rooms, so that
there are few in the army who have not heard it, but modesty
has sealed my lips, until now, my friends, in the privacy of
these intimate gatherings, I am inclined to lay the true facts
before you.

In the first place, there is one thing which I can assure you.
In all his career Napoleon never had so splendid an army as
that with which he took the field for that campaign. In 1813
France was exhausted. For every veteran there were five
children—Marie Louises as we called them, for the Empress
had busied herself in raising levies while the Emperor took the
field. But it was very different in 1815. The prisoners had all
come back—the men from the snows of Russia, the men from
the dungeons of Spain, the men from the hulks in England.
These were the dangerous men, veterans of twenty battles,
longing for their old trade, and with hearts filled with hatred
and revenge. The ranks were full of soldiers who wore two
and three chevrons, every chevron meaning five years' service.
And the spirit of these men was terrible. They were raging,
furious, fanatical, adoring the Emperor as a Mameluke does
his prophet, ready to fall upon their own bayonets if their
blood could serve him. If you had seen these fierce old veterans
going into battle, with their flushed faces, their savage eyes,
their furious yells, you would wonder that anything could
stand against them. So high was the spirit of France at that
time that every other spirit would have quailed before it; but
these people, these English, had neither spirit nor soul, but
only solid, immovable beef, against which we broke ourselves
in vain. That was it, my friends! On the one side, poetry,
gallantry, self-sacrifice—all that is beautiful and heroic. On the
other side, beef. Our hopes, our ideals, our dreams—all were
shattered on that terrible beef of Old England.

You have read how the Emperor gathered his forces, and
then how he and I, with a hundred and thirty thousand veterans, hurried to the northern frontier and fell upon the

Prussians and the English. On the 16th of June Ney held the English in play at Quatre Bras while we beat the Prussians at Ligny. It is not for me to say how far I contributed to that victory, but it is well known that the Hussars of Conflans covered themselves with glory. They fought well, these Prussians, and eight thousand of them were left upon the field. The Emperor thought that he had done with them, as he sent Marshal Grouchy with thirty-two thousand men to follow them up and to prevent their interfering with his plans. Then, with nearly eighty thousand men, he turned upon these "Goddam" Englishmen. How much we had to avenge upon them, we Frenchmen—the guineas of Pitt, the hulks of Portsmouth, the invasion of Wellington, the perfidious victories of Nelson! At last the day of punishment seemed to have arisen.

Wellington had with him sixty-seven thousand men, but many of them were known to be Dutch and Belgian, who had no great desire to fight against us. Of good troops he had not fifty thousand. Finding himself in the presence of the Emperor in person with eighty thousand men, this Englishman was so paralyzed with fear that he could neither move himself nor his army. You have seen the rabbit when the snake approaches. So stood the English upon the ridge of Waterloo. The night before, the Emperor, who had lost an aide-de-camp at Ligny, ordered me to join his staff, and I had left my Hussars to the charge of Major Victor. I know not which of us was the most grieved, they or I, that I should be called away upon the eve of battle; but an order is an order, and a good soldier can but shrug his shoulders and obey. With the Emperor I rode across the front of the enemy's position on the morning of the 18th, he looking at them through his glasses and planning which was the shortest way to destroy them. Soult was at his elbow, and Ney and Foy and others who had fought the English in Portugal and Spain. "Have a care, Sire," said Soult, "the English infantry is very solid."

"You think them good soldiers because they have beaten you," said the Emperor, and we younger men turned away our faces and smiled. But Ney and Foy were grave and serious. All the time the English line, checquered with red and blue and dotted with batteries, was drawn up silent and watchful within a long musket-shot of us. On the other side of the shallow valley our own people, having finished their soup, were assembling for the battle. It had rained very heavily;

but at this moment the sun shone out and beat upon the French army, turning our brigades of cavalry into so many dazzling rivers of steel, and twinkling and sparkling on the innumerable bayonets of the infantry. At the sight of that splendid army, and the beauty and majesty of its appearance, I could contain myself no longer; but, rising in my stirrups, I waved my busby and cried, *"Vive l'Empereur!"* a shout which growled and roared and clattered from one end of the line to the other, while the horsemen waved their swords and the footmen held up their shakos upon their bayonets. The English remained petrified upon their ridge. They knew that their hour had come.

And so it would have come if at that moment the word had been given and the whole army had been permitted to advance. We had but to fall upon them to sweep them from the face of the earth. To put aside all question of courage, we were the more numerous, the older soldiers, and the better led. But the Emperor desired to do all things in order, and he waited until the ground should be drier and harder, so that his artillery could manœuvre. So three hours were wasted, and it was eleven o'clock before we saw Jerome Buonaparte's columns advance upon our left and heard the crash of the guns which told that the battle had begun. The loss of those three hours was our destruction. The attack upon the left was directed upon a farmhouse which was held by the English Guards, and we heard the three loud shouts of apprehension which the defenders were compelled to utter. They were still holding out, and D'Erlon's corps was advancing upon the right to engage another portion of the English line, when our attention was called away from the battle beneath our noses to a distant portion of the field of action.

The Emperor had been looking through his glass to the extreme left of the English line, and now he turned suddenly to the Duke of Dalmatia, or Soult, as we soldiers preferred to call him.

"What is it, Marshal?" said he.

We all followed the direction of his gaze, some raising our glasses, some shading our eyes. There was a thick wood over yonder, then a long, bare slope, and another wood beyond. Over this bare strip between the two woods there lay something dark, like the shadow of a moving cloud.

"I think they are cattle, Sire," said Soult.

At that instant there came a quick twinkle from amid the dark shadow.

"It is Grouchy," said the Emperor, and he lowered his glass. "They are doubly lost, these English. I hold them in the hollow of my hand. They cannot escape me."

He look round, and his eyes fell upon me.

"Ah! here is the prince of messengers," said he. "Are you well mounted, Colonel Gerard?"

I was riding my little Violette, the pride of the brigade. I said so.

"Then ride hard to Marshal Grouchy, whose troops you see over yonder. Tell him that he is to fall upon the left flank and rear of the English while I attack them in front. Together we shall crush them and not a man escape."

I saluted and rode off without a word, my heart dancing with joy that such a mission should be mine. I looked at that long, solid line of red and blue looming through the smoke of the guns, and I shook my fist at it as I went. "We shall crush them and not a man escape." They were the Emperor's words, and it was I, Etienne Gerard, who was to turn them into deeds. I burned to reach the Marshal, and for an instant I thought of riding through the English left wing, as being the shortest cut. I have done bolder deeds and come out safely, but I reflected that if things went badly with me and I was taken or shot the message would be lost and the plans of the Emperor miscarry. I passed in front of the cavalry therefore, past the Chasseurs, the Lancers of the Guard, the Carabineers, the Horse Grenadiers, and, lastly, my own little rascals, who followed me wistfully with their eyes. Beyond the cavalry the Old Guard was standing, twelve regiments of them, all veterans of many battles, sombre and severe, in long blue overcoats, and high bearskins from which the plumes had been removed. Each bore within the goatskin knapsack upon his back the blue and white parade uniform which they would use for their entry into Brussels next day. As I rode past them I reflected that these men had never been beaten, and, as I looked at their weather-beaten faces and their stern and silent bearing, I said to myself that they never would be beaten. Great heavens, how little could I foresee what a few more hours would bring!

On the right of the Old Guard were the Young Guard and the Sixth Corps of Lobau, and then I passed Jacquinot's Lancers and Marbot's Hussars, who held the extreme flank of the line. All these troops knew nothing of the corps which was coming towards them through the wood, and their attention was taken up in watching the battle which raged upon their left. More than a hundred guns were thundering from each side, and the din was so great that of all the battles which I have fought I cannot recall more than half-a-dozen which were as noisy. I looked back over my shoulder, and there were two brigades of Cuirassiers, English and French, pouring down the hill together, with the sword-blades playing over them like summer lightning. How I longed to turn Violette, and to lead my Hussars into the thick of it! What a picture! Etienne Gerard with his back to the battle, and a fine cavalry action raging behind him. But duty is duty, so I rode past Marbot's vedettes and on in the direction of the wood, passing the village of Frishermont upon my left.

In front of me lay the great wood, called the Wood of Paris, consisting mostly of oak trees, with a few narrow paths leading through it. I halted and listened when I reached it; but out of its gloomy depths there came no blare of trumpet, no murmur of wheels, no tramp of horses to mark the advance of that great column which with my own eyes I had seen streaming towards it. The battle roared behind me, but in front all was as silent as that grave in which so many brave men would shortly sleep. The sunlight was cut off by the arches of leaves above my head, and a heavy damp smell rose from the sodden ground. For several miles I galloped at such a pace as few riders would care to go with roots below and branches above. Then, at last, for the first time I caught a glimpse of Grouchy's advance guard. Scattered parties of Hussars passed me on either side, but some distance off, among the trees. I heard the beating of a drum far away, and the low, dull murmur which an army makes upon the march. Any moment I might come upon the staff and deliver my message to Grouchy in person, for I knew well that on such a march a Marshal of France would certainly ride with the van of his army.

Suddenly the trees thinned in front of me, and I understood with delight that I was coming to the end of the wood, whence I could see the army and find the Marshal. Where the track comes out from amid the trees there is a small cabaret, where wood-cutters and waggoners drink their wine. Outside the door of this I reined up my horse for an instant while I took in the scene which was before me. Some few miles away I saw a second great forest, that of St. Lambert, out of which the Emperor had seen the troops advancing. It was easy to see, however, why there had been so long a delay in their leaving one wood and reaching the other, because between the two ran the deep defile of the Lasnes, which had to be crossed. Sure enough, a long column of troops—horse, foot, and guns—was streaming down one side of it and swarming up the other, while the advance guard was already among the trees on either side of me. A battery of Horse Artillery was coming along the road, and I was about to gallop up to it and ask the officer in command if he could tell me where I should find the Marshal, when suddenly I observed that, though the gunners were dressed in blue, they had not the dolman trimmed with red brandenburgs as our own horse-gunners wear it. Amazed at the sight, I was looking at these soldiers to left and right when a hand touched my thigh, and there was the landlord, who had rushed from his inn.

"Madman!" he cried, "why are you here? What are you doing?"

"I am seeking Marshal Grouchy."

"You are in the heart of the Prussian army. Turn and fly!"

"Impossible; this is Grouchy's corps."

"How do you know?"

"Because the Emperor has said it."

"Then the Emperor has made a terrible mistake! I tell you that a patrol of Silesian Hussars has this instant left me. Did you not see them in the woods?"

"I saw Hussars."

"They are the enemy."

"Where is Grouchy?"

"He is behind. They have passed him."

"Then how can I go back? If I go forward I may see him yet. I must obey my orders and find him wherever he is."

The man reflected for an instant.

"Quick! quick!" he cried, seizing my bridle. "Do what I say and you may yet escape. They have not observed you yet. Come with me and I will hide you until they pass."

Behind this house there was a low stable, and into this he thrust Violette. Then he half led and half dragged me into the kitchen of the inn. It was a bare, brick-floored room. A stout, red-faced woman was cooking cutlets at the fire.

"What's the matter now?" she asked, looking with a frown from me to the innkeeper. "Who is this you have brought in?"

"It is a French officer, Marie. We cannot let the Prussians take him."

"Why not?"

"Why not? Sacred name of a dog, was I not myself a soldier of Napoleon? Did I not win a musket of honor among the Vélites of the Guard? Shall I see a comrade taken before my eyes? Marie, we must save him."

But the lady looked at me with most unfriendly eyes.

"Pierre Charras," she said, "you will not rest until you have your house burned over your head. Do you not understand, you blockhead, that if you fought for Napoleon it was because Napoleon ruled Belgium? He does so no longer. The Prussians are our allies and this is our enemy. I will have no Frenchman in this house. Give him up!"

The innkeeper scratched his head and looked at me in despair, but it was very evident to me that it was neither for France nor for Belgium that this woman cared, but that it was the safety of her own house that was nearest her heart.

"Madame," said I, with all the dignity and assurance I could command, "the Emperor is defeating the English and the French army will be here before evening. If you have used me well you will be rewarded, and if you have denounced me you will be punished and your house will certainly be burned by the provost-marshal."

She was shaken by this, and I hastened to complete my victory by other methods.

"Surely," said I, "it is impossible that any one so beautiful can also be hard-hearted? You will not refuse me the refuge which I need."

She looked at my whiskers and I saw that she was softened. I took her hand, and in two minutes we were on such terms that her husband swore roundly that he would give me up himself if I pressed the matter farther.

"Besides, the road is full of Prussians," he cried. "Quick! quick! into the loft!"

"Quick! quick! into the loft!" echoed his wife, and together they hurried me towards a ladder which led to a trap-door in the ceiling. There was a loud knocking at the door, so you can think that it was not long before my spurs went twinkling through the hole and the board was dropped behind me. An instant later I heard the voices of the Germans in the rooms below me.

The place in which I found myself was a single long attic, the ceiling of which was formed by the roof of the house. It ran over the whole of one side of the inn, and through the cracks in the flooring I could look down either upon the kitchen, the sitting-room, or the bar at my pleasure. There were no windows, but the place was in the last stage of disrepair, and several missing slates upon the roof gave me light and the means of observation. The place was heaped with lumber—fodder at one end and a huge pile of empty bottles at the other. There was no door save the hole through which I had come up.

I sat upon the heap of hay for a few minutes to steady myself and to think out my plans. It was very serious that the Prussians should arrive upon the field of battle earlier than our reserves, but there appeared to be only one corps of them, and a corps more or less makes little difference to such a man as the Emperor. He could afford to give the English all this and beat them still. The best way in which I could serve him, since Grouchy was behind, was to wait here until they were past, and then to resume my journey, to see the Marshal, and to give him his orders. If he advanced upon the rear of the English instead of following the Prussians all would be well. The fate of France depended upon my judgment and my nerve. It was not the first time, my friends, as you are well aware, and you know the reasons that I had to trust that neither nerve nor judgment would ever fail me. Certainly, the Emperor had chosen the right man for his mission. "The prince of messengers" he had called me. I would earn my title.

It was clear that I could do nothing until the Prussians had passed, so I spent my time in observing them. I have no love for these people, but I am compelled to say that they kept excellent discipline, for not a man of them entered the inn, though their lips were caked with dust and they were ready to drop with fatigue. Those who had knocked at the door were bearing an insensible comrade, and having left him they returned at once to the ranks. Several others were carried in in the same fashion and laid in the kitchen, while a young surgeon, little more than a boy, remained behind in charge of them. Having observed them through the cracks in the floor, I next turned my attention to the holes in the roof, from which

I had an excellent view of all that was passing outside. The Prussian corps was still streaming past. It was easy to see that they had made a terrible march and had little food, for the faces of the men were ghastly, and they were plastered from head to foot with mud from their falls upon the foul and slippery roads. Yet, spent as they were, their spirit was excellent, and they pushed and hauled at the gun-carriages when the wheels sank up to the axles in the mire, and the weary horses were floundering knee-deep unable to draw them through. The officers rode up and down the column encouraging the more active with words of praise, and the laggards with blows from the flat of their swords. All the time from over the wood in front of them there came the tremendous roar of the battle, as if all the rivers on earth had united in one gigantic cataract, booming and crashing in a mighty fall. Like the spray of the cataract was the long veil of smoke which rose high over the trees. The officers pointed to it with their swords, and with hoarse cries from their parched lips the mud-stained men pushed onwards to the battle. For an hour I watched them pass, and I reflected that their vanguard must have come into touch with Marbot's vedettes and that the Emperor knew already of their coming. "You are going very fast up the road, my friends, but you will come down it a great deal faster," said I to myself, and I consoled myself with the thought.

But an adventure came to break the monotony of this long wait. I was seated beside my loophole and congratulating myself that the corps was nearly past, and that the road would soon be clear for my journey, when suddenly I heard a loud altercation break out in French in the kitchen.

"You shall not go!" cried a woman's voice.

"I tell you that I will!" said a man's, and there was a sound of scuffling.

In an instant I had my eye to the crack in the floor. There was my stout lady, like a faithful watch-dog, at the bottom of the ladder; while the young German surgeon, white with anger, was endeavoring to come up it. Several of the German soldiers who had recovered from their prostration were sitting about on the kitchen floor and watching the quarrel with stolid, but attentive, faces. The landlord was nowhere to be seen.

"There is no liquor there," said the woman.

"I do not want liquor; I want hay or straw for these men to lie upon. Why should they lie on the bricks when there is straw overhead?"

"There is no straw."

"What is up there?"

"Empty bottles."

"Nothing else?"

"No."

For a moment it looked as if the surgeon would abandon his intention, but one of the soldiers pointed up to the ceiling. I gathered from what I could understand of his words that he could see the straw sticking out between the planks. In vain the woman protested. Two of the soldiers were able to get upon their feet and to drag her aside, while the young surgeon ran up the ladder, pushed open the trap-door, and climbed into the loft. As he swung the door back I slipped behind it, but as luck would have it he shut it again behind him, and there we were left standing face to face.

Never have I seen a more astonished young man.

"A French officer!" he gasped.

"Hush!" said I. "Hush! Not a word above a whisper." I had drawn my sword.

"I am not a combatant," he said; "I am a doctor. Why do you threaten me with your sword? I am not armed."

"I do not wish to hurt you, but I must protect myself. I am in hiding here."

"A spy!"

"A spy does not wear such a uniform as this, nor do you find spies on the staff of an army. I rode by mistake into the heart of this Prussian corps, and I concealed myself here in the hope of escaping when they are past. I will not hurt you if you do not hurt me, but if you do not swear that you will be silent as to my presence you will never go down alive from this attic."

"You can put up your sword, sir," said the surgeon, and I saw a friendly twinkle in his eyes. "I am a Pole by birth, and I have no ill-feeling to you or your people. I will do my best for my patients, but I will do no more. Capturing Hussars is not one of the duties of a surgeon. With your permission I will now descend with this truss of hay to make a couch for these poor fellows below."

I had intended to exact an oath from him, but it is my experience that if a man will not speak the truth he will not swear the truth, so I said no more. The surgeon opened the trap-door, threw out enough hay for his purpose, and then descended the ladder, letting down the door behind him. I watched him anxiously when he rejoined his patients, and so did my good friend the landlady, but he said nothing and busied himself with the needs of the soldiers.

By this time I was sure that the last of the army corps was past, and I went to my loop-hole confident that I should find the coast clear, save, perhaps, for a few stragglers, whom I could disregard. The first corps was indeed past, and I could see the last files of the infantry disappearing into the wood; but you can imagine my disappointment when out of the Forest of St. Lambert I saw a second corps emerging, as numerous as the first. There could be no doubt that the whole Prussian army, which we thought we had destroyed at Ligny, was about to throw itself upon our right wing while Marshal Grouchy had been coaxed away upon some fool's errand. The roar of guns, much nearer than before, told me that the Prussian batteries which had passed me were already in action. Imagine my terrible position! Hour after hour was passing; the sun was sinking towards the west. And yet this cursed inn, in which I lay hid, was like a little island amid a rushing stream of furious Prussians. It was all important that I should reach Marshal Grouchy, and yet I could not show my nose without being made prisoner. You can think how I cursed and tore my hair. How little do we know what is in store for us! Even while I raged against my ill-fortune, that same fortune was reserving me for a far higher task than to carry a message to Grouchy—a task which could not have been mine had I not been held tight in that little inn on the edge of the Forest of Paris.

Two Prussian corps had passed and a third was coming up, when I heard a great fuss and the sound of several voices in the sitting-room. By altering my position I was able to look down and see what was going on.

Two Prussian generals were beneath me, their heads bent over a map which lay upon the table. Several aides-de-camp and staff officers stood round in silence. Of the two generals one was a fierce old man, white-haired and wrinkled, with a ragged, grizzled moustache and a voice like the bark of a hound. The other was younger, but long-faced and solemn.

He measured distances upon the map with the air of a student, while his companion stamped and fumed and cursed like a corporal of Hussars. It was strange to see the old man so fiery and the young one so reserved. I could not understand all that they said, but I was very sure about their general meaning.

"I tell you we must push on and ever on!" cried the old fellow, with a furious German oath. "I promised Wellington that I would be there with the whole army even if I had to be strapped to my horse. Bülow's corps is in action, and Zeithen's shall support it with every man and gun. Forwards, Gneisenau, forwards!"

The other shook his head.

"You must remember, your Excellency, that if the English are beaten they will make for the coast. What will your position be then, with Grouchy between you and the Rhine?"

"We shall beat them, Gneisenau; the Duke and I will grind them to powder between us. Push on, I say! The whole war will be ended in one blow. Bring Pirsch up, and we can throw sixty thousand men into the scale while Thielmann holds Grouchy beyond Wavre."

Gneisenau shrugged his shoulders, but at that instant an orderly appeared at the door.

"An aide-de-camp from the Duke of Wellington," said he.

"Ha, ha!" cried the old man; "let us hear what he has to say."

An English officer, with mud and blood all over his scarlet jacket, staggered into the room. A crimson-stained handkerchief was knotted round his arm, and he held the table to keep himself from falling.

"My message is to Marshal Blucher," says he.

"I am Marshal Blucher. Go on! go on!" cried the impatient old man.

"The Duke bade me to tell you, sir, that the British army can hold its own, and that he has no fears for the result. The French cavalry has been destroyed, two of their divisions of infantry have ceased to exist, and only the Guard is in reserve. If you give us a vigorous support the defeat will be changed to absolute rout and——" His knees gave way under him, and he fell in a heap upon the floor.

"Enough! enough!" cried Blucher. "Gneisenau, send an aide-de-camp to Wellington and tell him to rely upon me to the full. Come on, gentlemen, we have our work to do!" He bustled eagerly out of the room, with all his staff clanking behind him, while two orderlies carried the English messenger to the care of the surgeon.

Gneisenau, the Chief of the Staff, had lingered behind for an instant, and he laid his hand upon one of the aides-de-camp. The fellow had attracted my attention, for I have always a quick eye for a fine man. He was tall and slender, the very model of a horseman; indeed, there was something in his appearance which made it not unlike my own. His face was dark and as keen as that of a hawk, with fierce black eyes under thick, shaggy brows, and a mustache which would have put him in the crack squadron of my Hussars. He wore a green coat with white facings, and a horsehair helmet—a Dragoon, as I conjectured, and as dashing a cavalier as one would wish to have at the end of one's sword-point.

"A word with you, Count Stein," said Gneisenau. "If the enemy are routed, but if the Emperor escapes, he will rally another army, and all will have to be done again. But if we can get the Emperor, then the war is indeed ended. It is worth a great effort and a great risk for such an object as that."

The young Dragoon said nothing, but he listened attentively.

"Suppose the Duke of Wellington's words should prove to be correct, and the French army should be driven in utter rout from the field, the Emperor will certainly take the road back through Genappe and Charleroi as being the shortest to the frontier. We can imagine that his horses will be fleet, and that the fugitives will make way for him. Our cavalry will follow the rear of the beaten army, but the Emperor will be far away at the front of the throng."

The young Dragoon inclined his head.

"To you, Count Stein, I commit the Emperor. If you take him your name will live in history. You have the reputation of being the hardest rider in our army. Do you choose such comrades as you may select—ten or a dozen should be enough. You are not to engage in the battle, nor are you to follow the general pursuit, but you are to ride clear of the crowd, reserving your energies for a nobler end. Do you understand me?"

Again the Dragoon inclined his head. This silence impressed me. I felt that he was indeed a dangerous man.

"Then I leave the details in your own hands. Strike at no

one except the highest. You cannot mistake the Imperial carriage, nor can you fail to recognize the figure of the Emperor. Now I must follow the Marshal. Adieu! If ever I see you again I trust that it will be to congratulate you upon a deed which will ring through Europe."

The Dragoon saluted, and Gneisenau hurried from the room. The young officer stood in deep thought for a few moments. Then he followed the Chief of the Staff. I looked with curiosity from my loophole to see what his next proceeding would be. His horse, a fine, strong chestnut with two white stockings, was fastened to the rail of the inn. He sprang into the saddle, and, riding to intercept a column of cavalry which was passing, he spoke to an officer at the head of the leading regiment. Presently, after some talk, I saw two Hussars—it was a Hussar regiment—drop out of the ranks and take up their position beside Count Stein. The next regiment was also stopped, and two Lancers were added to his escort. The next furnished him with two Dragoons, and the next with two Cuirassiers. Then he drew his little group of horsemen aside, and he gathered them round him, explaining to them what they had to do. Finally the nine soldiers rode off together and disappeared into the Wood of Paris.

I need not tell you, my friends, what all this portended. Indeed, he had acted exactly as I should have done in his place. From each colonel he had demanded the two best horsemen in the regiment, and so he had assembled a band who might expect to catch whatever they should follow. Heaven help the Emperor if, without an escort, he should find them on his track!

And I, dear friends—imagine the fever, the ferment, the madness, of my mind! All thought of Grouchy had passed away. No guns were to be heard to the east. He could not be near. If he should come he would not now be in time to alter the event of the day. The sun was already low in the sky and there could not be more than two or three hours of daylight. My mission might be dismissed as useless. But here was another mission, more pressing, more immediate, a mission which meant the safety, and perhaps the life, of the Emperor. At all costs, through every danger, I must get back to his side. But how was I to do it? The whole Prussian army was now between me and the French lines. They blocked every road, but they could not block the path of duty when Etienne

Gerard sees it lie before him. I could not wait longer. I must
be gone.

There was but the one opening to the loft, and so it was
only down the ladder that I could descend. I looked into the
kitchen, and I found that the young surgeon was still there.
In a chair sat the wounded English aide-de-camp, and on the
straw lay two Prussian soldiers in the last stage of exhaustion.
The others had all recovered and been sent on. These were
my enemies, and I must pass through them in order to gain my
horse. From the surgeon I had nothing to fear; the Englishman
was wounded, and his sword stood with his cloak in a corner;
the two Germans were half insensible, and their muskets were
not beside them. What could be simpler? I opened the trap-
door, slipped down the ladder, and appeared in the midst of
them, my sword drawn in my hand.

What a picture of surprise! The surgeon, of course, knew
all, but to the Englishman and the two Germans it must have
seemed that the god of war in person had descended from the
skies. With my appearance, with my figure, with my silver
and grey uniform, and with that gleaming sword in my hand,
I must indeed have been a sight worth seeing. The two Germans lay petrified, with staring eyes. The English officer half
rose, but sat down again from weakness, his mouth open and
his hand on the back of his chair.

"What the deuce!" he kept on repeating, "what the deuce!"

"Pray do not move," said I; "I will hurt no one, but woe
to the man who lays hands upon me to stop me. You have
nothing to fear if you leave me alone, and nothing to hope if
you try to hinder me. I am Colonel Etienne Gerard, of the
Hussars of Conflans."

"The deuce!" said the Englishman. "You are the man that
killed the fox." A terrible scowl had darkened his face. The
jealousy of sportsmen is a base passion. He hated me, this
Englishman, because I had been before him in transfixing the
animal. How different are our natures! Had I seen him do
such a deed I would have embraced him with cries of joy. But
there was no time for argument.

"I regret it, sir," said I; "but you have a cloak here and
I must take it."

He tried to rise from his chair and reach his sword, but I
got between him and the corner where it lay.

"If there is anything in the pockets——"

"A case," said he.

"I would not rob you," said I; and raising the coat I took from the pockets a silver flask, a square wooden case, and a field-glass. All these I handed to him. The wretch opened the case, took out a pistol, and pointed it straight at my head.

"Now, my fine fellow," said he, "put down your sword and give yourself up."

I was so astonished at this infamous action that I stood petrified before him. I tried to speak to him of honor and gratitude, but I saw his eyes fix and harden over the pistol.

"Enough talk!" said he. "Drop it!"

Could I endure such a humiliation? Death were better than to be disarmed in such a fashion. The word "Fire!" was on my lips when in an instant the Englishman vanished from before my face, and in his place was a great pile of hay, with a red-coated arm and two Hessian boots waving and kicking in the heart of it. Oh, the gallant landlady! It was my whiskers that had saved me.

"Fly, soldier, fly!" she cried, and she heaped fresh trusses of hay from the floor on to the struggling Englishman. In an instant I was out in the courtyard, had led Violette from her stable, and was on her back. A pistol bullet whizzed past my shoulder from the window, and I saw a furious face looking out at me. I smiled my contempt and spurred out into the road. The last of the Prussians had passed, and both my road and my duty lay clear before me. If France won, all was well. If France lost, then on me and on my little mare depended that which was more than victory or defeat—the safety and the life of the Emperor. "On, Etienne, on!" I cried. "Of all your noble exploits, the greatest, even if it be the last, lies now before you!"

II—THE STORY OF THE NINE PRUSSIAN HORSEMEN

I told you when last we met, my friends, of the important mission from the Emperor to Marshal Grouchy, which failed through no fault of my own, and I described to you how during a long afternoon I was shut up in the attic of a country inn, and was prevented from coming out because the Prussians were all around me. You will remember also how I overheard the Chief of the Prussian Staff give his

instructions to Count Stein, and so learned the dangerous
plan which was on foot to kill or capture the Emperor in
the event of a French defeat. At first I could not have believed
in such a thing, but since the guns had thundered all day, and
since the sound had made no advance in my direction, it was
evident that the English had at least held their own and beaten
off all our attacks.

I have said that it was a fight that day between the soul of
France and the beef of England, but it must be confessed that
we found the beef was very tough. It was clear that if the
Emperor could not defeat the English when alone, then it
might, indeed, go hard with him now that sixty thousand of
these cursed Prussians were swarming on his flank. In any case,
with this secret in my possession, my place was by his side.

I had made my way out of the inn in the dashing manner
which I have described to you when last we met, and I left
the English aide-de-camp shaking his foolish fist out of the
window. I could not but laugh as I looked back at him, for his
angry red face was framed and frilled with hay. Once out on
the road I stood erect in my stirrups, and I put on the handsome black riding-coat, lined with red, which had belonged
to him. It fell to the top of my high boots, and covered my
tell-tale uniform completely. As to my busby, there are many
such in the German service, and there was no reason why it
should attract attention. So long as no one spoke to me there
was no reason why I should not ride through the whole of the
Prussian army; but though I understood German, for I had
many friends among the German ladies during the pleasant
years that I fought all over that country, still I spoke it with
a pretty Parisian accent which could not be confounded with
their rough, unmusical speech. I knew that this quality of my
accent would attract attention, but I could only hope and
pray that I would be permitted to go my way in silence.

The Forest of Paris was so large that it was useless to think
of going round it, and so I took my courage in both hands
and galloped on down the road in the track of the Prussian
army. It was not hard to trace it, for it was rutted two feet
deep by the gunwheels and the caissons. Soon I found a fringe
of wounded men, Prussians and French, on each side of it,
where Bülow's advance had come into touch with Marbot's
Hussars. One old man with a long white beard, a surgeon, I
suppose, shouted at me, and ran after me still shouting, but
I never turned my head and took no notice of him save to

spur on faster. I heard his shouts long after I had lost sight of him among the trees.

Presently I came up with the Prussian reserves. The infantry were leaning on their muskets or lying exhausted on the wet ground, and the officers stood in groups listening to the mighty roar of the battle and discussing the reports which came from the front. I hurried past at the top of my speed, but one of them rushed out and stood in my path with his hand up as a signal to me to stop. Five thousand Prussian eyes were turned upon me. There was a moment! You turn pale, my friends, at the thought of it. Think how every hair upon me stood on end. But never for one instant did my wits or my courage desert me. "General Blucher!" I cried. Was it not my guardian angel who whispered the words in my ear? The Prussian sprang from my path, saluted and pointed forwards. They are well disciplined, these Prussians, and who was he that he should dare to stop the officer who bore a message to the general? It was a talisman that would pass me out of every danger, and my heart sang within me at the thought. So elated was I that I no longer waited to be asked, but as I rode through the army I shouted to right and left, "General Blucher! General Blucher!" and every man pointed me onwards and cleared a path to let me pass. There are times when the most supreme impudence is the highest wisdom. But discretion must also be used, and I must admit that I became indiscreet. For as I rode upon my way, ever nearer to the fighting line, a Prussian officer of Uhlans gripped my bridle and pointed to a group of men who stood near a burning farm. "There is Marshal Blucher. Deliver your message!" said he, and sure enough my terrible old gray-whiskered veteran was there within a pistol shot, his eyes turned in my direction.

But the good guardian angel did not desert me. Quick as a flash there came into my memory the name of the general who commanded the advance of the Prussians. "General Bülow!" I cried. The Uhlan let go my bridle. "General Bülow! General Bülow!" I shouted as every stride of the dear little mare took me nearer my own people. Through the burning village of Plancenoit I galloped, spurred my way between two columns of Prussian infantry, sprang over a hedge, cut down a Silesian Hussar who flung himself before me, and an instant afterwards, with my coat flying open to show the uniform below, I passed through the open files of the tenth of

the line and was back in the heart of Lobau's corps once more.
Outnumbered and outflanked, they were being slowly driven
in by the pressure of the Prussian advance. I galloped onwards, anxious only to find myself by the Emperor's side.

But a sight lay before me which held me fast as though I
had been turned into some noble equestrian statue. I could not
move, I could scarce breathe, as I gazed upon it. There was a
mound over which my path lay, and as I came out on the top
of it I looked down the long shallow valley of Waterloo. I
had left it with two great armies on either side and a clear
field between them. Now there were but long, ragged fringes
of broken and exhausted regiments upon the two ridges, but
a real army of dead and wounded lay between. For two miles
in length and half a mile across the ground was strewed and
heaped with them. But slaughter was no new sight to me, and
it was not that which held me spell-bound. It was that up the
long slope of the British position was moving a walking forest
—black, tossing, waving, unbroken. Did I not know the bearskins of the Guard? And did I not also know, did not my soldier's instinct tell me, that it was the last reserve of France;
that the Emperor, like a desperate gamester, was staking all
upon his last card? Up they went and up—grand, solid, un-
breakable, scourged with musketry, riddled with grape, flowing onwards in a black, heavy tide, which lapped over the
British batteries. With my glass I could see the English gunners throw themselves under their pieces or run to the rear.
On rolled the crest of the bearskins, and then, with a crash
which was swept across to my ears, they met the British infantry. A minute passed, and another, and another. My heart
was in my mouth. They swayed back and forwards; they no
longer advanced; they were held. Great Heaven! was it possible that they were breaking? One black dot ran down the
hill, then two, then four, then ten, then a great, scattered,
struggling mass, halting, breaking, halting, and at last shred-
ding out and rushing madly downwards. "The Guard is
beaten! The Guard is beaten!" From all around me I heard
the cry. Along the whole line the infantry turned their faces
and the gunners flinched from their guns.

"The Old Guard is beaten! The Guard retreats!" An officer
with a livid face passed me yelling out these words of woe.
"Save yourselves! Save yourselves! You are betrayed!" cried
another. "Save yourselves! Save yourselves!" Men were rush-

ing madly to the rear, blundering and jumping like frightened
sheep. Cries and screams rose from all around me. And at that
moment, as I looked at the British position, I saw what I can
never forget. A single horseman stood out black and clear upon
the ridge against the last red angry glow of the setting sun.
So dark, so motionless against that grim light, he might have
been the very spirit of Battle brooding over that terrible
valley. As I gazed he raised his hat high in the air, and at the
signal, with a low, deep roar like a breaking wave, the whole
British army flooded over their ridge and came rolling down
into the valley. Long steel-fringed lines of red and blue, sweeping waves of cavalry, horse batteries rattling and bounding—
down they came on to our crumbling ranks. It was over. A
yell of agony, the agony of brave men who see no hope, rose
from one flank to the other, and in an instant the whole of that
noble army was swept in a wild, terror-stricken crowd from
the field. Even now, dear friends, I cannot, as you see, speak
of that dreadful moment with a dry eye or with a steady
voice.

At first I was carried away in that wild rush, whirled off
like a straw in a flooded gutter. But, suddenly, what should
I see amongst the mixed regiments in front of me but a group
of stern horsemen, in silver and grey, with a broken and tattered standard held aloft in the heart of them! Not all the
might of England and of Prussia could break the Hussars of
Conflans. But when I joined them it made my heart bleed to
see them. The major, seven captains, and five hundred men
were left upon the field. Young Captain Sabbatier was in command, and when I asked him where were the five missing
squadrons he pointed back and answered: "You will find them
round one of those British squares." Men and horses were at
their last gasp, caked with sweat and dirt, their black tongues
hanging out from their lips; but it made me thrill with pride
to see how that shattered remnant still rode knee to knee, with
every man, from the boy trumpeter to the farrier-sergeant, in
his own proper place. Would that I could have brought them
on with me as an escort for the Emperor! In the heart of
the Hussars of Conflans he would be safe indeed. But the
horses were too spent to trot. I left them behind me with
orders to rally upon the farmhouse of St. Aunay, where we
had camped two nights before. For my own part I forced my
horse through the throng in search of the Emperor.

There were things which I saw then, as I pressed through that dreadful crowd, which can never be banished from my mind. In evil dreams there comes back to me the memory of that flowing stream of livid, staring, screaming faces upon which I looked down. It was a nightmare. In victory one does not understand the horror of war. It is only in the cold chill of defeat that it is brought home to you. I remember an old Grenadier of the Guard lying at the side of the road, with his broken leg doubled at a right angle. "Comrades, comrades, keep off my leg!" he cried, but they tripped and stumbled over him all the same. In front of me rode a Lancer officer without his coat. His arm had just been taken off in the ambulance. The bandages had fallen. It was horrible. Two gunners tried to drive through with their gun. A Chasseur raised his musket and shot one of them through the head. I saw a major of Cuirassiers draw his two holster pistols and shoot first his horse and then himself. Beside the road a man in a blue coat was raging and raving like a madman. His face was black with powder, his clothes were torn, one epaulette was gone, the other hung dangling over his breast. Only when I came close to him did I recognize that it was Marshal Ney. He howled at the flying troops and his voice was hardly human. Then he raised the stump of his sword—it was broken three inches from the hilt. "Come and see how a Marshal of France can die!" he cried. Gladly would I have gone with him, but my duty lay elsewhere. He did not, as you know, find the death he sought, but he met it a few weeks later in cold blood at the hands of his enemies.

There is an old proverb that in attack the French are more than men, in defeat they are less than women. I knew that it was true that day. But even in that rout I saw things which I can tell with pride. Through the fields which skirt the road moved Cambronne's three reserve battalions of the Guard, the cream of our army. They walked slowly in square, their colors waving over the sombre line of the bearskins. All around them raged the English cavalry and the black Lancers of Brunswick, wave after wave thundering up, breaking with a crash, and recoiling in ruin. When last I saw them the English guns, six at a time, were smashing grape-shot through their ranks, and the English infantry were closing in upon three sides and pouring volleys into them; but still, like a noble lion with fierce hounds clinging to its flanks, the glorious remnant of the Guard, marching slowly, halting, closing up, dressing, moved majestically from their last battle. Behind them the Guards' battery of twelve-pounders was drawn up upon the ridge. Every gunner was in his place, but no gun fired. "Why do you not fire?" I asked the colonel as I passed. "Our powder is finished." "Then why not retire?" "Our appearance may hold them back for a little. We must give the Emperor time to escape." Such were the soldiers of France.

Behind this screen of brave men the others took their breath, and then went on in less desperate fashion. They had broken away from the road, and all over the countryside in the twilight I could see the timid, scattered, frightened crowd who ten hours before had formed the finest army that ever went down to battle. I, with my splendid mare, was soon able to get clear of the throng, and just after I passed Genappe I overtook the Emperor with the remains of his Staff. Soult was with him still, and so were Drouot, Lobau, and Bertrand, with five Chasseurs of the Guard, their horses hardly able to move. The night was falling, and the Emperor's haggard face gleamed white through the gloom as he turned it towards me.

"Who is that?" he asked.

"It is Colonel Gerard," said Soult.

"Have you seen Marshal Grouchy?"

"No, Sire. The Prussians were between."

"It does not matter. Nothing matters now. Soult, I will go back."

He tried to turn his horse, but Bertrand seized his bridle. "Ah, Sire," said Soult, "the enemy has had good fortune enough already." They forced him on among them. He rode in silence with his chin upon his breast, the greatest and the saddest of men. Far away behind us those remorseless guns were still roaring. Sometimes out of the darkness would come shrieks and screams and the low thunder of galloping hoofs. At the sound we would spur our horses and hasten onwards through the scattered troops. At last, after riding all night in the clear moonlight, we found that we had left both pursued and pursuers behind. By the time we passed over the bridge at Charleroi the dawn was breaking. What a company of spectres we looked in that cold, clear, searching light, the Emperor with his face of wax, Soult blotched with powder, Lobau dabbled with blood! But we rode more easily now and had ceased to glance over our shoulders, for Waterloo was more than thirty miles behind us. One of the Emperor's carriages had been picked up at Charleroi, and we halted now on the other side of the Sambre, and dismounted from our horses.

You will ask me why it was that during all this time I had said nothing of that which was nearest my heart, the need for guarding the Emperor. As a fact, I had tried to speak of it both to Soult and to Lobau, but their minds were so over-whelmed with the disaster and so distracted by the pressing needs of the moment that it was impossible to make them understand how urgent was my message. Besides, during this long flight we had always had numbers of French fugitives beside us on the road, and, however demoralized they might be, we had nothing to fear from the attack of nine men. But now, as we stood round the Emperor's carriage in the early morning, I observed with anxiety that not a single French soldier was to be seen upon the long, white road behind us. We had outstripped the army. I looked round to see what means of defence were left to us. The horses of the Chasseurs of the Guard had broken down, and only one of them, a grey-whiskered sergeant, remained. There were Soult, Lobau, and Bertrand; but, for all their talents, I had rather, when it came to hard knocks, have a single quartermaster-sergeant of Hussars at my side than the three of them put together. There remained the Emperor himself, the coachman, and a valet of the household who had joined us at Charleroi—eight all told; but of the eight only two, the Chasseur and I, were fighting soldiers who could be depended upon at a pinch. A chill came over me as I reflected how utterly helpless we were. At that moment I raised my eyes, and there were the nine Prussian horsemen coming over the hill.

On either side of the road at this point are long stretches of rolling plain, part of it yellow with corn and part of it rich grass land watered by the Sambre. To the south of us was a low ridge, over which was the road to France. Along this road the little group of cavalry was riding. So well had Count Stein obeyed his instructions that he had struck far to the south of us in his determination to get ahead of the Emperor. Now he was riding from the direction in which we were going—the last in which we could expect an enemy. When I caught that first glimpse of them they were still half a mile away.

"Sire!" I cried, "the Prussians!"

They all started and stared. It was the Emperor who broke the silence.

"Who says they are Prussians?"

"I do, Sire—I, Etienne Gerard!"

Unpleasant news always made the Emperor furious against the man who broke it. He railed at me now in the rasping, croaking, Corsican voice which only made itself heard when he had lost his self-control.

"You were always a buffoon," he cried. "What do you mean, you numskull, by saying that they are Prussians? How could Prussians be coming from the direction of France? You have lost any wits that you ever possessed."

His words cut me like a whip, and yet we all felt towards the Emperor as an old dog does to its master. His kick is soon forgotten and forgiven. I would not argue or justify myself. At the first glance I had seen the two white stockings on the forelegs of the leading horse, and I knew well that Count Stein was on its back. For an instant the nine horsemen had halted and surveyed us. Now they put spurs to their horses, and with a yell of triumph they galloped down the road. They had recognized that their prey was in their power.

At that swift advance all doubt had vanished. "By heavens, Sire, it is indeed the Prussians!" cried Soult. Lobau and Bertrand ran about the road like two frightened hens. The sergeant of Chasseurs drew his sabre with a volley of curses. The coachman and the valet cried and wrung their hands. Napoleon stood with a frozen face, one foot on the step of the carriage. And I—ah, my friends, I was magnificent! What words can I use to do justice to my own bearing at that supreme instant of my life! So coldly alert, so deadly cool, so clear in brain and ready in hand. He had called me a numskull and a buffoon. How quick and how noble was my revenge! When his own wits failed him, it was Etienne Gerard who supplied the want.

To fight was absurd; to fly was ridiculous. The Emperor was stout, and weary to death. At the best he was never a good rider. How could he fly from these, the picked men of an army? The best horseman in Prussia was among them. But I was the best horseman in France. I, and only I, could hold my own with them. If they were on *my* track instead of the Emperor's, all might still be well. These were the thoughts which flashed so swiftly through my mind that in an instant I had sprung from the first idea to the final conclusion. Another instant carried me from the final conclusion to prompt and vigorous action. I rushed to the side of the Emperor, who stood petrified, with the carriage between him and our enemies. "Your coat, Sire! your hat!" I cried. I dragged them off him. Never had he been so hustled in his life. In an instant I had them on and had thrust him into the carriage. The next I had sprung on to his famous white Arab and had ridden clear of the group upon the road.

You have already divined my plan; but you may well ask how could I hope to pass myself off as the Emperor. My figure is as you still see it, and his was never beautiful, for he was both short and stout. But a man's height is not remarked when he is in the saddle, and for the rest one had but to sit forward on the horse and round one's back and carry oneself like a sack of flour. I wore the little cocked hat and the loose grey coat with the silver star which was known to every child from one end of Europe to the other. Beneath me was the Emperor's own white charger. It was complete.

Already as I rode clear the Prussians were within two hundred yards of us. I made a gesture of terror and despair with my hands, and I sprang my horse over the bank which lined the road. It was enough. A yell of exultation and of furious hatred broke from the Prussians. It was the howl of starving wolves who scent their prey. I spurred my horse over the meadow-land and looked back under my arm as I rode. Oh, the glorious moment when one after the other I saw eight horsemen come over the bank at my heels! Only one had stayed behind, and I heard shouting and the sounds of a struggle. I remembered my old sergeant of Chasseurs, and I was sure that 'number nine would trouble us no more. The road was clear, and the Emperor free to continue his journey.

But now I had to think of myself. If I were overtaken the Prussians· would certainly make short work of me in their disappointment. If it were so—if I lost my life—I should still have sold it at a glorious price. But I had hopes that I might shake them off. With ordinary horsemen upon ordinary horses I should still have had no difficulty in doing so, but here both steeds and riders were of the best. It was a grand creature that I rode, but it was weary with its long night's work, and the Emperor was one of those riders who do not know how to manage a horse. He had little thought for them, and a heavy hand upon their mouths. On the other hand Stein and his men had come both far and fast. The race was a fair one.

So quick had been my impulse, and so rapidly had I acted upon it, that I had not thought enough of my own safety. Had I done so in the first instance I should, of course, have ridden straight back the way we had come, for so I should have met our own people. But I was off the road and had galloped a mile over the plain before this occurred to me. Then when I looked back I saw that the Prussians had spread out into a long line, so as to head me off from the Charleroi road. I could not turn back, but at least I could edge towards the north. I knew that the whole face of the country was covered with our flying troops, and that sooner or later I must come upon some of them.

But one thing I had forgotten—the Sambre. In my excitement I never gave it a thought until I saw it, deep and broad, gleaming in the morning sunlight. It barred my path, and the Prussians howled behind me. I galloped to the brink, but the horse refused the plunge. I spurred him, but the bank was high and the stream deep. He shrank back trembling and snorting. The yells of triumph were louder every instant. I turned and rode for my life down the river bank. It formed a loop at this part, and I must get across somehow, for my retreat was blocked. Suddenly a thrill of hope ran through me, for I saw a house on my side of the stream and another on the farther bank. Where there are two such houses it usually means that there is a ford between them. A sloping path led to the brink, and I urged my horse down it. On he went, the water up to the saddle, the foam flying right and left. He blundered once and I thought we were lost, but he recovered and an instant later was clattering up the farther slope. As we came out I heard the splash behind me as the first Prussian took the water. There was just the breadth of the Sambre between us.

I rode with my head sunk between my shoulders in Napoleon's fashion, and I did not dare to look back for fear they should see my moustache. I had turned up the collar of the grey coat so as partly to hide it. Even now if they found out their mistake they might turn and overtake the carriage. But when once we were on the road I could tell by the drumming of their hoofs how far distant they were, and it seemed to me that the sound grew perceptibly louder, as if they were slowly gaining upon me. We were riding now up the stony and rutted lane which led from the ford. I peeped back very cautiously from under my arm and I perceived that my danger came from a single rider, who was far ahead of his comrades. He was a Hussar, a very tiny fellow, upon a big black horse, and it was his light weight which had brought him into the foremost place. It is a place of honor; but it is also a place of danger, as he was soon to learn. I felt the holsters, but, to my horror, there were no pistols. There was a field-glass in one and the other was stuffed with papers. My sword had been left behind with Violette. Had I only my own weapons and my own little mare I could have played with these rascals. But I was not entirely unarmed. The Emperor's own sword hung to the saddle. It was curved and short, the hilt all crusted with gold—a thing more fitted to glitter at a review than to serve a soldier in his deadly need. I drew it, such as it was, and I waited my chance. Every instant the clink and clatter of the hoofs grew nearer. I heard the panting of the horse, and the fellow shouted some threat at me. There was a turn in the lane, and as I rounded it I drew up my white Arab on his haunches. As we spun round I met the Prussian Hussar face to face. He was going too fast to stop, and his only chance was to ride me down. Had he done so he might have met his own death, but he would have injured me or my horse past all hope of escape. But the fool flinched as he saw me waiting, and flew past me on my right. I lunged over my Arab's neck and buried my toy sword in his side. It must have been the finest steel and as sharp as a razor, for I hardly felt it enter, and yet his blood was within three inches of the hilt. His horse galloped on and he kept his saddle for a hundred yards before he sank down with his face on the mane, and then dived over the side of the neck on to the road. For my own part, I was already at his horse's heels. A few seconds had sufficed for all that I have told.

I heard the cry of rage and vengeance which rose from the Prussians as they passed their dead comrade, and I could not but smile as I wondered what they could think of the Emperor as a horseman and a swordsman. I glanced back cautiously as before, and I saw that none of the seven men stopped. The fate of their comrade was nothing compared to the carrying out of their mission. They were as untiring and as remorseless as blood hounds. But I had a good lead, and the

brave Arab was still going well. I thought that I was safe. And yet it was at that very instant that the most terrible danger befell me. The lane divided, and I took the smaller of the two divisions because it was the more grassy and the easier for the horse's hoofs. Imagine my horror when, riding through a gate, I found myself in a square of stables and farm-buildings, with no way out save that by which I had come! Ah, my friends, if my hair is snowy white, have I not had enough to make it so?

To retreat was impossible. I could hear the thunder of the Prussians' hoofs in the lane. I looked round me, and Nature has blessed me with that quick eye which is the first of gifts to any soldier, but most of all to a leader of cavalry. Between a long, low line of stables and the farmhouse there was a pig-sty. Its front was made of bars of wood four feet high; the back was of stone, higher than the front. What was beyond I could not tell. The space between the front and the back was not more than a few yards. It was a desperate venture, and yet I must take it. Every instant the beating of those hurrying hoofs was louder and louder. I put my Arab at the pig-sty. He cleared the front beautifully, and came down with his forefeet upon the sleeping pig within, slipping forward upon his knees. I was thrown over the wall beyond, and fell upon my hands and face in a soft flower-bed. My horse was upon one side of the wall, I upon the other, and the Prussians were pouring into the yard. But I was up in an instant, and had seized the bridle of the plunging horse over the top of the wall. It was built of loose stones, and I dragged down a few of them to make a gap. As I tugged at the bridle and shouted the gallant creature rose to the leap, and an instant afterwards he was by my side and I with my foot on the stirrup.

An heroic idea had entered my mind as I mounted into the saddle. These Prussians, if they came over the pig-sty, could only come one at once, and their attack would not be formidable when they had not had time to recover from such a leap. Why should I not wait and kill them one by one as they came over? It was a glorious thought. They would learn that Etienne Gerard was not a safe man to hunt. My hand felt for my sword, but you can imagine my feelings, my friends, when I came upon an empty scabbard. It had been shaken out when the horse had tripped over that infernal pig. On what absurd trifles do our destinies hang—a pig on one side, Etienne Gerard on the other! Could I spring over the wall and get the sword? Impossible! The Prussians were already in the yard. I turned my Arab and resumed my flight.

But for a moment it seemed to me that I was in a far worse trap than before. I found myself in the garden of the farmhouse, an orchard in the center and flower-beds all round. A high wall surrounded the whole place. I reflected, however, that there must be some point of entrance, since every visitor could not be expected to spring over the pig-sty. I rode round the wall. As I expected, I came upon a door with a key upon the inner side. I dismounted, unlocked it, opened it, and there was a Prussian Lancer sitting his horse within six feet of me.

For a moment we each stared at the other. Then I shut the door and locked it again. A crash and a cry came from the other end of the garden. I understood that one of my enemies had come to grief in trying to get over the pig-sty. How could I ever get out of this cul-de-sac? It was evident that some of the party had galloped round, while some had followed straight upon my tracks. Had I my sword I might have beaten off the Lancer at the door, but to come out now was to be butchered. And yet if I waited some of them would certainly follow me on foot over the pig-sty, and what could I do then? I must act at once or I was lost. But it is at such moments that my wits are most active and my actions most prompt. Still leading my horse, I ran for a hundred yards by the side of the wall away from the spot where the Lancer was watching. There I stopped, and with an effort I tumbled down several of the loose stones from the top of the wall. The instant I had done so I hurried back to the door. As I expected, he thought I was making a gap for my escape at that point, and I heard the thud of his horse's hoofs as he galloped to cut me off. As I reached the gate I looked back, and I saw a green-coated horseman, whom I knew to be Count Stein, clear the pig-sty and gallop furiously with a shout of triumph across the garden. "Surrender, your Majesty, surrender!" he yelled; "we will give you quarter!" I slipped through the gate, but had no time to lock it on the other side. Stein was at my very heels, and the Lancer had already turned his horse. Springing upon my Arab's back, I was off once more with a clear stretch of grass land before me. Stein had to dismount to open the gate, to lead his horse through, and to mount again before he could follow. It was he that I feared rather than the Lancer, whose horse was coarse-bred and weary. I galloped hard for a mile before I ventured to look back, and then Stein was a musket-shot from me, and the Lancer as much again, while only three of the others were in sight. My nine Prussians were coming down to more manageable numbers, and yet one was too much for an unarmed man.

It had surprised me that during this long chase I had seen no fugitives from the army, but I reflected that I was considerably to the west of their line of flight, and that I must edge more towards the east if I wished to join them. Unless I did so it was probable that my pursuers, even if they could not overtake me themselves, would keep me in view until I was headed off by some of their comrades coming from the north. As I looked to the eastward I saw afar off a line of dust which stretched for miles across the country. This was certainly the main road along which our unhappy army was flying. But I soon had proof that some of our stragglers had wandered into these side tracks, for I came suddenly upon a horse grazing at the corner of a field, and beside him, with his back against the bank, his master, a French Cuirassier, terribly wounded and evidently at the point of death. I sprang down, seized his long, heavy sword, and rode on with it. Never shall I forget the poor man's face as he looked at me with his failing sight. He was an old, grey-moustached soldier, one of the real fanatics, and to him this last vision of his Emperor was like a revelation from on high. Astonishment, love, pride—all shone in his pallid face. He said something—I fear they were his last words—but I had no time to listen, and I galloped on my way.

All this time I had been on the meadow-land, which was intersected in this part by broad ditches. Some of them could not have been less than from fourteen to fifteen feet, and my heart was in my mouth as I went at each of them, for a slip would have been my ruin. But whoever selected the Emperor's horses had done his work well. The creature, save when it balked on the bank of the Sambre, never failed me for an instant. We cleared everything in one stride. And yet we could not shake off those infernal Prussians. As I left each watercourse behind me I looked back with renewed hope, but it was only to see Stein on his white-legged chestnut flying over it as lightly as I had done myself. He was my enemy, but I honored him for the way in which he carried himself that day.

Again and again I measured the distance which separated him from the next horseman. I had the idea that I might turn and cut him down, as I had the Hussar, before his comrade could come to his help. But the others had closed up and were not far behind. I reflected that this Stein was probably as fine a swordsman as he was a rider, and that it might take me some little time to get the better of him. In that case the others would come to his aid and I should be lost. On the whole, it was wiser to continue my flight.

A road with poplars on either side ran across the plain from east to west. It would lead me towards the long line of dust which marked the French retreat. I wheeled my horse, therefore, and galloped down it. As I rode I saw a single house in front of me upon the right, with a great bush hung over the door to mark it as an inn. Outside there were several peasants, but for them I cared nothing. What frightened me was to see the gleam of a red coat, which showed that there were British in the place. However, I could not turn and I could not stop, so there was nothing for it but to gallop on and to take my chance. There were no troops in sight, so these men must be stragglers or marauders, from whom I had little to fear. As I approached I saw that there were two of them sitting drinking on a bench outside the inn door. I saw them stagger to their feet, and it was evident that they were both very drunk. One stood swaying in the middle of the road. "It's Boney! So help me, it's Boney!" he yelled. He ran with his hands out to catch me, but luckily for himself his drunken feet stumbled and he fell on his face in the road. The other was more dangerous. He had rushed into the inn, and just as I passed I saw him run out with his musket in his hand. He dropped upon one knee, and I stooped forward over my horse's neck. A single shot from a Prussian or an Austrian is a small matter, but the British were at that time the best shots in Europe, and my drunkard seemed steady enough when he had a gun at his shoulder. I heard the crack, and my horse gave a convulsive spring which would have unseated many a rider. For an instant I thought he was killed, but when I turned in my saddle I saw a stream of blood running down the off hind-quarter. I looked back at the Englishman, and the brute had bitten the end off another cartridge and was ramming it into his musket, but before he had it primed we were beyond his range. These men were foot-soldiers and could not join in the chase, but I heard them whooping and tally-hoing behind me as if I had been a fox. The peasants also shouted and ran through the fields flourishing their sticks. From all sides I heard cries, and everywhere were the rushing, waving figures of my pursuers. To think of the great Emperor being chivied over the countryside in this fashion! It made me long to have these rascals within the sweep of my sword.

But now I felt that I was nearing the end of my course. I had done all that a man could be expected to do—some would say more—but at last I had come to a point from which I could see no escape. The horses of my pursuers were exhausted, but mine was exhausted and wounded also. It was losing blood fast, and we left a red trail upon the white, dusty road. Already his pace was slackening, and sooner or later he must drop under me. I looked back, and there were the five inevitable Prussians—Stein, a hundred yards in front, then a Lancer, and then three others riding together. Stein had drawn his sword, and he waved it at me. For my own part I was determined not to give myself up. I would try how many of these Prussians I could take with me into the other world. At this supreme moment all the great deeds of my life rose in a vision before me, and I felt that this, my last exploit, was indeed a worthy close to such a career. My death would be a fatal blow to those who loved me, to my dear mother, to my Hussars, to others who shall be nameless. But all of them had my honor and my fame at heart, and I felt that their grief would be tinged with pride when they learned how I had ridden and how I had fought upon this last day. Therefore I hardened my heart and, as my Arab limped more and more upon his wounded leg, I drew the great sword which I had taken from the Cuirassier, and I set my teeth for my supreme struggle. My hand was in the very act of tightening the bridle, for I feared that if I delayed longer I might find myself on foot fighting against five mounted men. At that instant my eye fell upon something which brought hope to my heart and a shout of joy to my lips.

From a grove of trees in front of me there projected the steeple of a village church. But there could not be two steeples like that, for the corner of it had crumbled away or been struck by lightning, so that it was of a most fantastic shape. I had seen it only two days before, and it was the church of the village of Gosselies. It was not the hope of reaching the village which set my heart singing with joy, but it was that I knew my ground now, and that farmhouse not half a mile ahead, with its gable end sticking out from amid the trees, must be that very farm of St. Aunay where we had bivouacked, and which I had named to Captain Sabbatier as the rendezvous of the Hussars of Conflans. There they were, my little rascals, if I could but reach them. With every bound my horse grew weaker. Each instant the sound of the pursuit grew louder. I heard a gust of crackling German oaths at my very heels. A pistol bullet sighed in my ears. Spurring frantically and beating my poor Arab with the flat of my sword I kept him at the top of his speed. The open gate of the farmyard lay before me. I saw the twinkle of steel within. Stein's horse's head was within ten yards of me as I thundered through. "To me, comrades! To me!" I yelled. I heard a buzz as when the angry bees swarm from their nest. Then my splendid white Arab fell dead under me, and I was hurled on to the cobble-stones of the yard, where I can remember no more.

Such was my last and most famous exploit, my dear friends, a story which rang through Europe and has made the name of Etienne Gerard famous in history. Alas! that all my efforts could only give the Emperor a few weeks more liberty, since he surrendered upon July 15th to the English. But it was not my fault that he was not able to collect the forces still waiting for him in France, and to fight another Waterloo with a happier ending. Had others been as loyal as I was the history of the world might have been changed, the Emperor would have preserved his throne, and such a soldier as I would not have been left to spend his life in planting cabbages or to while away his old age telling stories in a café. You ask me about the fate of Stein and the Prussian horsemen! Of the three who dropped upon the way I know nothing. One you will remember that I killed. There remained five, three of whom were cut down by my Hussars, who, for the instant, were under the impression that it was indeed the Emperor whom they were defending. Stein was taken, slightly wounded, and so was one of the Uhlans. The truth was not told to them, for we thought it best that no news, or false news, should get about as to where the Emperor was, so that Count Stein still believed that he was within a few yards of making that tremendous capture. "You may well love and honor your Emperor," said he, "for such a horseman and such a swordsman I have never seen." He could not understand why the young colonel of Hussars laughed so heartily at his words—but he has learned since.

1821

X. The Last Adventure of the Brigadier

I WILL tell you no more stories, my dear friends. It is said that man is like the hare, which runs in a circle and comes back to die at the point from which it started. Gascony has been calling to me of late. I see the blue Garonne winding among the vineyards and the bluer ocean towards which its waters sweep. I see the old town also, and the bristle of masts from the side of the long stone quay. My heart hungers for the breath of my native air and the warm glow of my native sun. Here in Paris are my friends, my occupations, my pleasures. There all who have known me are in their grave. And yet the south-west wind as it rattles on my windows seems always to be the strong voice of the mother-land calling her child back to that bosom into which I am ready to sink. I have played my part in my time. The time has passed. I must pass also. Nay, dear friends, do not look sad, for what can be happier than a life completed in honor and made beautiful with friendship and love? And yet it is solemn also when a man approaches the end of the long road and sees the turning which leads him into the unknown. But the Emperor and all his Marshals have ridden round that dark turning and passed into the beyond. My Hussars, too—there are not fifty men who are not waiting yonder. I must go. But on this the last night I will tell you that which is more than a tale—it is a great historical secret. My lips have been sealed, but I see no reason why I should not leave behind me some account of this remarkable adventure, which must otherwise be en-

tirely lost, since I, and only I of all living men, have a knowledge of the facts.

I will ask you to go back with me to the year 1821. In that year our great Emperor had been absent from us for six years, and only now and then from over the seas we heard some whisper which showed that he was still alive. You cannot think what a weight it was upon our hearts for us who loved him to think of him in captivity eating his giant soul out upon that lonely island. From the moment we rose until we closed our eyes in sleep the thought was always with us, and we felt dishonored that he, our chief and master, should be so humiliated without our being able to move a hand to help him. There were many who would most willingly have laid down the remainder of their lives to bring him a little ease, and yet all that we could do was to sit and grumble in our cafés and stare at the map, counting up the leagues of water which lay between us. It seemed that he might have been in the moon for all that we could do to help him. But that was only because we were all soldiers and knew nothing of the sea.

Of course, we had our own little troubles to make us bitter, as well as the wrongs of our Emperor. There were many of us who had held high rank and would hold it again if he came back to his own. We had not found it possible to take service under the white flag of the Bourbons, or to take an oath which might turn our sabres against the man whom we loved. So we found ourselves with neither work nor money. What could we do save gather together and gossip and grumble, while those who had a little paid the score and those who had nothing shared the bottle? Now and then, if we were lucky, we managed to pick a quarrel with one of the Garde du Corps, and if we left him on his back in the Bois we felt that we had struck a blow for Napoleon once again. They came to know our haunts in time, and they avoided them as if they had been hornets' nests.

There was one of these—the Sign of the Great Man—in the Rue Varennes, which was frequented by several of the more distinguished and younger Napoleonic officers. Nearly all of us had been colonels or aides-de-camp, and when any man of less distinction came among us we generally made him feel that he had taken a liberty. There were Captain Lepine, who had won the medal of honor at Leipzig; Colonel Bonnet, aide-de-camp to Macdonald; Colonel Jourdan, whose fame in the army was hardly second to my own; Sabbatier of my own Hussars, Meunier of the Red Lancers, Le Breton of the Guards, and a dozen others. Every night we met and talked, played dominoes, drank a glass or two and wondered how long it would be before the Emperor would be back and we at the head of our regiments once more. The Bourbons had already lost any hold they ever had upon the country, as was shown a few years afterwards, when Paris rose against them and they were hunted for the third time out of France. Napoleon had but to show himself on the coast, and he would have marched without firing a musket to the capital, exactly as he had done when he came back from Elba.

Well, when affairs were in this state there arrived one night in February, in our café, a most singular little man. He was short but exceedingly broad, with huge shoulders, and a head which was a deformity, so large was it. His heavy brown face was scarred with white streaks in a most extraordinary manner, and he had grizzled whiskers such as seamen wear. Two gold ear-rings in his ears, and plentiful tattooing upon his hands and arms, told us also that he was of the sea before he introduced himself to us as Captain Fourneau, of the Emperor's navy. He had letters of introduction to two of our number, and there could be no doubt that he was devoted to the cause. He won our respect, too, for he had seen as much fighting as any of us, and the burns upon his face were caused by his standing to his post upon the *Orient*, at the Battle of the Nile, until the vessel blew up underneath him. Yet he would say little about himself, but he sat in the corner of the café watching us all with a wonderfully sharp pair of eyes and listening intently to our talk.

One night I was leaving the café when Captain Fourneau followed me, and touching me on the arm he led me without saying a word for some distance until we reached his lodgings. "I wish to have a chat with you," said he, and so conducted me up the stair to his room. There he lit a lamp and handed me a sheet of paper which he took from an envelope in his bureau. It was dated a few months before from the Palace of Schönbrunn at Vienna. "Captain Fourneau is acting in the highest interests of the Emperor Napoleon. Those who love the Emperor should obey him without question—Marie Louise." That is what I read. I was familiar with the signature of the Empress, and I could not doubt that this was genuine.

"Well," said he, "are you satisfied as to my credentials?"

"Entirely."

"Are you prepared to take your orders from me?"

"This document leaves me no choice."

"Good! In the first place, I understand from something you said in the café that you can speak English?"

"Yes, I can."

"Let me hear you do so."

I said in English, "Whenever the Emperor needs the help of Etienne Gerard, I am ready night and day to give my life in his service."

Captain Fourneau smiled.

"It is funny English," said he, "but still it is better than no English. For my own part I speak English like an Englishman. It is all that I have to show for six years spent in an English prison. Now I will tell you why I have come to Paris. I have come in order to choose an agent who will help me in a matter which affects the interests of the Emperor. I was told that it was at the café of the Great Man that I would find the pick of his old officers, and that I could rely upon every man there being devoted to his interests. I studied you all, therefore, and I have come to the conclusion that you are the one who is most suited for my purpose."

I acknowledged the compliment. "What is it that you wish me to do?" I asked.

"Merely to keep me company for a few months," said he. "You must know that after my release in England I settled down there, married an English wife, and rose to command a small English merchant ship, in which I have made several voyages from Southampton to the Guinea coast. They look on me there as an Englishman. You can understand, however, that with my feelings about the Emperor I am lonely sometimes, and that it would be an advantage to me to have a companion who would sympathize with my thoughts. One gets very bored on these long voyages, and I would make it worth your while to share my cabin."

He looked hard at me with his shrewd grey eyes all the time that he was uttering this rigmarole, and I gave him a glance in return which showed him that he was not dealing with a fool. He took out a canvas bag full of money.

"There are a hundred pounds in gold in this bag," said he. "You will be able to buy some comforts for your voyage. I should recommend you to get them in Southampton, whence we will start in ten days. The name of the vessel is the *Black Swan*. I return to Southampton tomorrow, and I shall hope to see you in the course of next week."

"Come now," said I, "tell me frankly what is the destination of our voyage?"

"Oh, didn't I tell you?" he answered. "We are bound for the Guinea coast of Africa."

"Then how can that be in the highest interests of the Emperor?" I asked.

"It is in his highest interests that you ask no indiscreet questions and I give no indiscreet replies," he answered, sharply. So he brought the interview to an end, and I found myself back in my lodgings with nothing save this bag of gold to show that this singular interview had indeed taken place.

There was every reason why I should see the adventure to a conclusion, and so within a week I was on my way to England. I passed from St. Malo to Southampton, and on inquiry at the docks I had no difficulty in finding the *Black Swan*, a neat little vessel of a shape which is called, as I learned afterwards, a brig. There was Captain Fourneau himself upon the deck, and seven or eight rough fellows hard at work grooming her and making her ready for sea. He greeted me and led me down to his cabin.

"You are plain Mr. Gerard now," said he, "and a Channel Islander. I would be obliged to you if you would kindly forget your military ways and drop your cavalry swagger when you walk up and down my deck. A beard, too, would seem more sailor-like than those moustaches."

I was horrified by his words, but, after all, there are no ladies on the high seas, and what did it matter? He rang for the steward.

"Gustav," said he, "you will pay every attention to my friend, Monsieur Etienne Gerard, who makes this voyage with us. This is Gustav Kerouan, my Breton steward," he explained, "and you are very safe in his hands."

This steward, with his harsh face and stern eyes, looked a very warlike person for so peaceful an employment. I said nothing, however, though you may guess that I kept my eyes open. A berth had been prepared for me next the cabin, which would have seemed comfortable enough had it not contrasted with the extraordinary splendour of Fourneau's quarters. He was certainly a most luxurious person, for his room was new-fitted with velvet and silver in a way which would have suited the yacht of a noble better than a little West African trader. So thought the mate, Mr. Burns, who could not hide his amusement and contempt whenever he looked at it. This fellow, a big, solid red-headed Englishman, had the other berth connected with the cabin. There was a second mate named Turner, who lodged in the middle of the ship, and there were nine men and one boy in the crew, three of whom, as I was informed by Mr. Burns, were Channel Islanders like myself. This Burns, the first mate, was much interested to know why I was coming with them.

"I come for pleasure," said I.

He stared at me.

"Ever been to the West Coast?" he asked.

I said that I had not.

"I thought not," said he. "You'll never come again for that reason, anyhow."

Some three days after my arrival we untied the ropes by which the ship was tethered and we set off upon our journey. I was never a good sailor, and I may confess that we were far out of sight of any land before I was able to venture upon deck. At last, however, upon the fifth day I drank the soup which the good Kerouan brought me, and I was able to crawl from my bunk and up the stair. The fresh air revived me, and from that time onwards I accommodated myself to the motion of the vessel. My beard had begun to grow also, and I have no doubt that I should have made as fine a sailor as I have a soldier had I chanced to be born to that branch of the service. I learned to pull the ropes which hoisted the sails, and also to haul round the long sticks to which they are attached. For the most part, however, my duties were to play écarté with Captain Fourneau, and to act as his companion. It was not strange that he should need one, for neither of his mates could read nor write, though each of them was an excellent seaman. If our captain had died suddenly I cannot imagine how we should have found our way in that waste of waters, for it was only he who had the knowledge which enabled him to mark our place upon the chart. He had this fixed upon the cabin wall, and every day he put our course upon it so that we could see at a glance how far we were from our destination. It was wonderful how well he could calculate it, for one morning he said that we should see the Cape Verde light that very night, and there it was, sure enough, upon our left front the moment that darkness came. Next day, however, the land was out of sight, and Burns, the mate, explained to me that we should see no more until we came to our port in the Gulf of Biafra. Every day we flew south with a favoring wind, and always at noon the pin upon the chart was moved nearer and nearer to the African coast. I may explain that palm oil was the cargo which we were in search of, and that our own lading consisted of colored cloths, old muskets, and such other trifles as the English sell to the savages.

At last the wind which had followed us so long died away, and for several days we drifted about on a calm and oily sea under a sun which brought the pitch bubbling out between the planks upon the deck. We turned and turned our sails to catch every wandering puff, until as last we came out of this belt of calm and ran south again with a brisk breeze, the sea all round us being alive with flying fishes. For some days Burns appeared to be uneasy, and I observed him continually shading his eyes with his hand and staring at the horizon as if he were looking for land. Twice I caught him with his red head against the chart in the cabin, gazing at that pin, which was always approaching and yet never reaching the African coast. At last one evening, as Captain Fourneau and I were playing écarté in the cabin, the mate entered with an angry look upon his sunburned face.

"I beg your pardon, Captain Fourneau," said he. "But do you know what course the man at the wheel is steering?"

"Due south," the captain answered, with his eyes fixed upon his cards.

"And he should be steering due east."

"How do you make that out?"

The mate gave an angry growl.

"I may not have much education," said he, "but let me tell you this, Captain Fourneau, I've sailed these waters since I was a little nipper of ten, and I know the line when I'm on it, and I know the doldrums, and I know how to find my way to the oil rivers. We are south of the line now, and we should be steering due east instead of due south if your port is the port that the owners sent you to."

"Excuse me, Mr. Gerard. Just remember that it is my lead," said the captain, laying down his cards. "Come to the map here, Mr. Burns, and I will give you a lesson in practical navigation. Here is the trade wind from the south-west and here is the line, and here is the port that we want to make, and here is a man who will have his own way aboard his own ship." As he spoke he seized the unfortunate mate by the throat and squeezed him until he was nearly senseless. Kerouan, the steward, had rushed in with a rope, and between them they gagged and trussed the man, so that he was utterly helpless.

"There is one of our Frenchmen at the wheel. We had best put the mate overboard," said the steward.

"That is safest," said Captain Fourneau.

But that was more than I could stand. Nothing would persuade me to agree to the death of a helpless man. With a bad grace Captain Fourneau consented to spare him, and we carried him to the after-hold, which lay under the cabin. There he was laid among the bales of Manchester cloth.

"It is not worth while to put down the hatch," said Captain Fourneau. "Gustav, go to Mr. Turner, and tell him that I would like to have a word with him."

The unsuspecting second mate entered the cabin, and was instantly gagged and secured as Burns had been. He was carried down and laid beside his comrade. The hatch was then replaced.

"Our hands have been forced by that red-headed dolt," said the captain, "and I have had to explode my mine before I wished. However, there is no great harm done, and it will not seriously disarrange my plans. Kerouan, you will take a keg of rum forward to the crew and tell them that the captain gives it to them to drink his health on the occasion of crossing the line. They will know no better. As to our own fellows, bring them down to your pantry so that we may be sure that they are ready for business. Now, Colonel Gerard, with your permission we will resume our game of écarté."

It is one of those occasions which one does not forget. This captain, who was a man of iron, shuffled and cut, dealt and played as if he were in his café. From below we heard the inarticulate murmurings of the two mates, half smothered by the handkerchiefs which gagged them. Outside the timbers creaked and the sails hummed under the brisk breeze which was sweeping us upon our way. Amid the splash of the waves and the whistle of the wind we heard the wild cheers and shoutings of the English sailors as they broached the keg of rum. We played half a dozen games, and then the captain rose. "I think they are ready for us now," said he. He took a brace of pistols from a locker, and he handed one of them to me.

But we had no need to fear resistance, for there was no one to resist. The Englishman of those days, whether soldier or sailor, was an incorrigible drunkard. Without drink he was a brave and good man. But if drink were laid before him it was a perfect madness—nothing could induce him to take it with moderation. In the dim light of the den which they inhabited, five senseless figures and two shouting, swearing, singing madmen represented the crew of the *Black Swan*. Coils of rope were brought forward by the steward, and with the help of two French seamen (the third was at the wheel) we secured the drunkards and tied them up, so that it was impossible for them to speak or move. They were placed under the forehatch, as their officers had been under the after one, and Kerouan was directed twice a day to give them food and drink. So at last we found that the *Black Swan* was entirely our own.

Had there been bad weather I do not know what we should have done, but we still went gaily upon our way with a wind which was strong enough to drive us swiftly south, but not strong enough to cause us alarm. On the evening of the third day I found Captain Fourneau gazing eagerly out from the platform in the front of the vessel. "Look, Gerard, look!" he cried and pointed over the pole which stuck out in front.

A light blue sky rose from a dark blue sea, and far away, at the point where they met, was a shadowy something like a cloud, but more definite in shape.

"What is it?" I cried.

"It is land."

"And what land?"

I strained my ears for the answer, and yet I knew already what the answer would be.

"It is St. Helena."

Here, then, was the island of my dreams! Here was the cage where our great Eagle of France was confined! All those thousands of leagues of water had not sufficed to keep Gerard from the master whom he loved. There he was, there on that cloud-bank yonder over the dark blue sea. How my eyes de-

voured it! How my soul flew in front of the vessel—flew on
and on to tell him that he was not forgotten, that after many
days one faithful servant was coming to his side! Every instant
the dark blur upon the water grew harder and clearer. Soon
I could see plainly enough that it was indeed a mountainous
island. The night fell, but still I knelt upon the deck, with my
eyes fixed upon the darkness which covered the spot where I
knew that the great Emperor was. An hour passed and another one, and then suddenly a little golden twinkling light
shone out exactly ahead of us. It was the light of the window
of some house—perhaps of his house. It could not be more
than a mile or two away. Oh, how I held out my hands to it!
—they were the hands of Etienne Gerard, but it was for all
France that they were held out.

Every light had been extinguished aboard our ship, and
presently, at the direction of Captain Fourneau, we all pulled
upon one of the ropes, which had the effect of swinging
round one of the sticks above us, and so stopping the vessel.
Then he asked me to step down to the cabin.

"You understand everything now, Colonel Gerard," said
he, "and you will forgive me if I did not take you into my
complete confidence before. In a matter of such importance
I make no man my confidant. I have long planned the rescue
of the Emperor, and my remaining in England and joining
their merchant service was entirely with that design. All has
worked out exactly as I expected. I have made several success-
ful voyages to the West Coast of Africa, so that there was no
difficulty in my obtaining the command of this one. One by
one I got these old French man-of-war's men among the
hands. As to you, I was anxious to have one tried fighting man
in case of resistance, and I also desired to have a fitting companion for the Emperor during his long homeward voyage.
My cabin is already fitted up for his use. I trust that before
tomorrow morning he will be inside it, and we out of sight of
this accursed island."

You can think of my emotion, my friends, as I listened to
these words. I embraced the brave Fourneau, and implored
him to tell me how I could assist him.

"I must leave it all in your hands," said he. "Would that I
could have been the first to pay him homage, but it would not
be wise for me to go. The glass is falling, there is a storm
brewing, and we have the land under our lee. Besides, there

are three English cruisers near the island which may be upon us at any moment. It is for me, therefore, to guard the ship and for you to bring off the Emperor."

I thrilled at the words.

"Give me your instructions!" I cried.

"I can only spare you one man, for already I can hardly pull round the yards," said he. "One of the boats has been lowered, and this man will row you ashore and await your return. The light which you see is indeed the light of Longwood. All who are in the house are your friends, and all may be depended upon to aid the Emperor's escape. There is a cordon of English sentries, but they are not very near to the house. Once you have got as far as that you will convey our plans to the Emperor, guide him down to the boat, and bring him on board."

The Emperor himself could not have given his instructions more shortly and clearly. There was not a moment to be lost. The boat with the seaman was waiting alongside. I stepped into it, and an instant afterwards we had pushed off. Our little boat danced over the dark waters, but always shining before my eyes was the light of Longwood, the light of the Emperor, the star of hope. Presently the bottom of the boat grated upon the pebbles of the beach. It was a deserted cove, and no challenge from a sentry came to disturb us. I left the seaman by the boat and began to climb the hillside.

There was a goat-track winding in and out among the rocks, so I had no difficulty in finding my way. It stands to reason that all paths to St. Helena would lead to the Emperor. I came to a gate. No sentry—and I passed through. Another gate—still no sentry! I wondered what had become of this cordon of which Fourneau had spoken. I had come now to the top of my climb, for there was the light burning steadily right in front of me. I concealed myself and took a good look round, but still I could see no sign of the enemy. As I approached I saw the house, a long, low building with a veranda. A man was walking up and down upon the path in front. I crept nearer and had a look at him. Perhaps it was this cursed Hudson Lowe. What a triumph if I could not only rescue the Emperor, but also avenge him! But it was more likely that this man was an English sentry. I crept nearer still, and the man stopped in front of the lighted window, so that I could see him. No; it was no soldier, but a priest. I wondered

what such a man could be doing there at two in the morning. Was he French or English? If he were one of the household I might take him into my confidence. If he were English he might ruin all my plans. I crept a little nearer still, and at that moment he entered the house, a flood of light pouring out through the open door. All was clear for me now, and I understood that not an instant was to be lost. Bending myself double I ran swiftly forward to the lighted window. Raising my head I peeped through, and there was the Emperor lying dead before me!

My friends, I fell down upon the gravel walk as senseless as if a bullet had passed through my brain. So great was the shock that I wonder that I survived it. And yet in half an hour I had staggered to my feet again, shivering in every limb, my teeth chattering, and there I stood staring with the eyes of a maniac into that room of death.

He lay upon a bier in the center of the chamber, calm, composed, majestic, his face full of that reserve power which lightened our hearts upon the day of battle. A half-smile was fixed upon his pale lips, and his eyes, half-open, seemed to be turned on mine. He was stouter than when I had seen him at Waterloo, and there was a gentleness of expression which I had never seen in life. On either side of him burned rows of candles, and this was the beacon which had welcomed us at sea, which had guided me over the water, and which I had hailed as my star of hope. Dimly I became conscious that many people were kneeling in the room; the little Court, men and women, who had shared his fortunes, Bertrand, his wife, the priest, Montholon—all were there. I would have prayed too, but my heart was too heavy and bitter for prayer. And yet I must leave, and I could not leave him without a sign. Regardless of whether I was seen or not, I drew myself erect before my dead leader, brought my heels together, and raised my hand in a last salute. Then I turned and hurried off through the darkness, with the picture of the wan, smiling lips and the steady gray eyes dancing always before me.

It had seemed to me but a little time that I had been away, and yet the boatman told me that it was hours. Only when he spoke of it did I observe that the wind was blowing half a gale from the sea and that the waves were roaring in upon the beach. Twice we tried to push out our little boat, and twice it was thrown back by the sea. The third time a great wave filled it and stove the bottom. Helplessly we waited beside it until the dawn broke, to show a raging sea and a flying scud above it. There was no sign of the *Black Swan*. Climbing the hill we looked down, but on all the great torn expanse of the ocean there was no gleam of a sail. She was gone. Whether she had sunk, or whether she was recaptured by her English crew, or what strange fate may have been in store for her, I do not know. Never again in this life did I see Captain Fourneau to tell him the result of my mission. For my own part I gave myself up to the English, my boatman and I pretending that we were the only survivors of a lost vessel—though, indeed, there was no pretence in the matter. At the hands of their officers I received that generous hospitality which I have always encountered, but it was many a long month before I could get a passage back to the dear land outside of which there can be no happiness for so true a Frenchman as myself.

And so I tell you in one evening how I bade goodbye to my master, and I take my leave also of you, my kind friends, who have listened so patiently to the long-winded stories of an old broken soldier. Russia, Italy, Germany, Spain, Portugal, and England, you have gone with me to all these countries, and you have seen through my dim eyes something of the sparkle and splendour of those great days, and I have brought back to you some shadow of those men whose tread shook the earth. Treasure it in your minds and pass it on to your children, for the memory of a great age is the most precious treasure that a nation can possess. As the tree is nurtured by its own cast leaves, so it is these dead men and vanished days which may bring out another blossoming of heroes, of rulers, and of sages. I go to Gascony, but my words stay here in your memory, and long after Etienne Gerard is forgotten a heart may be warmed or a spirit braced by some faint echo of the words that he has spoken. Gentlemen, an old soldier salutes you and bids you farewell.